BROKEN
PLACES

BROKEN PLACES

László Petrovics-Ofner

A MORGAN ENTREKIN BOOK

THE ATLANTIC MONTHLY PRESS

NEW YORK

Published simultaneously in Canada
Printed in the United States of America

Library of Congress Cataloging-in-Publication Data

Petrovics-Ofner, László, 1948–
Broken places / László Petrovics-Ofner.
ISBN 0-87113-359-8
1. Hungary—History—20th century—Fiction.   I. Title.
PS3566.E8585B76   1990   813'.54—dc20   89-78227

The Atlantic Monthly Press
19 Union Square West
New York, NY 10003

FIRST PRINTING

Dedication

To the Simon Wiesenthal Center, Los Angeles, Mr. Marvin Gimprich, Dr. Mordecai Paldiel of Yad Vashem, Dr. Gaurie Bar-Shaked, director of the Hungarian Section, Mr. Efraim Zurof, director of the Simon Wiesenthal Center in Jerusalem, to the many who helped us seek witnesses over a period of six years, and, most importantly, to the witnesses themselves, gratitude is expressed for making possible the Ceremony on behalf of my parents, Zsuzsanna and Dr. László Petrovics, 19 May 1988, as Righteous Among the Nations. This work is also dedicated to the grandchildren and offspring of those rescued from the Holocaust whom I was blessed to see playing in the meadows outside Budapest and to the living Memorial, Yad Vashem, a place of remembering and revival, where keening songs rake the trees, and the Maytide chorus peals for our southern sun. Among the lights of the Children's Memorial, Yeats rushes back, Romanticism a castaway here:

> Ponder a little how love then fled
> Paced cragged peaks, washed-white, stark-bled,
> Hid amid floes of stars afar their birth
> Love's form fleeing from orbs of Earth.

Bless the many who bring life back, the hope and the memory.

Who helped my sister and myself reach across a dark veil to light, to find our parents, parents to life.

20 május 1988
Jerusalem
LPO

They lived by backward glances—toward the old sun, the old shade, the old breeze.

—ERIK H. ERIKSON

The world breaks everyone, and many grow stronger in the broken places.

—ERNEST HEMINGWAY

Contents

PREFACE

The Return
1976

Thirty years ago, during the cold October of 1956, my friends and I on Damjanich Street hoarded fallen chestnuts, the missiles for our battles in the park. I was still a youngster, much too small for my seventeen years and had only recently abandoned childish games. Though I was an adolescent, possessed by teenaged interests, especially in girls, my frame was that of a child of perhaps thirteen or fourteen years old. During folk dances, the *csádárs* and other dances we learned in school, the girls in the countryside towered above me and grew bewildered when I asked them to dance. They seemed to have memorized the phrases. "Well, really, I mean I am flattered. But I am nearly at the third form in high school."

My father, my Apu, and I went for the rides at the city amusement park that autumn, and we walked through the turning barrel together. We braced each other by the forearms so we would not fall. Sharing a knowledge still new to me, I laughed at the girls as hard as he.

The barrel kept rolling, and Apu and I shuffled along. Holding each other by the arm, we moved our ankles as the barrel turned and scraped the wood as we slid back to the center. Most people held the sides of the churning barrel so as not to fall; Apu and I had perfected our own method of helping each other. After many trips over a period of several years, Apu and I looked like we were simply walking along, sideways, sidewalking along.

Now and then strong bursts of air shot up from below. This was of little distraction to men, but the girls and women had to let go of the barrel in order to hold down their skirts. They were lost either way, for both Apu and I got a good look when they fell or, better yet, when they chose to stay upright, the skirts billowing above their waists, sometimes even above their heads, muffling their shrieks. My laughter was as deep as Apu's and seemed incongruous for my size. After the girls fell, they sat up and puzzled over the manly excitement in my child's frame.

That October, the fallen leaves drifted into piles. I watched with fascination as my younger friends galloped through them, neighing loudly like a herd of wild horses. At the snorting from the lead stallion, they fell and rolled, sinking into the blanket of dead leaves, their heaving chests devouring the bittersweet fragrance of autumn.

The autumn was just as exciting for us older boys. We were treated as men for the first time. We helped the workers from the factory fill seltzer bottles full of kerosene. We lugged these to the rooftops and arranged them in neat rows, as though they were preserves stored for winter. The older boys on our block were the ones to join the poetry readings at the Petőfi Writer's Club, and we were the ones to rip up the cobblestones to make barriers against the Russian tanks. They were gone now, but they were expected back any day.

Flushed from my own adventures preparing for the Russian invasion, I returned to the softness of a familiar apron and the woman who caressed me, arching like the bough of a tree heavy with fruit at fall harvest. I was not ashamed to hug Anyu close like that, even though I sometimes thought of myself as a young man. We just fit together that way. "Spoon in spoon," she had said many times.

From that cold October of awakening life, I was called to the painful journey. What beckoned was remote and mysterious—better opportunity, *minden lesz*, and prosperity, *ott minden lesz*—things I hardly cared about and did not understand. I still do not understand. Prosperity? Better opportunity? They were twin brothers to capitalism, a philosophy that would triumph over Marxism. But I learned only briefly what it meant to defend oneself, to live for oneself alone and not for someone else. I had been socialized into a selflessness by Hungary that was not appropriate when I eventually matured in America. Capitalism always struck me as a form of Darwinism, the big dog doing it to the little dog; although plenty of Americans were kind, they were motivated by a self-interest that I could not decipher.

The caller of that October was history, some far-removed, unknowable beast without substance. A shadow to the senses of the young and the trusting. But I felt its menace, rending all that was familiar, while I was still green and waiting to ripen.

I departed from Keleti Station. Across thirty years, I can still smell the coal from the soot-black engines. I see the rhythmic bursts of steam from between the mesh of giant wheels. The train slowly pulls westward. I hear the exertions increase. The siss and hiss deepen to the snorting of a boxer in the ring. I kneel on the seat. I look out the window. Mother hastens by the train. "There is prosperity there!" she calls. Where is there? I wonder. "Prosper, my little one."

I do not understand the tears that redden the faces of my parents. We would be soon united. They stand arm in arm, waving. They grow smaller, figurines that continue to wave. The caller intones coldly: "Liberty." The dots dissolve into nothingness. They are gone and I can already hear the cry of loss: "What will be?"

After the last station, Angi, my older sister, and I walk for three days, mostly at night. Toward the end of the third day I can walk no farther. Through a break in the trees covering the mountainside I look out over the plain. Lit by a half-moon, the muddy fields heave and swell, the black horizon convulses. Angi and I move on. Later that night, we cross into Austria. We sing our anthem.

> O God, the Magyar people bless,
> Plagued by woe as pelting rain,
> Give generous protectiveness,
> A nation tossed on seas of pain.
> To those whom sorrow ever rends,
> Bring now Maytide's joyous amends.
> The people have long paid the sum
> For sins of past and all to come.

For twenty years I grew and changed, tried to become American, to take root in arid soil grown barren from the curse "Prosper. Leave us and prosper!"

Once processed at Camp Kilmer in New Jersey, the first priority was a quick trip to Macy's so that Angi and I might look American at once. I got lost in the furniture department, which I did not mind. I had never seen anything like it—the Colonial style, I later learned. It was at the height of fashion back then. The manager, having a foreign-speaking youngster on his hands, pondered his dilemma, muttering uselessly, *"Qué llamo? Qué llamo, pocito?"* I was frightened by a passing lady's bright red dress. *"Ruski damoy!"* I yelled. The manager was startled and started rattling the one word, "Magyar. Magyar." Soon the loudspeaker blared, "Magyar youngster, Magyar youngster, lost on floor three, Colonial Furnishings."

For lunch, crosstown, a first steak, rare, New York cut . . . and nausea. Raw meat, of all things. Of course everyone was upset, a filet mignon, and I had eaten only two mouthfuls. To cheer me, a first dollar bill from Uncle Ervin, who finished my steak with zeal.

My wardrobe had been made over from head to toe. Scratching my neck endlessly from the new winter coat, I felt uncomfortable and alien. Back across town, Ervin explained the advantages of radios in taxis. "Bet you don't have that in Hungaria?" he commented in a forgotten tongue. "Do you know what capitalism is? It's that György Washington, right there in your hand." I was bewildered. Had he only pronounced it "Gehorgeh Vashinghtun," I would have recognized the dollar at once.

Then among all the great excitement and strangeness—of glass everywhere, and concrete, the crush of people and blaring traffic, my neck chafed and shoes too tight, overwhelmed by a one-day transformation—I cried. I felt ashamed because I was an adolescent, but I could not keep my tears back. People huddled round, fretting as a gaggle, "Don't cry. Don't cry. How can it be? Why cry? Don't cry." Which I had never heard: "No, don't cry."

The soil was rich. Surely not barren. The land, the air, even the water was bountiful. Uncle would look at me in wonder when day after day during the spring I came home from Kawlis Creek with my limit of brook trout. I told him how they danced energetically after I landed them, reflecting the noon light. In April, when the maple sap was flowing freely, I collected buckets of the clear liquid for the forester up by the reservoir. He boiled it down in a tub and sold it to locals in milk bottles that he had saved over winter. I befriended local dogs as Aunt did not allow me to have my own. A sheepdog named Blackie became a good friend. I was learning English in school, and to the marvel of my friends soon mastered the homophones *to*, *too*, and *two*. It struck me as a minor miracle when the kids on my team for the spelling bee cheered. My schoolmates and I hunted for red squirrels, and Blackie accompanied our games in the woods.

The water was bountiful, the soil rich.

It was *I* who was accursed. Leave us and prosper. Which was the same as becoming fallow.

But I knew nothing of it for some time.

Until I returned, over ten years ago today. Twenty years after I had left. It was summer.

At Frankfurt I transferred to the Hungarian airline, Malév, flying in a small plane with wings that were active in the wind. We made an unexpected stop in Austria. Dr. Lásoi, an engineer from London who sat next to me, commented dryly, "One must presume metal fatigue under these conditions. We're only fifteen minutes from Budapest." I had no idea what he meant. He sipped a martini, one finger extended. "The wing might rip off at three thousand meters," he explained. "We're in for a wait, I'm afraid. It can only be tested electronically."

He looked out the window and in great alarm put down the martini. "Say, there's a mechanic bobbing on the wing."

Eventually, the exhausted plane hovered over the heart of Budapest, the Paris of Eastern Europe, as the travelogue said. But as we descended, I saw a vast grayness enveloping the city. Buildings lacked color, cars were few, and only a sprinkling of people were about on the streets. As the plane angled to land, the center of the metropolis moved in a lethargic circle, like a worn carousel.

Broken friend Budapest, I thought. Your moments of freedom infuse with pain the thousand-year wound. Crossroads for the wars of Europe, city of the gray mask, what does it mean to be Magyar now?

My outlook soon proved prejudiced. No, not merely prejudiced, rancorous.

As my mind revolved with the carousel, the happy throngs in the plane applauded the pilot for having brought us in safely. He waved to us, smiling broadly, aware of the joke at his expense, but still laughing. He lifted his captain's cap.

I waited in the lobby after being cleared at customs. The place overflowed with workers. The odors raised by the noonday heat made it difficult to breathe. The workers were dressed like the proletariat from the futuristic films of a generation ago. Gray pants, soiled-gray or off-white shirts wet in the back and bulging over khaki trousers. Streams of sweat poured down their faces. "Do not judge," I muttered. "Who are you?"

Then, on the far side of the room, amid the blur of black and gray, I saw a rich red color. I looked closer. There, standing arm in arm with Father, Mother held poppies. When she took off her glasses, I saw her eyes shadowed with grief. Creases lined Father's face. Twenty years, I thought. They had been parents without children.

Then they saw me, and the keening years gathered in a moment. My mother held her flowers, and Father cried out, "Pisti! Pisti!"

I ran to them. I did not stop to think, You. You too felt loss, were wanting. I just ran, feeling tightness grow supple, and I wrapped my arms around their necks.

It was fantasy, as though nothing had happened. No awkward silence or tears. Just joy, as if I had returned from the countryside after a summer outing and had been missed.

We returned to the apartment. The taxi driver talked about dollars and about the fare to Kennedy. "Twenty dollars, dearest God," he prattled. "Just one trip, one trip a week. I'd have the *kert*, the garden, and what goes with it." When we arrived, my father, who knew a few words of English, spoke sternly to me: "Two. Only two. No more." The driver was very happy.

I walked through the gate, the walls always in mind: they were the same, the courtyard and stairwells as though they had been awaiting me, as if alive and perpetually suffering. The plaster missing and scaling like the skin of a leper, unable to recover from war. My father saw me looking. "Not enough cement for patch-work even, let alone for housing."

I still remembered the air of the night. Its warmth and fullness held one lingering near the window, expectant, and helped bring laughter as we drank Gray Friar wine.

Grandmother, nearing ninety, sat knitting in the rocker by the window. She finally looked toward me. I kissed her. She looked up, "Oh, my kitten. Little kitten."

I felt good for her endearment.

"Mici . . . Mici . . . ," she went on.

"Do you remember me?" I asked. "Or do I look different?"

"You are Torda," she said, flicking the yarn with her finger. "Our chieftain from the Great Plains."

"Mici is her cat from childhood," Mother explained in answer to my alarm.

Later, I walked into Grandmother's room. I stood surrounded by her embroidery. The matching needlepoint above the mantel offered baskets of fruit bloated with peaches and grapes. Sparkling gooseberries overflowed the basket in the picture and gnarled pears rested on their sides. *Nagymama*, give me some of them, I thought. It was all she did, or could do: sew for the last twenty years of her life.

The couch abounded in her pillows. Some, sewn in the Mátyo style, were embroidered with the gentle curves of many-colored flowers. One had a red rose in the center, surrounded by orange short-pistiled daisies.

We sat in the room together. The curtain billowed, and the evening whispered. We both heard it.

She raised her eyes from her sewing and smiled. She adjusted her glasses. "Pisti," she smiled. Her face grew smooth again. She rubbed her neck and returned to the needle.

Her back rounded over her sewing, her crossed knee bobbed slowly. She looked up at me, her weak eyes swollen by the thick lenses. She did not smile at me. She did not respond or even seem to notice me. She resumed her chore.

My gaze rested on the pillows.

Can such flowers ever wilt? I wondered.

Only fade. Maybe that's worse: to be forgotten.

The question again surfaced: What does it mean to be Magyar? Am *I* Magyar, part of the main? The next day I would go rowing upriver with my cousin, and we would swim the width of the Danube. In the nude no less, he had bragged on the phone. Two girls would come with us. This was new for me, skinny-dipping, but it was a custom the Magyar had gotten from the Americans, he assured me.

Before retiring, I browsed through János Arany, the epic poet of Magyar myth. I turned sleepily to the section on the tribal migration from Asia.

Old Taltos, do we scatter
throughout the fallow earth,
the golden hind lead to our rebirth?
Past Salt Sea's brine and matter,
to River Kur, her tundra dome,
yield us a Danubian home?

Will Tisza's ripples prance
in April's abounding rain?
Bounty harvest, golden-grain,
ripe the seed, one stance:
One house? Earth's One-house?
Tisza, Duna, Dráva, Száva,
waters to quaff, and infant douse.

Ancient times of youth. . . . The cry of the ice vendor echoing off corridor walls, now the hum of electric freezers; the rhythmic clomping of hooves against cobblestone streets in early morning, now the scream of rubber on asphalt; the lonely songs of fishers dancing among the reeds on the shores of Badacsony, now poor reception from a Korean radio.

New shoes fit tightly and hurt the feet. But eventually they grow comfortable.

Don't wait! Can't wait! To be Magyar now meant to rush forward, headlong, *előre*. As the statue replacing Stalin's fallen monument on Liberty Square, the statue *Előre* runs headlong, nearly supine, into a brave new future. The sense of momentum and energy is striking. Stalin's mammoth memorial, a study in socialist realism, stood stiff and mummified, heavily weighing down, history pinned helpless beneath his boots like a landed fish. *Előre* looks forward, seeks an ideal, tries to undo the self for the common good.

Much gain. And much good, I thought, looking at this proletarian statue surging forward.

It was 1976, I recall.

Crowds gathered around Premier Kádár, peasant women kissing him and the throng pressing close. A Jew? With the surname Csermanek? Many people still thought so. Though he, too, was imprisoned by Rákosi, Kádár disavowed Jewish roots.

I experienced the new future as the crowds gathered around Kádár. Perhaps his promises of 1956 would come true, I imagined. Multiparty systems, greater freedom, more prosperity.

I cried out with the old ones who welcomed me, the few who remained; Rózsi, Gizella, and Erzsi. With soft kisses and frail arms they enveloped me, caressed me, took back the curse. With their laughter they enriched the garden bed so I knew from what soil I sprang and could join in the chorus as part of the main.

On the last day of my first trip back, I sat at the very table where Anyu had drawn her family tree so long before. The same red roosters still crowed from the wallpaper. My mind turned again.

In a world of sorrow and endings, desire still grows in all places, here as everywhere. New forms awaken, as does my own desire: to remember and to never forget. My source, among the old shades and familiar air.

I asked again: Was it anybody's fault, our dispersion? Was it even a fault? Or the world as it is? It is only the few who can be the history makers, and often they undo history. I had never ceased to yearn for belonging. But out of the chaos of being I found a new desire simply for context. Was it Premier Rákosi who hurt? Perhaps. But Anyu had lost most of her relatives to the "Good War." So it was the Holocaust as well. And to know that helped. One does not feel less pain, but one feels less crazy.

The Holocaust? An abstraction? It was real, had a presence in the room among us as we ate the creamed chicken, when we went to the café or strolled at dusk, the city blaring with National

Television and the streets abandoned, as in the United States during Super Bowl telecasts. The Holocaust was also with us into the night as we dreamed the dreamless sleep.

I was eating goose crackling, of all things, unaware, dipping them into salt as I had on the day Rózsi lost hope in her grief over our family tree. "Bereft of foliage" as she put it. And I was there when a short while later her hope revived. "The Messiah tarries," she had said then. "But there is will to persist. And there is the persistence of will."

The last day. Desire persistently unfolding—at the airport, on a wooden bench, hunched intensity with the used envelope, Mother's desire to be let be:

> *Life calls and you must answer,*
> *But the will is hard to find.*
> *Your youth, on the threshold*
> > *just once . . .*
> *Looks behind.*

She still wore her mourner's glasses. At first, I could not see her brightening eyes. I grew impatient. I said, "Speak your memory, Anyu." I looked at her. "Do not write our good-bye. Dead words to scare a bird."

"Another time, Pisti," she said. Her smile was pleasing. "There will be many other times."

I handed her Arany's mythology. I did not want it anymore. They too now struck me as dead words hung on sticks.

I lifted her mourner's glasses and saw her gaze glistening. I kissed her eyes. I was taken by the exchange: the mythology for her dark glasses, which I pocketed. And which she forgot.

The flight was announced for boarding. I kissed her again and hurried off. I saw all around me a lightness, the ease of the people, and heard laughter I had not heard upon arriving.

The plane was over the Alps when I recalled with a start that

I had left my luggage by Anyu's side. I knew she had laughed after noticing it, the laughter of *röhög*, laughter that would frighten most people in America. I could see her doubled over on the bench, laughing the cleansing laugh, and afterward able to go home, clutching the bundle to her side.

I pictured her walking alone, past the guards at the entrance to the airport and up the Ferihegy Road, a long, sloping climb. Exhausted, she flags the express bus and falls asleep, the luggage secured on her lap. She awakens, full of dreams, at Engels Square.

I reclined the seat and dozed with her image, clutching the glasses in my jacket pocket. In the twilight consciousness I heard words resounding.

Speak, memory. Speak, I pray.

I dream I stand on Buda's shore, up on the cliffs, and a mist rises from the Danube. It rises high, enveloping me and extending eastward. I feel myself rising with the mist, slowly rising, past the plains of Pest and the quiltwork of buildings, through the open markets of Pécel at the outskirts of the city, over checkered fields of alfalfa and wheat. I see the mist flowing between the rows of pear trees and sour cherry at Nagykőrös onto the Puszta, the Great Plain where grazing horses move amid the green seas of tall grass, and farther . . . overflowing the River Tisza and enveloping the yellow and red fishing boats, then turning north to the collective farms of Szabolcs and Zemplén where the peasants bend in unison to primitive pentatonic songs of harvest, past the whitewashed cottages of Lonya and through the locust trees and broad-leafed tobacco that line the border to Russia . . . over all this and from all this, the gray mist thickens and grows . . . to the barren steppes of a foreign land, from Ere, the tribal name of nether darkness, to Asu, region of the sun . . . over the waters of Rivers Oka and Káma and up the gentle Ural slopes, the divider between Europe and Asia and cradle of the Magyar race.

* * *

The stewardess rouses me to fill the customs forms. I had bought nothing, I tell her, groggy from sleep. Just took whatever I wanted from the house. I hand back the forms and she gives me a pillow. I had forgotten my luggage, but Apu's used satchel was secure under the seat, filled with embroidered pillowcases, a yellow ceramic rose, a painted water pitcher, used tablecloths decorated with the red threadwork of the Zala district, and old watercolors of peasant cottages.

My earliest memories are of such things, I realize as I rest my head. Not of war, but of the country. I recall a time when I am not yet able to walk but already know a few sentences. "Dog gone," I say of Rózsi's puli, a Hungarian sheepdog she got from relatives in Zalavég in the countryside of western Hungary, as it runs from the room. "Pigeon fly bye," I point to Uncle Kálmán's white tufted tumbler on the farm up north as it takes to wing. I soon learn the names of colors and can elaborate on the brown matted hair of the puli and describe the homing pigeons as red or white.

From that time, when I walked straight but could not yet hop, let alone skip along, my recollection also encompasses the very large and unseeable—the steady pounding in the distance, like thunder at dusk, the smell of freshly cut wheat on cooperatives so vast that the eye could not see the tractors, only a film of dust rising at the horizon's edge. Most keenly, I recall a constant press, a wanting. I spent a lifetime reclaiming what I lost, and what I have found is history, the history of a second generation, stretching back in time to before our birth.

Our prayers, the prayers of the second generation after World War II, have long gone unheard. In part, we disown our right to them. But they will echo down the centuries, as the cry of Ionesco's exiles: "Let these sufferers of our pains be gone. Give us back our dreams. Give us back the dreams we lent them. And let them be gone."

* * *

The stewardess rouses me. "You were tossing about," she says. "Are you all right?" She hands me a seltzer. I sip it slowly, still rooted in thoughts. Do I deceive myself even in the one truth I know? I want a child, to have a family. I realize my hunger is for that. Not merely context, dead words to scare birds, but to surrender to life. I want a child, to be a good caretaker. Good enough, just to be good enough, I think. That will do. Would I ever have a family?

I had gained one way to meaning: faith. I had received it from both Father and Mother. Apu had always compared life to a tree that needed tending. For some reason I never understood, he worried endlessly about the roots, hardly thinking of the foliage. "Take root. Be a good tree," he muttered once after planting a cherry sapling behind Uncle Kálmán's cottage in Dunaalmás. "Bear fruit. Be blessed." And whenever he read, either from the Old or New Testament, it was as though he were dreaming the Big Dream, millennia deep, with roots that sucked sustenance from darkest night. Were he Jewish, he would, I knew, kiss the hands of the Hassidic *rebbe*.

But Mother always worried about the foliage, as did I, about the leaves on the topmost branches. It bode ill if they dried. It was a first sign of dying when the uppermost leaves of the hemlock or oak, those nearest the sun, withered away.

Anyu worried about the spring green leaves, young and just born. I saw them as children.

I was deceiving myself. I wanted a desire beyond context, I knew, to become a part of the earth. And that meant to belong, to have a family. I could even picture my tiny child and gazed upon Him in wonder, a point of hope and a point of light from millennia's depth and darkness.

Szülők lesznek, I thought. All children will be parents someday.

Either to a living child, their own flesh, or else they will breathe life into an inner child, their vision and hope. A child within, a voice they had lost somewhere, that was playful, and clear, and laughing the big Yes. YAH! The only YAH-way. It came as a startle. *Ruach*, breath. The breath, the wind, Adam rising from dust, his chest heaving and eating at the air. The child will resurrect. My own child. The angels at the four corners of the earth had stood guard over death long enough, silent and in awe, even as the gusts roared. Now they will revel.

There is a dawning on the Duna, I knew, darkness yielding to a pastel dawn. The day of the totalitarian over. God bless! Their days over. And yielding to a faith, *my* way to faith. I had a child, a song. A song I could sing. And it rose with Easter and slept in the glow of the Sabbath afternoon. It would be a song with one word: "Yes."

Say yes, I beg myself. Yield to it. A breath, a soul. Say yes and surrender. Bring it back. You are among the leaves closest the sun. Revive. Bring it back, damn you. What else are you good for?

1

Through Fields of Poppies
1942

"It is well past noon," I heard Kálmán, my uncle from the countryside, saying as he entered the bedroom. I thought I was still sleeping, for although I had told my eyes to open, all was still pitch black. But when I heard his gruff voice and the bang of the door against the wall, I knew that I could not see. I could not open my eyes, and I sat up with a start and a rush of fear. "Uncle!" I cried. "I am blind!"

I was flooded with panic and screamed out loud. But he grabbed me and held me tight. "Shush, you hear! No need to be frightened. Your eyes were tearing in the night, that's all, Pisti." His voice seemed so certain. "It's just your eyelids shut from tearing." He laid me back onto the down bedding, left for a moment, and returned to place a damp cloth over my eyes. "Now just shush," he comforted me. "Leave that over your eyes for a minute." The cloth was warm. He had heated water for it.

When Uncle removed the cloth, I could open my eyes again. The picture of the Virgin Mother loomed from across the room, next to the crucifix where the six-pointed star had once hung. It had hung there for years and had kept the stucco surface free of summer's dust. Although Ibolya, Kálmán's wife, had tried to wash away the dust surrounding the spot where the star had protected the stucco, the silhouette of the Star of David could still be seen behind the crucifix. Later, after the Liberation of 1945, the same spot on the wall would be covered first by Admiral Horthy and then, finally, by Stalin's broad smile. And so it went, one stain covering the other—the relief of the Star of David covered by the cross, to be later covered by the official portrait of the Hungarian leader and then by Stalin's propagandist icon.

I grew quiet and thankful after my sight returned. As I looked at the colorful Virgin with ruddy cheeks and golden halo, I thought that next to my parents, I loved God most, and then I loved Admiral Horthy, the leader of our nation for all my three years, and many years before. "I love you as much as the Admiral Horthy," I told my uncle, full of gratitude for his healing and thinking it would please him.

He broke into laughter. "Imagine," he laughed. "That's meant as an endearment."

I was born in Budapest on 11 május 1939, a week after the Second Anti-Jewish Law was passed. It was a blessing she had converted, Anyu used to say. A blessing that her parents had converted right after her, Apu added. Now the lineage was protected. Angi, my older sister, laughed: "And so on and so on."

I spoke early. But according to my parents' expectations, I spoke late. I was truly precocious, having spoken my first imperative sentence before I could walk. Actually, it was only a word, a grunt at that—"Ko-ko." But everyone took it to be a command and ran to fetch the hot chocolate, reinforcing my grunting. Apu, my father, and Anyu, my mother, both in their late thirties, and even Angi, nearly five years older than I, could understand my grunts and gestures and quickly shaped my language. "Ugh," a groan, a circular wave of an arm, and I got the cookies from the cupboard, thin squares with apricot topping or butter balls that dissolved in my mouth and eased my teething. But even as an infant, I know I felt the need for expression. My first words were uncommon words at that, *lepke,* "butterfly," and *labda,* "soccer ball." I could soon speak well beyond my age, knowing when to use the proper "thou," and the informal *te,* or "you."

* * *

My earliest memories are of Uncle Kálmán and the countryside and not of the war, though they are hard to separate. The great estates in the Komárom district in northern Hungary were so vast that they curved around the bend of the earth. The peasants from three villages shared one combine and marveled at the efficiency of the monstrous machine. I recall climbing Round Hill, holding my uncle's hand, and looking out over the checkered fields of rye and wheat and the golden squares of sunflowers, poplars lining the road in the distance like tiny soldiers marching in rows across the fertile plain.

From this time, when I was only three years old, my recollection draws on small things: the color of my cocoa cup (which was mostly used for tea), the smell of cinnamon from Aunt Ibolya's baked muffins, the baby chickens that wriggled from my hands, and the crow of the rooster at dawn, which I did not heed, covering my head with the overstuffed down pillow and returning to sleep.

Less immediate but more ominous are my recollections of very large things, too large to comprehend, and shrouded in mystery and confusion—a steady pelting in the distance that Kálmán eventually told me was from shellfire. Of course, I thought at once of freshwater oyster shells from the southern lakes, and I could not understand how they made such a pounding sound. I had heard the ocean's steady humming in the conch that Kálmán kept on the mantel. Only later did I learn that the sounds were explosions. I first thought of them as the popping of Christmas bulbs when they fell from the tree.

From the city where my parents lived came recollections of horse-drawn wagons, slowly crowded out by the auto, and the fouled yellow cobblestones gradually clearing of dung. The direction signals for cars did not blink then—an orange arm pivoted from the auto's side to indicate a turn. We were fascinated more by this little arm than by the whole of the auto. They were fragile, and few of them worked, and those that did soon broke from our fussing with them. I also remember the playground out back, the huge spruce with the swings and the tire dangling low, and playing in the sandbox with my sand car, indicating my sharp turns with a waving arm that I shot out in either direction like a real turning signal.

The city was gray, always crowded and clamoring, even in the early morning. The cry of the tinker and ice vendor often woke me when it was still dark. "Pots to mend, pots to mend." "Ice, ice, burn to freeze, dry ice, and cubes and chunks." These cries were more effective than the rooster's crow in rousing me. The city was loud and gray, and I longed for it.

I felt a constant longing, a feeling of want, especially when out in the country and apart from my parents. Perhaps that's why I spoke early and why my first words were not the common "Papa" or "Mama." My parents were constant in one way: in absence. And that, perhaps, would be my most persistent inheritance—an unending sense of loss, of feeling apart and in exile, even in the arms of love.

My first trip to the country took place in 1942 when Apu, a commissioned officer in the medical corps, was stationed at Kaposvár. He was there for only five months before contracting typhoid, whereupon he was recalled to Budapest. Only the immediate family knew his role in contracting the illness. He had injected himself with infected milk after he received word that he was being transferred to the Russian front. In Budapest he obtained a position as a physician for Jewish forced labor at the Páva Street Synagogue, the Lutheran high school, the National Textile factory in the Ninth District, and finally at the Melocco Cement factory on Gubácsi Road. After 1944 he was a medical officer for the ghetto for a short time before we had to flee. But all this would happen later.

My time in Kaposvár turned out to be even shorter than my father's. Soon after we arrived, Hungary declared war on the United Kingdom; five days later, it declared war on the United

States. Because bombings were expected, Angi and I were evacuated to Uncle Kálmán's in Dunaalmás, well behind the front. Of course, Kaposvár was not attacked, only the capital, but no one could predict that. It mattered little that Kaposvár was nearly two hundred kilometers from the capital, or that it was hardly larger than a hamlet. It also did not matter that the bombers eventually came from Russia. In the prevailing state of hysteria, everything was imagined.

"Now what the hell did they do that for? Joining a Three Power Pact against the world," Apu kept repeating. "We have nothing to gain by that damned agreement. For one thing, we're hardly a power. Three Powers, hah!"

When Angi and I were ready to leave Kaposvár, Apu consulted with Uncle Oti on the route to Ukk, where the trains were still running. Most of the railways farther north and closer to the city had been bombed, and Oti described seeing rolling stock in the city railyards scattered about the tracks like toy trains. A ruddy, jovial sort, Oti had been instrumental in getting a three-piston Skôda on loan from the mayor of Kaposvár. Military vehicles would not do for our trip.

"A moving target is still a target," Apu insisted. He put on his civilian clothes and, cranking the tiny car, told us we were headed around Lake Balaton. Angi's favorite summertime uncle, Kálmán, would meet us at the station at Ukk and take us back to Dunaalmás, his village.

Apu dared not travel with Mother, who stayed behind. He feared her papers might be questioned. "Needless exposure," he said. "At least Kálmán is well known at the lower-end church." I grew confused. The only papers I knew of were for drawing. Then I grew agitated as Apu started muttering about all the fussing and the many arrangements. "That jackass pact," he said, gripping the wheel. "We'll be fighting Eskimos next."

Despite his warnings of much danger on the trip, Apu also kept repeating that Angi and I should just think of this as our regular summer vacation. Even though winter still jealously held

on, I kept trying to imagine picking cherries with abandon, as
Angi had described doing in summers past, Angi up in the tree
throwing down the cherries, which I would collect into a basket.

But a cold rain was falling, and the leafless trees in the woods
by the road cast doubt on my cheerful expectations. The poplars
lining the road had only just begun to bud, and their thin yellow
branches clawed at the air as the trees shook in the storm.

At Ukk we met Uncle Kálmán, who had arrived earlier by the
morning train and was pacing the platform. He wore a sheepskin
cloak, a *suba*, puffed on his curved pipe, and stomped his high
boots. "Felt sure they'd last through the summer." He considered
his boots. "But as I've paced here, past the concrete to the oiled
beams and down the gravel path, I feared they'd wear a hole." Now
and then he smacked his pipe against his heel to empty the bowl.

Apu asked him to reassure us. "Tell the children it will be like
vacation, Kálmán." Kálmán repeated Father's phrases. "Sure, sure,
it will be like summertime. A regular summer."

The cold rain continued to wash my tousled hair across my
face.

On the train to Kálmán's hamlet, a peasant shared our
compartment. He had a bottle with a straw cover clasped between
his boots. He smiled a toothless smile and held up the sealed wine
bottle proudly, repeating, "For Cili Néni. For Aunt Cili." We could
not tell from this if the wine was for his wife or for an older
relative. The ticket collector sat next to him; beside him sat a
soldier on leave, his pinky stuck in the barrel of his rifle, holding
the gun precariously upright. Uncle Kálmán was serving them
coffee from a jar.

Later, the peasant uncorked the bottle and drank it down
with zeal, almost swimming in it, like a landed fish returned to
water. This made us all uneasy. For one, he had just drunk
someone's gift. Uncle was also worried that the man would get
sick. Which soon he did, sweating all the while and growing
increasingly pale.

Kálmán, who sat uneasily next to the peasant, tried to ignore the vomit. He joked with Angi about the cows grazing in the meadows we passed. "Come on, Angi. Look at that foolish cud chewer. It's pure black."

"No." Angi readjusted me on her lap.

"In the name of dear God, why not?"

"I don't feel like it. I feel sort of sick."

"Well, all the more reason to ignore . . . it."

"Ignore what?"

"In the name of the merciful Father, Angi, you want me to actually talk about *it*?" Kálmán was familiar with Gentile phrases and used them freely.

"Sir, really, must you invoke the name of the Lord?" the soldier quipped. His rifle, pivoting around his little finger, swayed to and fro.

Kálmán made an awkward gesture toward the floor, pulling his legs to the side like a schoolgirl. A trail of blood mixed in the vomit near his feet.

My sister and Kálmán joked about the cows routinely, but in the heavy stink of the room she did not feel like playing. I sat uncomfortably in her lap, staring blankly at the strange man slouched over and moaning, his hair matted and wet.

At Dunaalmás, the peasant did not take his bottle but left it lying on the floor. It was empty, the straw covering tattered. He held onto the sides of the car as he left the train, guiding his staggering gait.

His Cili Néni, his wife, round faced and pudgy, with blue kerchief and flowered shawl, spotted him from afar but did not notice his condition. "Niki, love." The flowered shawl waved. Her five children, gathered around her, greeted him on cue, "Dear one and only father."

"Niki, love." She stood on her toes, waving. They were all waving when, having finally heard them, the peasant leaned forward, clasping the handrail, and focused his eyes.

Seeing the drunkard staggering toward his family, who were standing with arms outstretched, ready to catch him if he collapsed, aroused my longing. The scene reminded me of my return from the playground, weary with play, when I would fall into Mother's open arms.

Aunt Ibolya, Kálmán's wife, had gone to the sanatorium in Debrecen to care for her brother. Ibolya's brother had contracted TB, Kálmán explained, and she would be gone for months. "Only money can save him, the doctors said," Kálmán told us. "So she will nurse him back to health." Kálmán rubbed my hair. "Some woman, that Ibolya. The will to persist, and the persistence of will." I looked up at him in confusion. The dark holes of his nostrils flared.

The glass factory with its many boarded windows dwarfed the clay houses at Dunaalmás. The long, shingled roof glistened in the soft light of the cloud-veiled sun. The building appeared mysterious, like an abandoned castle from King Arpád's ancient reign that had succumbed to foreign legions and was haunted by defeat. Electric bulbs no longer lighted the village, Uncle Kálmán said as he guided the horse along the bumpy road around the wire fence. The outline of the factory was hard to make out in the waning light. A scent of kerosene came from the faintly glowing windows of the cottages we passed.

Kálmán pulled back on the reins of the four-in-hand and pointed with a whip at the green-hued cottage glowing amid the rowan at the far side of the field. The stucco collected the weak light from the sunset after the rain. But he was not one to linger on pretty pictures. He suddenly lifted his head and cupped an ear. He pulled the reins in, stopped the team, and sat listening.

"No, it wasn't anything. I thought I heard the shelling," he said. He drove on, continuing his banter. Since December, he said, the black iron gates of the factory had been closed. Most of the men in the village now slept till noon.

Then he pulled the reins again, abruptly this time. Listened again. "It is shelling, all right. They have started up again."

"What shelling, Uncle Kálmán?" I heard nothing.

"It's from the Ukraine. Can you imagine? Over five hundred kilometers around the bend of the earth. And still one can hear it."

"What do you hear?" Angi wondered.

"Why, can't you hear it? It's a popping sound, then a rumble. Like distant thunder."

Angi and I heard nothing. Kálmán drove on slowly, as though entranced by the sounds. I wondered why we didn't hear them. Were Kálmán's big ears more sensitive?

But Kálmán became his jovial self again when Pityu, his son, two years older than I, ran up to us as we neared the cottage. Kálmán pointed out a section of green wall where we could kick the soccer ball I had brought from Pest. Pityu had never seen a leather ball. I was so tiny, my arms hardly circled the ball, and I could not really throw it to him. And if I kicked it, it was as likely to be with a knee as with my foot. But Pityu was beside himself as the ball bounced back to him with force, and Kálmán laughed when the boy missed an easy header. As night fell, Pityu kicked the ball onto the roof and sent the rooster squawking in flight. We went to bed late, exhausted.

As we extinguished the flame of the kerosene lamp, I heard the faint popping and eruptions I had heard in the city. The sounds came from the east and mixed with the song of the sleepy hamlet. "Do you hear that?" I asked Angi, alarmed. Had my ears suddenly grown to the size of my uncle's or had the war grown closer? I wondered.

Angi sat up at once, motionless. The nighttime insects buzzed outside. Angi did not answer me, but the way she suddenly jumped up gave her reply.

I imagined the popping sounds as the smooching of lovers in the movies. (I had once accompanied Angi to a show and a couple behind us had kissed for over an hour. Angi kept smacking my hand whenever I turned around, gaping.) The sounds also reminded me of my mother in a playful mood, kissing my face all over, slowly kissing my cheeks and lips and neck when I had been younger and she had tucked me in. Distant thunder brought rain onto my bedroom window back then. And she sang, *"Tente, tente, little, my."*

The war was in the Ukraine and the faint pelting did not wake us. The sporadic sounds were from shelling, Kálmán kept saying. "They can be heard round the world," he said, scratching his ears, flat saucers that hung from his head, almost as big as plates. I felt sure those ears could hear everything. "The proletariat is of this world. Not like the fascists. The Russians will win us this war for sure. Not the fascists. That's the truth."

"What's the truth?" I asked.

"Ain't it the truth, Angi?"

"Yes, Uncle. The people are the salt," Angi said.

"What salt?" I asked.

"Why the kind you sprinkle on schmaltz," Uncle laughed.

School was closed here in the hamlet and we slept late, never thinking to close the curtains before going to bed. At ten-thirty every morning, the sun shone over the lilacs in the garden and lighted our room. Angi woke before me, and as she fussed and slammed the drawers to her dresser I awakened also. We had our breakfast with Uncle Kálmán. At one time, years earlier, when he had owned a plot of land at the outskirts of the hamlet, he had risen at four with the song of the lark, when it was still nearly pitch. But now he too slept late.

One day Angi painted our initials on two white cups. On hers was a big red *A*, and on mine was a smaller blue *P*, which looked like a *B* because the paint had run. Angi and I had tea from these mugs and toast with honey. Once we had cocoa four days straight. But to get that we had to barter Ibolya's ruby ring with the well-laden and brash gypsy who had pitched camp at the crossroads of the village for two weeks. Kálmán justified the exchange: "Can't eat a ring, can we?"

Uncle Kálmán browned thick slices of bread on the wood stove, turning the pieces with a fork. He drank black coffee and spread reduced chicken fat on his toast. He had once given me a drink of his coffee and reared back in laughter as my face screwed up from the bitter taste. Before he ate his toast, he got the salt jar from the cabinet and with small pinches spread the crystals evenly over the schmaltz.

"Your mother taught me that," he laughed. He leaned back in his chair, lit his pipe, and opened to the middle pages of *Népszava*, the People's Voice. That was where the dairy report and weather forecast were located. This day he quizzed Angi about dairy products.

"And the brown cows. What do they give?" Kálmán asked.

"Cocoa," Angi said.

"And the black ones?"

"Coffee."

"The ones with black spots give coffee with cream," I added. I was jealous of the attention Angi received.

We all laughed loudly and felt good and happy to be together.

My ears had grown attuned to the background noise, and I heard the pelting sound again. I knew Kálmán noticed it, too, for he lifted his head from *Népszava* and looked far away, his eyes glazed.

Then, still chewing his toast energetically, he flipped the paper over and glanced at the front page. "Well, well," he said. "I was mistaken. It should be out of Stalingrad soon enough."

"What will?"

He smacked and scraped his pipe carefully and blew through the stem. "The sounds will get louder then. You may want to pull the curtains closed at night."

The weeks passed and the light breezes of spring filled the air. Eventually, Kálmán showed me the loft on the roof for the homing pigeons he bred. I had never been allowed on the roof, only up to the attic, which had no windows.

Kálmán sat on a rung of the steep ladder that led to the roof and told of how his own father had grown gentle only around doves. " 'Twrit, twrit, twrit,' he would sing to them, petting them all the time, while with us he ranted loudly about chores undone, tools unmended, whatever came to his mind."

He talked on about the doves, growing brighter as he talked. "Did you know, Pisti, Noah was alerted to nearby land by a dove." His eyes widened before my face. "Even the Holy Spirit of the Gentiles took the shape of a dove."

He went on as though I understood him. "The Greeks and the Romans bred pigeons. That's how they'd win wars. And that's how the Rothschilds made their fortune. Even Shakespeare admired them and wrote about them. His writing shows accurate knowledge of the birds."

He looked down at me. "Do you see why they are important, Pisti?"

I had stopped listening. I still held his hand, but I was absorbed in exploring the loft. It was like a shanty, made of rough wood and boards. A grid of coops was fastened at the far end. Uncle Kálmán pointed to the hospital at the side of the shed where sick birds were isolated, the wooden bars of the cage painted white.

The best nesting, Kálmán went on, was long-needled pine, but if hay had to be used, some benefit could be derived from alfalfa. Coops quarantined not just sick birds, but also those returning from shows. The baby squabs, or *tóllatlan*, the featherless, were also quarantined. He explained the hereditary patterns, which I understood only to the extent that a blue male squab usually got its blueness from the father and a brown crested female got its color and markings from the mother. This was plain enough to see.

Kálmán loved the pigeons almost as his children. In some respects they were preferable to children because almost all the pigeons he trained returned and remained faithful to him and bred and kept the roost full, for trading as well as racing. Their faithfulness to him recalled my yearning for my parents, and I imagined returning to them after these many months, running and flying into their waiting embrace.

Kálmán had won two awards in races on the plains. The Kecskemét Buga, a crested bird with a brown tuft at the peak of its head, had been one of the winners. It was "combed" with white rosettes running from side to side on its head. It had been released at Beius in the Bihar Mountains of Romania and had flown four hundred kilometers home clear across the plains. As Kálmán petted the bird, stroking its neck so that it cooed, I thought, *Repülj galamb.* Fly pigeon. Fly home. And I relished the thought that Budapest was less than four hundred kilometers away, within easy reach of the bird.

"How fast could it fly to Pest?" I asked.

"Pest is nothing." Kálmán was unaware of my longing. "Probably half a day."

And I thought, *Repülj galamb.* Fly. Fly.

The other prizewinner was a Bácska tumbler, an old hen and a high flier that could stay up five hours at a time and then dive, helter-skelter, tumbling. It carried itself on the ground horizontally, pecking with the boxed beak under its high-placed crest. It was a frightening bird to behold because of its "bull's-eye"—a black pupil sat at the center of its bright yellow iris, surrounded by orange skin. It made me think of pain, of agony.

I peered at it closely, enchanted by its gnarled appearance and riveted by the eyes. It looked at me also, its head cocked and still, as though it saw something in me equally striking.

The birds demanded Kálmán's devotion as much as his family. In sickness or health, they needed tending, exercising twice a day, and feeding, bathing, and healing.

Pityu, however, was Kálmán's first love. He was a handsome child with golden hair and blue eyes. When he ran in the tall grass by the stream, his bright hair glowed amid the lush colors of the meadow. The field, marked by black-eyed Susans, pink and blue wild poppies, and an occasional sunflower standing tall, could never absorb the brightness of Pityu's head bobbing as he galloped about chasing grasshoppers. The delight Uncle took in him, the glint in his eyes as they followed the boy, again aroused in me a longing for my parents, their eyes following me running after the wrens in the park or looking after me laughing as I chased the length of the playground for the helium balloon that had slipped from my fingers, skipping and jumping as they had never seen me, the string just out of reach.

We went to the brook every morning except Friday, when we followed the trail past the slow-flowing waters to the hardwood forest where we gathered mushrooms. It was nothing like the streets of Pest. It would have been difficult not to love the glistening rocks and thick moss, but I missed the city anyway. Soon my feet would ache from the sharp stones on the trail, and on the way home Angi would carry me on her back all the way from the bridge to Kálmán's cottage, a good kilometer. Kálmán would deep-fry the mushrooms for dinner.

The woods were quiet and deep, but the stream was a busy place. The African stork and its young fished on its banks, mostly for frogs. They stalked cautiously, moving slowly, their beaks pointed like javelins, and then lunged in spasms, splashing the water high.

The stream thronged with toothed carp, or *ponty*, which had been introduced from Lake Balaton. They were the ruination of our flimsy nets, which we eventually abandoned in heaps by the barn door after Kálmán refused to mend them anymore. We also caught perch, crayfish, and a few black bass. Of course the place was abundant with frogs, and the tiniest of them, no bigger than a nail, would stray over fifty meters from the stream after a rain.

All the community animals that were herded—including Gray Hungarian longhorns and the red-skinned Palodian cattle, sheep, and Worsted Merino sheep with thick wool and curved horns— would be driven in the evening to the corner of town where the stream pooled. Cows cooled themselves there, as did goats. But to us, the children, it was first and foremost a swimming hole, the only one we had. We called it *A Jó Isten Egyháza*, the Good Lord's One-House.

None of us begrudged the animals because we believed that animal wastes floated and were washed away by moving water. Angi and Pityu used to have long arguments about whether this was really true.

The countryside was strange and beautiful, yet I felt a longing for the city. I wondered if Apu and Anyu missed Angi and me. I knew I missed them. I would readily trade my new adventures for their familiar hugs. Even with the city's smell of soot mixing with summer's sweat, I preferred to be close to my parents. Even as the cool breezes of the country blew around me and we basked in our swimming hole, I had already learned that only warmth can cure pain.

One afternoon after several months with Kálmán, Angi, Pityu, and I took the shortcut through the fields to go to the military hospital. Uncle Kálmán had told us the day before that the soldiers there were lonely. "They enjoy children," he had said. "I want the three of you to visit them." Angi and Pityu thought that perhaps the soldiers would give us chocolate. I grew hopeful, too.

The budding poppies shone bright red in the sunlight. Angi chased the frogs that had strayed from the river. As soon as the big green ones wet in her hand, she dropped them. But the little brown ones, which measured no bigger than the nail of her thumb, she put in her shirt pocket, thinking that their wetness was only water. Her pocket grew moist as we walked.

At the hospital, the geraniums were in bloom. Their petals stuck out irregularly from between the bars that covered every window.

An old nurse met us in the lobby. "They'll be tickled to death. *Milyen boldog lesznek*," she said without as much as a smile when she took our hands to lead us to the infirmary. She had a bad limp, and my arm jerked with each of her steps. Against the back wall of the lobby was hung a huge flag under which was a copper plaque with the names of all the soldiers who had died from wounds received in action during the Prezmysl Campaign in Poland during World War I. A green film had collected in the indentations of the names. The inscription was largely worn away, except for a phrase or two, "and . . . twilight . . . the silence there . . . velvet."

The soldiers were glad to see us.

In the infirmary, the nurse took us from bed to bed, starting from the back of the room. The men did not give us chocolate, but we did not let our disappointment show. They gave us rock candy and bits of fruit chews from boiled-down raspberries and pears. They told Angi what a pretty woman she would be some- day. One of the soldiers handed me a cigarette, but the nurse slapped it from his hand, knocking it to the floor.

"Private Nagy, he is only a child," she said.

"*Yay, jó édes anyám,*" the private replied. "Oh, mother dearest."

"What do you think?" the nurse snapped at him. "Don't you know that we are aware that smoking is the only acceptable way to commit suicide?"

"Up yours!" The soldier was screaming.

The other soldiers laughed, and the private seemed pleased with their laughter, thinking he had somehow outwitted the nurse.

I quickly crawled under the bed to retrieve the cigarette, but the nurse grabbed it from my hand, saying that it had been on the floor and was dirty. The private laughed again.

"A month of gangrene and I have to be careful of the goddamned dust." He looked at Angi. I could see he felt tense. The bandage of his leg leaked, and a sharp odor rose from the infection. He knew we were aware of it because it was hard to hide our reaction. I recognized the odor as the same as the carcass of some small animal left in the gutter of the road in the summer heat. The smell followed us down the hall, cloying, as though we had turned the carcass over with a stick and watched the maggots underneath scurry and writhe in the sunlight.

By the time we reached the corporal, our pockets were lumpy with rock candy, but still no chocolate. Angi's face was red from the fruit jelly, and she whispered that Uncle Kálmán would be angry if our pockets were to stick together. Some candy had even gotten into Pityu's hair. The corporal gave me his army hat. It was big and would not balance on my head but fell to one side. I saluted him, snapping my heels. His right arm was missing below the elbow, and he answered my salute with his left hand.

Then the nurse took us through the dimly lit corridor to the recovery room. "Now I'll take you to Major Király. He's just been operated on."

There was a white birch outside the window at the end of the hall, and patches of sunlight shone through the leaves. We walked to the room nearest the window. The wind shook the branches of the birch, sending the shadows of leaves into a dance across the marble tiles. The nurse said that just the week before the major's leg had been amputated below the knee. She added that we should try to be especially nice to him. She did not come into the room with us but opened the door and told us to enter.

The room had a small window with dark green curtains, which had been pulled back. We stood in a row in front of the door, awkwardly looking at the major, at the window, at one another. The long-suffering walls of the building had not been rebuilt since the Ottoman reign. The paint was flaking in places and the light screened by the curtains gave the walls an olive tint. Where they were flaking, they appeared sodden and yellow, discolored like an infection. The soldier lay on his back, staring at the ceiling, and did not look at us when we approached. He had heard the nurse, and I thought he might feel indignant at receiving special attention. Over his head hung a picture of a bunch of red flowers. They were hard to make out in the dim light. The room was stuffy and dark, and I feared our candy would soon melt. The soldier wore only his underwear. The smell of sweat came from his body, and I knew he was uncomfortable. A leather patch covered the stub of his leg. We were standing at the foot of the bed, and from the temperature graph I could make out his name: Major Király.

Pityu noticed some papers and pencils and said, "Do you want to play a game?"

The major propped himself up on an elbow. "Who sent you?" he asked.

"The nurse. She told us you needed special attention," Angi said.

"Crippled bitch." He looked away.

The sugar was melting in my pocket and I wanted to leave, but I remembered what the nurse had said.

"Do you want to play battleship?" Pityu said finally. "Angi is real good. She always wins." Király looked down at me. "Do you want some jelly?" I said, extending my palm toward him.

Angi also went to him and reached into her pocket. The rock candy came out in lumps and stuck to each of her fingers. Major Király smiled at the sight, and we laughed, too.

"No," he said. "Let me see you play battleship."

I pulled open the curtains and opened the window and a breeze blew the dust from the sill into my face. Major Király was a young man with a neat red mustache and curly orange hair and clear blue eyes. The sweat of his body evaporated in the fresh air. He sat against the head of his bed while Angi and Pityu knelt on either side. We had encircled his bed, like in the pictures Apu had shown me of the angels at the corners of the earth. Fending off evil, Father had said.

Angi won the first game because she placed her submarine and battleship in one corner. She started to brag.

"If you would have kept to the corners I would have lost," she said to Pityu. I was still too young to understand the game, let alone what the corners had to do with it. Angi sucked at the jelly that stuck to her fingers.

"What is the matter with you?" Pityu asked Király.

"What do you mean?"

"I mean what is your sickness?"

The major laughed again. "I have the war disease," he said and laughed louder.

Király joined them for the second game. It went well: Pityu sank Angi's destroyer and Király sank two of her submarines.

"What do you want to be when you grow up?" the major asked me after the game.

"I want to be a soldier," I said.

"Let me tell you," Király said, suddenly growing somber. "They move you from place to place and you don't go anywhere. Three times they moved me before deciding I needed an operation. Maybe my leg could have been saved. You wouldn't want to lose a leg, would you?"

I had always wanted to be a soldier, and the idea of riding in trains or vehicles that could go through mud still pleased me, in spite of the major's warning. But Pityu was the best wing in soccer for his class, even though he was just a first grader, and he grew alarmed at Király's question. "My class would go to defeat if I were to lose a leg," he said. "No, I wouldn't want that."

"Then you can be an admiral in the Hungarian navy," Király laughed. His joke only slowly settled in as we found it difficult to imagine a submarine in the shallow waters of the Danube.

A knock came from the door and a man entered. He had shiny buttons on his coat and small gold arrows crisscrossing his military hat. Across his brown shirt were black straps, and his black arm band bore thick arrows. When he clicked his heels, one of the buttons shook. He had stars on his shoulders and I imagined him a general.

I had started playing the general with my friends in autumn when the chestnuts had fallen and we could use them as missiles for our battles in the park. As with language, I seemed to skip over stages of normal development. Anyu used to marvel at how I never played alone, but had joined in group play as soon as I could walk. I was the smallest and would be assigned to stand in the rear, out of range of the enemy, and give the command to move from behind the trees to fire. But I had never met a general in real life. Major Király saluted lying down.

"I see you have company, Major," the man said.

"Yes, sir."

"I hate to break things up, but we'll be repositioning soon. The Russians will retake Kursk and Kharkov. Sure as sure. The blitzkrieg has lost some thunder, I'm afraid."

Király winked at me. "Let's just hope some of the lightning is left in the blitz, if there is no thunder. I'm used to moving."

I stood looking up at him, dumb, and rested my weary head on his mattress.

"I see you lost a leg. In the east?"

Király did not respond.

"In the east?"

Király still did not respond but continued to look at him helplessly.

"You'll come through, Király. Just wait. I've seen many come through well. My chef lost a leg at the front. Frostbite, of all things. Now you'd never know it, he's so jovial. Plays the goalie for the unit, even rides a bicycle."

The sound of motorcars came from outside. The trucks that were to take the men away were just arriving, and one of the drivers cursed at a pig that lay in the mud of the road. Light shone brightly on the brown leather patch covering Király's thigh.

"I would rather have my leg," Király said.

The Arrow Cross left. The major continued to stare at the ceiling, as though the man were present, still looming over him. He would not play cards or eat candy or talk of soldiers and trains. He did not even say good-bye when we made motions to leave.

At the door I turned toward him. "Aren't we friends?" I asked.

He looked at me straight, startled, his blue eyes icy. "It is not good to be friends at times like these," he said. "My leg was like a friend, you see. And in my dreams I still run through fields of poppies laughing aloud. I can tell when my knee bends, which toe is moving, feel the press of my calves against my snug boots. But then I wake up." His hardened eyes turned sad and he looked away from me.

* * *

The three of us took the long way home and stopped on a small bridge that crossed the stream. I suddenly became aware of the stillness of the afternoon. No cawing of the crows, the wind had died, the poplars were perfectly still, and the leaves of the oak were frozen. The pelting, the backdrop to our daily activities, for Kálmán and Pityu and Angi and myself, had quieted, and a silence blanketed the day. I pictured Kálmán jubilant, speaking his strange language of metaphors: "The blitzkrieg will stop. The tide will turn."

Angi took the little frogs from her shirt pocket and leaned over the railing. They were dry and limp and had bits of jelly stuck to their skins. She returned them to the stream and they floated upside down, their white bellies breaking the surface of the water.

Squatting there by the railing, I looked across the bridge to the furrowed and winding road that disappeared behind a knoll. And the words might have come to me back then for the first time, as they often do now: Who will drive me home along the bumpy road?

"Hop on, little one," Angi said to me cheerily. She squatted to make it easier. "They just got dried out," she said, anticipating my confusion. "They're just silly frogs."

I climbed up, and she carried me slung on her hip to the side, as women carry produce home in a basket from the open market. She would carry me throughout her life that way, my weight imprinted on her spine, even though we would scatter as seed cast to the wind, thousands of miles apart, at the corners of the world, mute and in awe, forever arrested as children, as angels, mute witness unto death, in the Good Lord's One-House.

The sounds echoed again, the first time I had heard Apu in his absence. YAH. And then softer. Yah. And finally in refrain, words I never heard and a strange name: Rayless as a leper, Yeats lies with Everyman. And as I look back upon it, the words became true, for it would take just a short while, less than a year, from the spring of 1944 when the Jews were branded until winter of the same year, with the death march to Hegyeshalom in October and November, the last of Magyar Jewry, the young the old the lame and the pregnant, the castaway useless, those seen unfit even for Auschwitz—these men, women, and children—were loaned to Germany as labor to build "the invincible defense" around Vienna against the approaching Allies. Two hundred kilometers on foot in winter's cold. A week to do it: two hundred kilometers. With only three meals all week: thin turnip soup, thin as in the camps.

What twisted mind could order the downcast, the homeless, to walk? To walk in winter? To build a wall? A defense? Ditches to trap the onrush of tanks and trenches to hide in and embankments to protect.

And when Kálmán, husband to Aunt Ibolya, refused to march from the Swiss Protected Territory of St. István Park in northern Budapest, the Arrow Cross Guard grew fearful. As a horde, they jumped him, bludgeoning him quickly lest his refusal infect everyone.

It was only years later, when Ibolya finally told of walking past his fallen frame on the stoop, without as much as daring to look down, that she was able to weep. She wept ceaselessly as she recalled that within a few minutes Wallenberg had dragged her from the line. Accursed, she lived. A firm hand gripped her arm, saying, Keep still. Keep still. You will be safe. And the arm led her down a long street, deep into the street, and then turned to rip her Star away and left at once, a voice saying, "Remove the threads as well."

"There were ten of them, at least," Ibolya wept. The realization came to her slowly and her tears flowed freely, like waves from a turgid sea beating the shoreline into wefts and warps. Her life soon withered, and even today, well past eighty, she is still alone, sitting by herself in a room and looking at her past.

2

By Backward Glances

Shahnda
Decrees 1.240 and 1.450
5 április 1944

I was constantly losing Father. This happened as soon as I could
crawl from the crib and turn the corner into the other room.
Without his face before me, his image faded and I lost him. When
I grew older and could walk to the far side of the house, his face
would linger longer. But as I sat to play marbles, or by the time I
had arranged my clay soldiers, I lost him again, for what seemed
forever. I would panic and call out, "Papa! Paaaw!" With repeated
experience, he gained the wisdom not to fetch me and would
simply respond, "Yup, little one. Ya." As I recall, that was the first
time I had heard the Lord's name, "Yah," and even then it had been
affirmative and a source of comfort. Throughout my toddler years,
our house echoed and resounded with our refrain. My urgent
song: "Paaaw! Paaaw!" And his response: "Ya. Ya." That was all I
needed for some time, for many decades as it turned out, hardly a
touch or embrace, just the sound of his voice, to know that he was
there: "Ya."

When Angi and I were at Dunaalmás with Uncle Kálmán for
those many months in the country, I remember that Apu's image

began to fade again, while Mother's continued to glow clearly, as did Grandmother Freund's. Angi and I were finally reunited with our family at Kaposvár in Southern Hungary, a small town back then. We were there for a brief time, and Apu's gaze and smile again gained constancy.

But Apu soon received notice that he was to be shipped to the front. After the messenger arrived, he began to pace up and down the foyer, wringing his hands and growing so agitated that he began to holler and yell, stomping about, "Yoodle-yup. Yup-yup-yoodle." I hardly understood him, and he had grown too preoccupied to notice my confusion. I could not see what could be wrong with the front or why he got upset.

I had just learned the words for locations and thought that the front was a pretty good place. I liked being in front of the line when my friends and I played choo-choo. Sitting up front in the barn that served as our makeshift school, near the nursery teacher and the coop for the chickens, was something I liked. And when we sat at the front of the church, I could see the peaceful smile of Our Mother and the open heart of Christ radiating gold light.

But I was forever losing our father, I knew as much. And so I did the best I could to be like him, so as not to lose him. I became a little man, not the little Caesar who ate endlessly and with zeal, but the handyman and the provider, even by age five. I undid the doors of our kitchen cabinets as Grandmother stirred the stewing fruit, her back to me, humming pentatonic tunes happily over the sweet mixture. When she turned around and saw me with screwdriver in hand, all four doors undone and neatly stacked, the pans and dishes in the cupboard revealed, her jaw fell noticeably. And then she laughed aloud, not quite the robust *röhög*, but doubled over still.

Adults had always been charmed by my precocity, and this pleased me to no end. It was a way to win a smile or a laugh, which in my child's mind was the same as affection, as warm as any embrace. I soon started taking the trolley alone, going nowhere in particular—here and there, but always only there and back, over and over. People on the trolley were amazed, and sometimes the driver would not let me on. "A toddler, of all things. A preschooler, no less. What the hell is the world coming to?" His brows furrowed as he worried aloud. "Sorry, little brother, *öcsém*, but I can't risk my job, you getting lost."

As food ran low in the city, I was given another opportunity to play the provider. The breadlines, as well as the milklines, as all lines in the Good Lord's One-House, as I eventually grew to know the world, meant hours of waiting. Anyu got on line early for produce or paper products, while Aunt Rózsi took me to Dob Street and placed me on line for bread and then led Angi to Wesselényi Street for milk, while she stood in line for odds and ends, kerosene for lamps, hardware, soap, whatever was needed at the time. This forethought saved half a day, because Anyu would simply pick me up as I neared the baker and then meet Angi as she neared the milkman.

We returned home while it was still morning, while Rózsi, the last to get on one line or another near some corner, would arrive much later, usually midafternoon. Of course the length of the lines could not be judged precisely, and sometimes I ended up in front of the baker before Anyu had arrived. This made for much confusion, just as it would in the breadlines many years later, in 1956. People were aghast at a small child standing in line. "He will surely grow hard chested," a topknot complained. "Such a dear little thing."

"He looks like a midget to me, pretending to be a youngster," the black shawl commented. "Doesn't his head seem swollen?"

"Horrifying," the man in the full beard muttered. "What horrors greet us even while shopping. Hard chested is right. A young boy, of all things, living his wounds."

It was all my way to avoid loss, to hold onto the image I had of Father as a child would see him—provider, protector, independent, a soft-hearted man living his wounds.

* * *

It was in mid-1942 when I was three that Father was called away from Kaposvár to the eastern front. As I had enjoyed his presence only sporadically, I was again threatened by his loss. Very few people knew what was happening in the Ukraine where the Second Army, of over two hundred thousand men, was being sent. This would bring the number of Hungarians on the front to nearly a quarter of a million men, an entire generation. No one knew for sure what was happening either to the infantry or to the auxiliary Jewish servicemen. Only victories were reported, upbeat and bombastic. But Apu had firsthand information from evacuees he had treated from the front. He was to be shipped out only a few days after Angi and I had returned to Kaposvár from Dunaalmás. But Apu injected himself with milk so that he developed typhoid. He was immediately transferred from the southern front back to Budapest.

I was not there when he injected himself because I went to bed by seven. But Angi, who was eight at the time, had seen the hypodermic—seen him do it—and she told me the story in detail. The day he got notice he had grown increasingly outraged at the thought of going to the front. By dinner he was muttering to himself aloud. "Cocking rifles from World War I against Russian canister missiles." He rolled his eyes up as though he could see through the ceiling. "What the hell do they take us for?"

Angi told me how he had invoked his late mother's name into the night: "Didn't Mama keep my own father out of the White Army in 1920? Simply by feeding him saffron until he turned yellow. Didn't Ibolya tell us—Oti, Sándor, and myself—never to go to war? To prick our fingers before the urine test and pee down the blood?"

The thought of him jabbing his thigh with the hypodermic drawn up with milk from a cup disturbed me. Of course, Apu had tasted the milk first, as Angi elaborated, to make sure it had not soured. "If he would have injected himself with bad milk, he surely would have died," Angi told me, and her explanation made sense.

Her story was troublesome, and I grew all the more frightened during the ensuing weeks when I saw Apu sick, sweltering with fever, his stomach and chest covered with red patches. After he recovered, he was reserved in Budapest as a doctor for the Jewish forced labor battalions from 1942. Both Angi and I quickly forgot the incident. We did not miss the country and continued our games of tag and hide-and-seek in the city. The bellowing of the oxen and the swaying tail that led our farm wagon was replaced by the trolley that ran clackety-clack along the cobblestones of the city's bumpy roads. Instead of the meadow, we now had the tar-covered square; instead of the endless fields, we had Városliget, the city park.

It went that way for nearly two years, all the way till 1944, time frozen in an upbeat bravado, the news from the front always chipper and good like the warbling of a songbird at dusk. Dusk still held a peacefulness as we sat on the shores of the Danube, the fading light playing on the smooth-flowing waters. But the daylight hours were troubled. Shortages became routine, and the banter on the long lines served to fill time, a welcome distraction from the vague worry that seemed to loom over everything. Everyone knew that the news from the front could not always be good.

The melody of the songbird at dusk soon changed to the racket of the sparrows, hungry in winter; by 1944, when reality was shattered for everyone, especially for the Jews, only the carnivorous, cawing crows remained.

Each Thursday, I went fishing up by Obuda, beyond the brick-yards and factories, where the water was fresh and where there were good-sized black bass. József, my favorite relative, mother's cousin from Zalavég in western Hungary, always joined me. We became friends one day over marbles and cocoa, which I recall he drank with a finger lifted. He rambled endlessly, and I soon knew all about him.

In the late 1930s, just before I was born and after economic restrictions on Jewish city businesses had spread to hide and wholesale milk, József had abandoned his goat farm. For a time he had become a writer, but he was too practical to stay at it long. He ended up a tinker.

Knowing full well the value of a mended pot, he often bragged to me, "No housewife, clever or not, can boil water in a leaking pot." He winked. "Either the fire will quench or the water leak." He brushed my hair. "Remember that, Pisti. Put that among the noodles in your head, sweet kugel, little one. You with the big head. It's a good thing to know."

A mist rose from early dawn until midmorning above the calm waters of the Danube. Whenever József cast out, I could hear only the bait land, a sudden plop some twenty meters away. The line was drawn tight by the current. He had a special way of hooking the bait, doubling it over, and pinning the end straight down. But because of the mist, we could never see his cast to see if the bait had loosed, if he was fishing empty. So I was in constant doubt, continually asking him to reel back in to check and double check.

In April, the peaks of the higher mountains to the west were the first to be lit by the sun, their granite faces pale in the early light. On Buda's side of the divided city, Sun Hill fell sharply to the Danube, and János Mountain, ranging west to the upper peaks, was covered by heath and scrub, dead dry for years. The conical peaks, blighted with fungus, discolored the leaf-green April.

It was still before nine, and I had already bravely taken the early trolley out alone. On the banks of the river, I amused myself with my makeshift fishing pole, hardly more than a stick with a thread. I had just changed to using this contraption as a flag, waving it about, when József made his way through the reeds to join me on the boulder. The sun quickly warmed the morning, and József's forehead was beading sweat.

"My favorite, you are the first to see me in this thing." He was covering his chest. I saw a yellow star beneath his hand.

"It's been brewing unbelievable two weeks, these many decrees." He removed his hand, and I saw the six-pointed star.

The usual glint in his eyes was gone. "How could I fish on a day like this, tell me?" he moaned. "But I wanted to see you." Though not quite forty, he smacked his lips like an old man, slurring his words. "They say we won't be able to drive cars or even ride the trolley."

He was wearing a thin jacket, stark black, more like a vest, since the sleeves were torn away. I saw the bright star in bold yellow sewn on his chest.

"What's that thing?"

"Law 1.240."

I continued to gaze at the star. How do numbers mean that? I wondered. And then I recalled that József used to bring his torn shirts around to Mother. He did not know how to sew.

"Who sewed that on?" I asked.

"The super's wife. Said the super told her to. 'It was I to do it, or he,' she said."

The neatly sewn yellow felt stood out against the black vest.

"She was quite eager, really, licking at the thread," he continued. "She objected when I said that my understanding of Law 1.240 was that I had to do it myself."

"But why are you wearing that star, József?" I asked.

"She kept arguing, 'What would a little one do, say someone five or six years old,' she argued. 'The law makes no sense. Ten centimeters by ten centimeters exactly, and six pointed at that. That's no easy work,' she went on, quite eager." József ignored me completely, caught up in the memories of the early day. "And she did a good job." His nostrils disappeared as he turned his head to look down at me. "Look, Pisti. Double stitches and all."

"But what's the star for?" I finally raised my voice.

"My grandmother from Zalavég was Jewish and I was not baptized. Records show these things, somehow or other," he said. "Maybe from your grandfather, the bookkeeper for the lot of us. The viper tongue."

"You mean Father's father?" I was puzzled. "He's down by the plains."

"No matter. Everybody will get it."

"Get what?"

"Ah, never mind. It's nothing for you to bother with."

He sat next to me on the sunny boulder. "At least you now know who I am, Pisti. Have a good look."

My unease grew.

"I'm Uncle József. You never did know I was Jewish."

"But you're *not* Jewish," I said. "You go to church."

"Pisti, this is the marking." He put an arm around my shoulders and whispered as if telling a secret. "The city is cordoned. They've already arrested three thousand trying to flee. Just a week ago, Decree 1.140 deprived us of owning phones. The first step is isolation, and now the second step, marking. Understand?"

I did not. There was much I could not understand. Why did Father have to get sick to stay out of the war? Why had Major Király rejected us? And now I pondered the star. What did it have to do with phones or riding the trolley? I stood mute, as an angel witnesses death, and shook my head.

József did not respond to my confusion.

But before I could ask, he turned abruptly and spit out, "*Ez a Messiás? Mondom, ez a nagy semmiség.* Is this our vision? Nothingness, I tell you."

Given his bitterness, it surprised me when he picked up his pole and cast. He fished with a plug now, which was heavy and carried out nearly thirty meters. A gust caught his painted lure and sent the line arching downwind. He grew quiet. He sat squatting over the pole, his shoulders hunched and sagging, as though even now he were carrying used crates to his dwelling.

"Why are you fishing?"

"Your father can't help us," he brooded, deaf to my questions. "He's put me in the hospital twice. Saved me from the front, from being shipped out. The fascists did not want sick Jews then, especially in work battalions. Now they're even searching *him*."

"But why you? You haven't said." My questions grew increasingly feeble.

"Now they want everybody, young, sick. Any small part Jewish."

József was a distant relative, a close friend of the family. He went to mass every Sunday with Mother. How could he be Jewish?

I recalled then how Apu, as a medical officer for the ghetto, had admitted József "for emergencies" to St. István Hospital, where he had rights of admission as a private physician. "This gives József time," I recalled Apu saying. "Nowadays time is not money, it can mean life." Even as I denied József's direct statement earlier about his Jewish identity, an unformed awareness grew from my memories, just as the light of late day all red and gold spills toward night.

This day József got a bite quickly, gave a flick of his wrist, and set the hook. With a turn of the mind, he became absorbed in the moment, in fishing. The bamboo pole bent sharply. A huge carp, at least three kilos, broke the smooth water. As it jumped and struggled in the air, its yellow belly caught the sun. József played the fish, and in a short while the carp surfaced near shore. He grew frenzied, far more excited than usual. He pleaded for me to get the net. Agitated, he grabbed the line, pulling hand over hand, as though this provided some solution.

"The reel is working," I said. "Use the reel. You'll lose the fish."

But he paid no heed, and like some primitive fisherman he kept pulling the line by hand.

"I thought I told you to get the net," he snapped. "Get the net, Pisti, in the name of God." He was pulling the line by hand and cursing. "Don't be a dolt. What if we lose the fish? Dear God! Help us not lose the fish."

Finally, by raising the line well over his head, he brought the carp onto the rock, and then, at once, ran to the flopping fish near the water's edge, pinning it with one hand.

Deftly balanced on a foot, he raised his heel and let it fall with an awful force.

"This small blessing won't get away." His speech was slurred.

Heel meeting flesh, a dull tearing. A marble-sized yellow fish eye slid out from under his boot, smooth as glass from Araby. Yet the fish kept writhing, hungry for life. As blood leaked from the empty socket, its lips bit at the air.

József let his foot fall again.

He picked up the eye and threw it into the bucket with the rest of the fish. "It'll be good in the soup," he laughed freely. "Hear that! Cholent, and then gefilte fish. Hear that! At least three kilos." He pulled at his beard, laughing, and left several nickel-colored scales by his chin.

Finally slumping, he wept in sudden release. He covered his face with his wet and soiled hands, sobbing. "For your Anyu, it will be all right. It is likely that 1.450 will follow in a day or two. For her it will be all right. She's married to your father."

I was gripped by a sudden desire to run away. To do something. Perhaps rip my clothes off. But all I could do was rock from foot to foot, overheated with what I felt must surely be a fever. Confused and uncomfortable, I focused my concern on József. "Why don't you take your vest off, József?" Even then, I was far better at caring for others. "You're sweating," I added.

"It's against the law." As he said this, his sadness turned. Passing through a range of emotion, he stopped weeping and began to laugh. "Sweltering," he laughed. "And it's against the law." He stopped then, again as quick, and grew quiet, panting.

Just as suddenly, he was somber and melancholy.

"My favorite. You must know everything. Be the winner, Pisti. Study! And study hard." His eyes drifted, as though loose in their sockets. "I tried. Beside the farm, even tried writing . . . you know that. You have my books on trees, flowers, even leaves according to shape, as though everything were important." He shook his head. "Books on leaves, good God, imagine. And just look at these April leaves." He cast his eyes across the river. "Milk green."

Then his gaze cut my face. "But you, you will not fail, Pisti, will you?" He put his hands to my shoulders. "You will have everything." His hands weighed heavily, an irrevocable burden. "You will have all. Wealth and fame. All that you desire."

"Am I Jewish, like you?" was all I asked.

His face fell flat. "It goes by the mother for the Jew."

* * *

Following the river, the trail home passed a cliff where a female osprey nested on a ledge against the gray stone surface. The male circled near the cliff in long loops, its movements deliberate. The African winds had brought a high pressure system, humid and enveloping, which heated our climb up the slope to the road. Threatening clouds darkened on the horizon. The osprey disappeared. I looked for its wings, both north and east, but it was gone. The female had vanished as well.

As we approached the main thoroughfare, people were already running for cover. They huddled under awnings and grouped in the shelter of doorways. In the dirty light, József's jacket melded with the drab color of Pest. But the Star of David, so neatly sewn on some, merely dangling on others, glowed brightly in the crowd.

I saw a star run by, then another and another, fireflies signaling with quick yellow flashes at dusk. Running for shelter under some tree or huddling against a building where the lintel protruded, giving protection. It had begun to spit. They were running for shelter. They stood huddled in masses, already waiting and lined against the walls. Then the cold northern winds cut the body of heat from the south and the sky exploded in lightning and downpour.

We hurried through the city. The driving rain pelted the boulevard, and the wind blew strong. The gutters overflowed, and we waded through pools at every corner. Soaked, we finally entered the apartment, József's bucket, heavy with the fish, swinging to and fro. Hearing voices from the examination room in the back, József pushed the door open.

I saw a brightness. Most of my relatives were wearing stars.

Gizella and Rózsi, Cili and Eszter, all great-aunts, the Rózsi I used to call Tanta Rózsika, and Kálmán, my uncle with the homing pigeons, and his wife Ibolya. Even Pityu, my friend, Kálmán's bright-haired son, wore a small shirt with a star that covered most of his chest. They had arrived in the city only recently. Varga, a shepherd from the plains, had arrived that day. The room was lost in turmoil, the uproar of voices, commotion, and Pityu's wailing.

There was much talk of what to do and more of what could no longer be done. The stars seemed a patchwork of color, appearing and reappearing as the adults walked about. I sat in the corner, unraveling father's surgical tape and casting glances toward my parents. Pityu tugged at his shirt.

Anyu, draped in a lace shawl, sat by the window in the oak rocker.

"Rózsi and Gizella can stay in the nunnery," Apu said. "I showed the mother superior the letter from Archbishop Spellman of the Archdiocese of New York."

Then I saw, just as suddenly, that our family stood out from the others. Angi wore her pink ruffled dress and stroked her Korean doll with the bone face. Apu was dressed in a summer suit with his watch chain looping across his stomach. And I was in my sailor outfit, soaked through and clinging to my flesh.

Rózsi and Gizella were muttering to Father, their gray top-knots undone, layers of hair hanging in shreds from their heads.

Kálmán stood. "And I can use the travel papers with Ibolya and Pityu, don't you think?" He cast about for some response. "The Yugoslavian border is still a possibility if we can get out of the city," he continued with forced confidence. Ibolya sat next to him and tried to embrace his massive torso, but her arms could not encircle him. It was as though she were hugging a big tree.

"It would be helpful, Kálmán, if you took my uniform," Father said.

"Kind and generous. How will I fit into it?"

"That's the least worry. How about willpower." Apu's laughter was awkward.

My thoughts raced in confusion. No one in my immediate family was wearing a star.

My mother then spoke without turning. "Katalin sent word about Jenő. The note was delayed a month, and Utci just brought it today." Katalin was mother's cousin in Canada, and Jenő was Katalin's nephew. Utci was the clerk in Anyu's old sweetshop before she lost the business.

"For God's sake," my father snapped. "Don't you think we're risking enough with so many relatives? He'll stand out. He's well known."

The word *vérrokon*—blood relation—buzzed in my ear. Amid the urgency and confusion of the room, it rang clearly.

"He is only sixteen. And both his parents have been taken already."

"So what am I supposed to do? I'm assigned to the ghetto, but other physicians are of help there as well. I can't do more, I'm sorry."

"He is the lead apprentice in the National Opera. And Katalin said they would care for him," Anyu persisted. "He's got a life, maybe a good one."

"It would be foolish, even dangerous. A celebrity of all things."

Anyu fell silent.

In the light of the waning day, her white shawl fought off the darkness. She looked into the rain, across the square and down to the Millennial Monument. She had stopped listening.

Kálmán lit the table lamp with the blue tinted shades. The stars were suddenly illumined. Mother's smooth silk shawl, still set apart, now looked darker and as textured as wool.

No one spoke of József, I realized. He sat on the floor by Pityu, calming the boy. "It's nothing to be afraid of," he said, stroking Pityu's hair.

The lamp gave little light. In the murkiness, the Stars of David paced back and forth, leaf green. Anyu, ghostlike, rocked back and forth by the window, as though patient and waiting.

I went up to her and I knelt before her, my clothes stifling. Thick odors rose in the closed room. The tepid rain failed to cool the city. When I looked up at her, Mother's shoulders were hunched, as though carrying the same weight I had seen on József by the river.

"Am I Jewish?" I asked. "Will we wear stars, too?"

I wanted her to say it, to say we were Jewish, to lift some burden from my own back. Perhaps the same burden that curved her own spine or weighed down on József.

She looked at me, startled, a quick frown forced back into a smile. "Never were we Jewish, Pisti, my sweet." Her smile was distant. "There's no trace of it in our blood."

"But these are our relatives."

"No. No. Don't say that. They're friends," she chided. "Don't we go to church, take communion? Don't we all—Apu, me, you, Angi?"

From her twisted smile, a mask lifted, and I gazed into the depth of her fear, an abyss that could swallow worlds. I knew at once she was frightened not for herself but mainly for me. Still, I thought, *Anyám fia vagyok*—I am my mother's son.

"József took communion, didn't he," I declared. "And now he's wearing a star."

I felt the unrelenting press within me to hear her say it. "You are my mother," I continued. "You are my mother."

"Yes, I am, my dear."

"And it goes by the mother for the Jew." I repeated by rote what József had said earlier on the river's edge, having little understanding of what it meant.

Her eyes burned. A fat vein rose on her forehead. Rocking forward, she grabbed the skin at the side of my neck, pulling it taut and yanking me to her lap. "Don't you dare ever say that," she shouted. "Not in school, not with neighbors, nor friends, no one." She was writhing. "Tell them the truth. You're Catholic, you hear. *Katolikus!* As I am."

Suddenly standing, she forced me to slump back onto my knees. She rushed about the assembly, which had stood mute witness to my conversion.

"Danger in shame!" she shouted. She pulled at Eszter's star, ripping it off in a sweep, and then snatched at Rózsi's and tore at Gizella's. "There is danger in shame," she sobbed. "*Shahnda.*"

I started on hearing the word. And I suddenly saw myself from some distance, kneeling as in prayer. A Yiddish word, I knew that much. I rubbed my neck. I heard again. *Shahnda*. The shame. The shameful.

Hallowed the Profane
The Third and Second Anti-Jewish Laws
2 augusztus 1941
4 május 1939

I remained preoccupied for days after I saw my relatives wearing the star. Why had my questions haunted Anyu so, to the point of evoking cruelty? As my mind recreated the scene, I felt a continual chafing in my chest and was constantly coughing, as though a fish bone had caught in my throat.

The city was truly cordoned, the star-marked Jews could not ride the trolleys, and enormous yellow stars painted on the facades isolated the Jewish buildings. The thin, yellow paint usually ran, streaking the walls, so that the symbols only remotely resembled stars. After a while, the Arrow Cross, the Hungarian ultra-fascists who favored the Nazis, abandoned any concern for aesthetics and merely threw the paint onto the walls, calling the buildings *Sárga Házak*, the Yellow Houses. Anyu quipped that the people were reduced to isolation and then marked with the weakest of colors, canary yellow. They were lured to genocide just as the fox outwitted the songbird. "The buildings are not as neatly done up as the stitchings," she repeated over and over.

It is only now I know that there was really no cleverness to the Nazi's systematic work. It was just logic and method, cold and calculated—the loud and self-assured voice on behalf of those pained, the mass propaganda and the mass psychology that presaged media not as mere message, but as the unrelenting tool of genocide.

Jews were not sheep led to slaughter. Their resistance remains a miracle that broke from the laws of large groups, where some small minority is cast as scapegoat and still resists and fights back, even if only in a cry from the street. And there was much more than a cry from the street. It was a time then also when silence meant death, and while many remained silent, many others acted for good.

Since no one could travel, the families remained put. And they remained separated from one another. It was an irony that made Father laugh, in fact actually *röhög*, the belly laugh common in Eastern Europe that cleanses the conquered of rancor and lifts them above despair, above the conqueror. I suppose it kept him from weeping helplessly—*böhög*, "to weep," a similar word. Apu would mutter to himself, "Remain put and be dispersed," as though rethinking some well-worn joke. Or he would laugh at a fragment of thought: "Hurry, hurry and wait and wait—those damned long lines for bread, just like mealtime in the army." I never understood his meaning, let alone the sudden bursts of anxiety-laden laughter that followed his words.

Within a week after the stars appeared, Apu's father came to visit. Old Man Boszor. We called him that behind his back because none of us liked this blacksmith with the wizened and raw hands. Angi and I had given him the nickname because it had a lewd ring to it.

One Thursday evening he knocked and entered our kitchen. Earlier, I had returned with two black bass and was now gutting and scaling them onto newspaper.

Mother was taken aback when he entered. "Why, Pisti, it's Grandfather." She pushed me toward his looming frame in the doorway, silhouetted against the hall lights. "Give Grandpapa a kiss hello." I felt awkward since she herself had not yet greeted him.

"Where's that son of mine?" Boszor did not greet her either. His back hunched and he wheezed through a gnarled nose, inhaling heavily as though he were starving for breath. When he exhaled, it was equally labored, and a thin stream of saliva ebbed and flowed across his lips.

"In the office," Anyu said, motioning.

"I'll greet him good then." He tipped his worn hat. "Now excuse me."

Anyu began pacing as soon as the old man had closed the door. "He's going to mock me, I'm sure. Maybe bring up Adám again. And complain to Apu of Angi not being his own daughter." In fact, the strain between Apu and my sister Angi had only recently begun to ease. I had grown accustomed to her cornering me in the back room and pummeling me with awful stories of real and imagined cruelties he had inflicted on her before I was born.

Apu, *my* Apu, had been heavily in debt after a prolonged education that was largely financed through loans. He had supported himself by tutoring, and in wealthier homes he was also given food in addition to his fee. Grandfather Boszor had been of no help to him. The old man practiced his rough trade in a hamlet on the plains. He had been a school teacher in his youth, but found the pay poor and the work demeaning. "My doctor tells me repeatedly: 'If you can't do anything else, well then, go teach,'" he quoted his physician from the plains. This venerated authority, Dr. Sándor Radó, was the only prodigy of Freud who had established a practice in the hinterlands of Hungary. He was known by the local peasants as "the healer of poor folk."

Grandfather had taken part in the Pogrom of Kisszeged during the White Terror of 1919. Boszor went as far as to brag about his exploits. "It's because of Béla Kun that Hungary drinks anti-Semitism even from mother's milk," he often repeated, and he was quick to point out the many historians down the years who agreed with him.

"We went into Kisszeged with pitchforks, and hoes, and whatever else," he went on loudly in front of Anyu after he returned to the kitchen. She had already heard the tale, and he knew it.

"The town emptied in short order." Mother stomped from the room, muttering and flushed, her hands clenched, and left me alone with the withered heathen.

Boszor had initially opposed any possible marriage of his son, especially to a *meshumed*.

"A *meshumed*, of all things, bleached from Jew to Gentile," he cursed Apu again.

"You fool," he kept at Apu. "Do you know what that means in their tongue? A turncoat, a troublemaker, whatever else. Not one good word can be said of such an apostate." He looked in my direction as I stood in the middle of the kitchen floor. I did not dare look directly at him, but I could see his reflection in the puddled water left from Mother's abandoned mopping. The bright red face of the devil himself, I imagined.

Before I had a chance to blurt out my question about the new word, Apu grabbed the old man by the arm and thrust him into the examining room, slamming the door shut. They yelled at each other for what seemed an hour, until they both grew hoarse and weary.

When the old man came out, his red face sagging, he held a hundred-pengö note clasped to his chest. Looking at his feet waddling below him, he muttered, "Son of mine. My, mine."

Apu followed him out, his shirt soaked through, walking in much the same way as the old man, his feet pointing outward. His beige summer suit was no longer crisp, and his straight dark hair hung to the side. Anyu came to him, and they embraced. "It's just a bribe, you know," she said. "He'll be back."

Anyu wanted Angi to call Father Apu, a term of affection, even before he moved in. This had upset Angi greatly, and she had always complained to me about it. She even told me long stories of having to sit on his lap just to please Mother, or of having to cook him breakfast while Anyu was pregnant with me, things even

I couldn't do as a child. "As though my own father, Adám, had never existed," she fumed as she trapped me in a corner.

Family folklore had it that Adám immigrated to America in 1937 to escape the war. He was one of those who had foresight, but why he left everyone behind remained a mystery. It was hard for Angi to understand his disappearance. She was only three years old at the time, and Adám simply announced his intention to leave one morning over breakfast, as though he were merely going on an outing. They had eaten a full breakfast of yellow pepper and cheeses; gulping his tea, he had packed off before the bells tolled noon. Angi believed for some time that he had merely gone shopping. When she first started telling me the story, which seemed as long ago as I could remember, perhaps even before I could understand speech and lay in my crib with closed eyes, she still believed it, I think.

"And will he ever return?" I used to ask, wondering at the confusion two fathers would bring to our household.

"The Man," as Angi now referred to her vanished father, lived somewhere in Florida. My Uncle Ervin, who had moved to the Adirondack Mountains of New York to live the dignified life of a country doctor, had traced him there. After finishing medical school in Padua during the days of *Numerus Nullus*, the anti-Semitic quotas of the 1920s, Ervin had made contact with Adám in New York. *Numerus Nullus* barred most Jews from advanced degrees.

Ervin had traced "The Man" to Florida when Anyu was about to remarry in early 1939. There was need for some urgency. She was already pregnant with me, well into her second trimester. But what mattered more were the required annulment papers that Adám had to sign in front of a priest. The papers gave consideration to conditions concerning my religious upbringing as well. At the time, Church decrees were to be honored, more so than any civil decrees, because religion had come to mean race. Ervin was enlisted on the first count, to get Adám to sign. Later, his role would be extended, much to his sorrow, to include raising my sister and myself as not only refugees in a new land but also as aliens in his own Jewish home. Apu had made him promise to raise us as Catholics. The era of our own One-House had not yet come.

Ervin finally flew Adám up to New York to meet with Church officials, and he, himself, served as witness to Anyu's signature. Although she lived three thousand miles away, Ervin swore he could recognize his sister's signature. "I taught her to write long-hand," he asserted. "Weaned her from printing when she was just in first grade."

Archbishop Spellman was the one to sign the papers. The letterhead of the Archdiocese of New York signed by the arch-bishop proved invaluable during the war. No one could read the English, except for the headings, the signature, and the title, but those were a source of great entitlement by which relatives were placed in nunneries and protected from persecution. In the end, "The Man" proved a blessing even in his absence, and had, in a way, truly "returned" to bless Angi.

Angi took her time talking to Apu. "A starched, very impor-tant man with a handkerchief in his pocket, the ends folding over even like a tongue, and his necktie with that strange knot." She went on endlessly as though she were dressing some imaginary doll for a formal dance. "This man whom Anyu brought home from Péterfi Hospital one day, six months before you were born, took me by surprise and I knew at once he could never be a real father, my *real* Apu. Not for me anyway," Angi droned. She had avowed a faith that her real father would return someday.

Yet Apu, my Apu, *my* Apu first and *our* Apu second, had a gentle way, as when we went to the gardens and he bent over each flower. Angi recalled how she was won over by him slowly during the course of a year, as the two of them took turns pushing my stroller in the park on Sunday afternoons, pretending Angi was my mother. "What a good Mommy you'll make," she recalled Apu praising her as she wiped my drool. He brought her a helium balloon and raspberry sherbet or pink cotton candy on each outing. Slowly she started calling him Apu with less prompting.

The unending thirst Apu and Anyu felt for each other frightened my sister at first. I understood Angi's complaints about him well, because I also reacted to Apu's impish ways. I grew jealous whenever he ran into the kitchen, grabbed Anyu away, and pretended to bite her neck, "Gobble. Gobble." I felt this way even after I became aware that he was playing. But Anyu loved Apu as she wanted. Anyu cared for him because he cared for her.

It was a supportive relationship, and they balanced each other. Even though Apu was a recent graduate of the University of Debrecen and heavily in debt, Anyu knew how to add a penny to a pence, or fillér to pengö. And much later, when Father was about to be court-martialed for sending Angi and myself out of the country during the revolution of 1956, I learned that they had role-played the trial late into the night for three days straight. At critical points in their fabricated cross-questioning, Apu practiced blaming Mother. He held that his position as a breadwinner was more important, and she had a reputation for hysteria that would account for many sins, including hysterically sending her children G–d knows where—if not to a land of bounty, then perhaps to a netherland that in her woman's mind was a step up from Magyar soil, can one imagine, a step up from the motherland. "What can one do with a wife like that?" Apu argued, and the Magyar judges understood him well.

That night, five days after the star decree, Boszor decided to spend the weekend with us. It was an especially tense few days for Anyu. After expressing admiration for Apu, his son, the old man had gone out, shuffling down the corridor as I looked after him through the door he had left ajar. When he returned, he could not open the warped door. As he banged on it, I knew he was tipsy.

He seemed to taunt Mother intentionally, actually bragging about his exploits. "It's because of Béla Kun that Hungary drinks anti-Semitism even from mother's milk," he blurted out.

Angi and I exchanged anxious glances. Boszor looked bleary-eyed, and tiny veins pocked his nose.

"You shouldn't have wasted the money," Apu told him. "We have plenty of wine."

"But not vodka."

Boszor looked toward the kitchen. "A *meshumed*, of all things, bleached from Jew to Gentile." He cursed Apu again, this time over our dinner of fried fish.

That Friday dinner, Anyu refused to eat with us. After Apu had said grace—"Bless us O Lord for these thine gifts"—she returned to the kitchen. "You fool," Boszor went on, even more belligerent in Mother's absence. "Do you know what that means in their tongue—a turncoat, a troublemaker, whatever else. Not one good word can be said of such an apostate."

I did not know then the difference between *meshumed* and *Marrano*, but I am certain now that Boszor would have preferred mother to be *Marrano*, simply so that she should suffer. And she would suffer in the name of Boszor's sweet Savior, a Savior not of the cross, the cross as Apu described it where Christ taught humankind to surrender. It would have been a twisted cross, a broken cross, a fitting symbol for warriors of aberrance, not humanity; like those of the Arrow Cross, with their cross of arrows, or the Nazis with their swastika—a broken mandala of hopelessness. Only with Anyu on the rack of his words, or on the torture wheel of his taunting, the blinding rod waving before her eyes, could Boszor rest. As a tortured *Marrano*, Anyu would have perhaps only then ceased to be a threat to Boszor.

The following day, Saturday, Anyu woke early and was nervous all morning. The old man had announced loudly the night before his intention to spend the weekend before returning to his hamlet on the Great Plains.

Before the war, Anyu had made a lavish display of her preparations for the Saturday meal. But now she just talked about it, so vivid in her descriptions that the Sabbath came to life. It was a most curious game she played, doing one thing and talking about another, a game that was not so much contradictory as extremely confusing. But as a child I think I understood it to be like the make-believe games I played—make-believe friends, and make-believe gifts, and make-believe tea parties. These tea ceremonies, I remember, were held under the waters of Lake Balaton in summertime. We would sit with our legs crossed and gently pour out the tea into make-believe cups and pass all the saucers around so that no one was without. As a child, a little boy, I thought it sissy to hold a tea party. The tea party was made more manly by being underwater so we had to hold our breath, letting bubbles out with each drink from the cup.

All morning I watched Anyu cook, and she kept shushing me even though I remained silent, as in a church. She blanched the loin of pork in a pan on our wood-burning stove and dipped it in flour and paprika and set it on the heat again.

"We used to grind the pike with onions from Ibolya's garden," she said, her untidy black hair falling across her forehead. Anyu brushed a strand away with the back of a hand. She cut away the excess fat from the loin of pork on the table, even as she spoke kosher: "We then boiled a broth with three more onions and the head, skin, and bones of the fish."

She spoke dreamily of those days, of her own mother's careful preparations, drifting in and out of her reverie. Sometimes she even talked with me as though I were in her past, cast as some distant figure she wanted to protect and educate. "Preparing itself was a ritual. For we prepare to greet the Messiah," she said often.

"What is the Messiah?" I asked, sitting on the stool by her feet. The soft light of the dining room was cupped in a blue lamp the shape of an orchid.

"The anointed one."

"What?"

"Anointed with oil, both head and feet."

"The way to prepare for the Messiah is how one lives daily," she continued. "But especially on the Sabbath." I could not imagine how the routines of my days—playing with my hoop, chasing after the orange glow glinting in the noon sun, or hiding under the rain barrel with my gypsy friend, Zsóka—could be so hallowed.

"Grandmother always had silken linens for the table, pure

white and smooth, no stains ever," she spoke from her reverie. "And the best flatware was used, only steel, but bright and polished."

"This is what is done if an honored guest is to arrive, isn't that so?" she quizzed.

"I remember how we prepare for Karácsonyapo, Father of Christmas," I lifted my brow in wonder at the memory of the Christmas tree lit with candles and decorated with white angels. Anyu leaned forward and mocked me, lifting her own brows and widening her eyes: "Oh, I am glad for your memories."

"I like Mikulás." I wanted to preserve him from the past.

"Yes, Santa," she continued. "Mikulás. Understand, Pisti, this is to prepare for the coming of the Lord. A world in peace. And this was how we prepared, by living out a little preparation each week. In fact, every day. Preparing makes things happen." Here her words struck me for the first time, for though she seemed perpetually to be preparing for something—dinner, or an outing— I never knew her to be preparing for peace. But I now know she was. Preparing as my inheritance an eternal rest.

As I recall her bent over the preparations for the meal, I now see how her bearing down, her exhortations would lead me to achieve, and overachieve, as I also prepared endlessly, ceaselessly for a tomorrow that was just beyond reach. And her image also helps me to understand why I never lived in the present, instead skipping the moment and the day and rushing from the past headlong into tomorrow. Which is another way of saying that I remained stuck in a perpetual past, all along like this, up until now, ép most, just now.

She turned the loin and sprinkled it with caraway seeds. "It is important to grind the fish well to get fluffy fish balls. At least twice." She sprinkled the sweet paprika onto the roast. "Three, if the blades are dull."

"We put on our finest clothes. I remember Ervin's first suit. Beige, a British cut."

"Your Grandmother Ilona, my mother, lit the white Sabbath

candle," Anyu added. "White as the linens. I remember everything as white, as though it had a glow to it. Always the candles had to be lit first. Mother always invited the light by brushes of the hand, and sometimes she brushed the light also in my direction. It was quite strange as I think of it. I actually felt a warmth covering me."

And then she drifted off, talking now to her past, as though she were really there. "His voice was soft and he spoke rapidly. Leo, you even asked me to cover the challah on my thirteenth birthday. And I lit the candles and said the Amen. Where did you go? Out of the land of Egypt, an exodus from us still in the land of Egypt." And then, to my alarm, she began sobbing, but she kept talking through her tears. The grease from the roast was popping and spraying, and a hot splatter from across the room hit my hands.

"It was evening and it was morning. Blessed art Thou, Lord our G–d, King of the Universe. When shall the Messiah come, dear G–d? It is still men who rule. And the haughtiness of man shall be humbled when? The cypress felled as the oak of Bashan, and the pride of men brought low. Men are hard chested and cannot live in their wounds."

She looked down at me through glistening eyes. And then she knelt before me, on both her knees as though praying. "You, sweet little one, are the salvation, G–d bless. You, our own Peacemaker. Bring comfort to my heart." She was weeping freely. "We waited for you long enough." Tears she did not wipe away wet her cheeks. "In your eyes alone I can see G–d."

"But what about Angi?" I was curious but fearful. I felt the burden of her words once again. What did it mean for me to be a peacemaker?

She had stopped crying. "Of course, in hers, too. But your eyes are darker. And I mirror in them."

I never thought that she might be looking at herself even as she gazed into my eyes. I felt her warmth, and the early day gained a glow.

* * *

Heavy knocking shook the door. Anyu ran into the parlor. I heard her talking with the super.

"Really, madame," the super said urgently. "They have threatened to paint the Star on the building unless the doctor sees no more Jewish patients in his office."

"The building is below the quota. It's still ten percent, yes?"

"That's what it's been for at least a month." The super stroked my hair gently as he spoke to Anyu.

"Well, tell them the patients don't live here."

"I already did."

She raised her voice in indignation. "Then do so again. What are laws for?" And she shut the door on the man.

She returned, heated with rage, drank some water, spilled the coffee grinds into the sink, and washed them away with a stir of her hand, muttering to herself. Finally she settled down to cooking again, which for her was a form of meditation. She finally sprinkled the black pepper onto the roast. "Not like days before the Flood, but for Viennese pork chops, it'll do."

I then saw myself with her back in the days before the flood, imagining it to mean the days before the war, a time before I was born. Her memories gained life as she conveyed them, lighting the candle and welcoming the light and inviting the light to enter her soul with sweeps of her hand, and on Saturday laying out the white linen cloth. I imagined watching her preparations for Saturday with fascination. First scaling the fish, gutting it smoothly, then breaking the eggs and getting out all of the whites with a finger. At last, mixing in the matzoh. I felt sure she would have let *me* drop the fish balls into the boiling stock. Why had she denied my Jewishness? Even the entire building was about to be condemned as yellow because of my parents, a nurse and a doctor treating the Yellow Stars, *Sárga Csillagok*.

"Why did you say that all those people here last week are not relatives, Anyu? Who are they?"

"They are dear friends. Almost as close as relatives."

"How are they different?"

She lifted the lid from the oven and I could see the glow of the cinders. "Your grandpapa, rest his soul, would get all dressed up, his red silk tie tucked behind his black vest, and he always gave the blessing." She threw in more tinder, ignoring my question. "It was not until I was a young woman, a few years older than Angi, that I joined in," she recalled, paying no attention to the pork sizzling before her, her voice hushed. "Let us inherit the day which shall be wholly a Sabbath, and let us inherit the day which is altogether good." Initially, my biting confusion was not tamed by the prayer, but it soon grew more quiet, and more still, and was finally at rest.

I picture the Saturday meals as a half dream, the image unclear and blurred, the special foods, the glow of the candles, the soft *niggunim*, a wordless chanting, grinding the fresh horseradish, the smell of herbs and sweet wine, the washing of hands, and falling unfalteringly toward a peaceful land of intimacy and rest. I pictured it, true, but never made the connection to the Sabbath.

Shabbat, our island in time that was washed away by history. G–d's bride in the billowing dress that made one digress, on walks and in talks, gently speaking in the soft light of Saturday morning, faded for us with the grinding of time.

After all, Apu was Catholic, and Angi and I went to church regularly, along with Mother, at least during the war. For our family, G–d's day of rest had moved to Sunday even before I was born. And after the war, G–d seemed to disappear completely. When the Stalinists took over in 1948, not only was my International Scout troop banned, but so was G–d. Many of the churches and synagogues became warehouses for surplus grain, an image for the proletarian youth: the factory was ours, the goods were ours, and G–d was mere chaff.

Even as a young child, I was already looking backward, rarely looking toward a tomorrow, as though I had no future. But memory can be the wellspring for renewal and return. And the more important part of memory is faith and belief, not fact.

Having experienced love, remembering it can become one way to affirm life. A friend can be a comfort, and a comforter can be a friend. But the teddy bear comes to imaginary life only to the degree it represents human warmth, the hug and embrace and the song of human beings as the lallation and lullabies my parents sang to me.

> Like celestial stalks of grain
> dawn's sparkle flies.
> Help me sunlight
> sing it plain
> your praises in refrain.

By remembering, my constant longing, which I never understood, eased somehow. It was as though part of my desire to belong could be eased by desire itself, a wish that came truly simply by wishing, even if hope proved fruitless.

Living by backward glances, without a tomorrow, I hardly needed self-definition. And I eventually realized that tomorrow was defined, at least in part, by hope, and that the daily preparation for the Sabbath was really a preparation not just for peaceful rest, but for peace itself. Perhaps one reason I hardly grew was that I lived without a tomorrow. My early years proved a training in hide-and-seek and hide-again, a peekaboo game where I could see no one, but where no one could see me either and I could feel safe somehow, cloistered. Much of my life became a game of imagining in which definition of self was left to myself. I was the pirate with my imaginary crew, the teacher with my own class, a tinker with a helper. In the absence of parents one comes to be parented by history, the mere flow of general events, and the streaming of people. But I eventually realized that tomorrow was defined by hope, and that the daily preparation for Sabbath was really a preparation not just for peaceful rest, but for peace itself.

A hope in tomorrow requires a surrendering to others, to all who are part of that world of tomorrow. But by the will to persist and the persistence of will, I wove memories of real and imagined kindness into a comforter of bright colors, fluffed full with down filling, Scandinavian down. Oti bought me toy cars. Sándor bought me colored marbles. And Grandmother always made me poppy noodles whenever I wanted, or even *díos tészta*, the nutted noodles, to satisfy my slightest whim.

My mind skipped along even as my body merely tottered. Language and thought, and very soon the ability to look at my own behavior—how I tied a shoe and which finger went under which or the way I kicked a ball with my toe and then with my heel—all came to me early. I finally became able to describe thought, and this skill became the knife that could carve a way through the Magyar wilderness. My body grew slowly, a sapling in the arid soil of war and a land constantly enslaved, but my mind quickly developed and overreached its bounds in an effort to make sense of the twisted world.

My limbs still retained baby fat and strangers took liberties in poking my belly. This would trouble me when I saw Angi growing into young adolescence while I remained puny even for five. Apu's explanation that I had an illness that could not be understood did not satisfy me.

I had a past at least, I knew that much. There had been the time when the peekaboo game began, a time when I, Pista, as they called me when I was a baby, played with Apu, who let me climb his back and who walked around like a horse, on all fours, and even neighed or pretended to be grazing. *"Kófboj! Kófboj!"* I cried out, riding him until he started bucking and I fell off.

I was not yet three then, and I recall Apu's joy when I made him laugh. I put marbles under the pillow and laughed wildly as they reappeared when I took it away.

Apu understood this game and would join in my play. But he would never actually hide. He just stood over me with an enchanted smile, then covered his face. When he revealed it again, it had changed completely to the downturned lips of a sad clown. And then back to the broad smile, then to sorrow again.

I stared up at him in wonder, too involved to laugh. I felt my forehead knot with worry, then ease again, mirroring Apu's changing face. He kept it up until my mouth was gaping and my lips drooled. Then I laughed in release, flailing with my arms. I felt sure I understood something but did not know what. It was not for many months that I learned the game was called peekaboo, and when I wanted to play it I said, "A-boo. A-boo," which sounded like "Apu." The first lessons in hide-and-seek were adventurous, and I repeated them with joy.

The ragged piece of cloth that I dragged around was also a topic in the family, till today. I used to call it Tanta after my great-aunt, Tanta Rózsika, Aunt Rose. The blanket eventually wore out, reduced from comforter to cloth to rag. But the comforter I wove from imagination, a quilt with many colors, endured always, even today. Even now.

When all that remained of Tanta was mere threads, I still would not part with it and tied it around a stick. Other than using it as a flag, I often sat on the cabinet near the dining table waiting and fishing with the strings until Anyu came out with the Saturday meal. She would laugh as she put the platter on the table: "My fisherboy, eat the real thing."

Mother told of when she and Apu were courting, during days before the flood. Apu would kiss her hands as she swept the light of the flames before his eyes. "Praises to you, my one and only," she recalled him cooing. And when Anyu told of their meeting, I knew that the larger part of devotion was to life with people, a life here and now. They met in the countryside by Lake Balaton one August weekend. The stars streaked the horizon, peppering consciousness, and they lay for hours in the dark in a field of alfalfa that was in bloom and hardly spoke and mostly breathed in the country air.

Now Apu, too, denied Sabbath. But this Saturday, his anger having healed and his heart softened like Pharaoh's, even though Anyu refused to eat with us and sat alone in the kitchen, Apu actually invited his father to read from the Bible during the meal. Boszor waved him off. Apu then instructed Angi and me from the Old Testament and read to us from Genesis. As he read, Boszor gave him little peace. We were prepared for the quizzing from Apu, but Apu had not anticipated Boszor. "What are you reading there?" Boszor quipped. "The Good Book? The Old Mumbo Jumbo?"

Apu ignored him. "Birds according to their kind, animals according to their kind, of every creeping thing according to its kind." He looked over his spectacles. We waited.

"Now what does that mean?"

"Animals and birds are different," Angi snapped in reply.

I raised my hand, grunting eagerly as though in my nursery, anxious to outdo my sister. I imagined Apu pleased by my effort. Unable to wait, I blurted out my observation: "Animals and birds are really the same."

In making my point, I leaned well into the table and knocked over a glass of water. I pretended nothing had happened, quickly threw my napkin over the puddle, and went on, "I mean, they all live outdoors. But an animal or bird isn't creeping and crawling like any lizard. A bird doesn't creep on the ground."

"In the name of the Heavenly Father!" Boszor blurted. "Look at the table."

Apu took off his glasses and scowled. "For crying out loud, Pisti, quit blithering. You've soaked all the linen. Now get the sponge."

I was crushed. Not only had I failed to please him, I had also made a fool of myself.

Angi took advantage. "Nya, nya, nya," she chanted, her emphasis falling on the third note as though she were singing a peasant song with a pentatonic melody.

"Get the sponge!"

By the time I returned, Boszor had apparently changed his mind about refusing to read. His voice cawed and crowed from Revelation like the cry of the osprey on the road to Szigliget, flying so low its yellow eyes glowed in the dusk. I tried to ignore his gaze and fixed my eyes on the circular sweep of my hand as I sponged the table.

> The stars of the sky fell to the earth as the fig tree sheds its winter fruit. . . . After this I saw four angels standing at the four corners of the world, holding back the four winds of the earth. And I heard the number of the sealed: out of every tribe of the sons of Israel, twelve thousand sealed out of the tribe of Judah, twelve thousand from Reuben, twelve thousand of the tribe of Gad. . . . And when they have finished their testimony, the beast that ascends from the bottomless pit will make war upon them, and conquer them and kill them. And those who dwell on earth shall rejoice over them and make merry and exchange presents, because these prophets had been a torment to those who dwell on the earth.

Boszor then turned to Angi and me. "Now what does that say?"

We were speechless. What a horrid thought, people being destroyed by beasts. I grew increasingly anxious as Boszor kept prodding: "Now tell me who that story is about. Tell me that, will you." Angi started playing with the silverware, moving it about and replacing it. "Tell me the meaning there!"

"Father, Father, calm down," Apu consoled the old man. Then he winked at us, "Is jus de mumbo jumbo in de mid'dull ov de jongle."

That broke the tension, and Angi and I laughed wildly, relieved of the awful picture Boszor had painted.

Still, toward the end of the meal, the happy, full feeling would not come and I could not rest. Apu looked over, smiling. "Your answer was really quite good, Pisti. It *was* a matter of things being the same. All creatures are one to God." He continued smiling, and finally respite came and I dozed off on the sofa.

*   *   *

Apu was a good father to me. He taught me about the saints and about history. He took me to the castle in the park on Sunday afternoons after church. The castle was built in a Gothic style, as was Our Lady's Church, which after the war we attended only twice a year, at Easter and Christmas. During those holidays, the national anthem, Kölcsey's march, could be sung for what it was, a sad lament that filled one with longing for a peaceable time when the nation would be delivered to G–d's graces. At soccer matches, and at all sporting events, such as the ones on May Day or at the celebration of the country's liberation by Stalin, the song was double-timed, almost as quick as the mambo.

Apu explained how the many straight lines in the facade of the castle reached upward, to heaven. "The building sanctifies God, as the Eucharist sanctifies your soul," he repeatedly explained, as though I could understand him. But when he told me that the building reached upward like a hand clasped in prayer, I could see what he meant. He had taught me the Lord's Prayer, *Mi Apánk*, with the same close attention to detail with which he described the workings of the medieval weaponry and jeweled armor at the castle.

He worried about my stunted growth and purchased quantities of milk, hoping I would grow. He examined me, checked my blood, gave me iron supplements. He marked my growth with a pencil line near the door as I tried to stand tall. He measured the circumference of my waist, my chest, my head. "You're growing, all right," he tried to reassure me. But invariably, month after month, the point fell on the same spot, darkening the line that measured my height at ninety-nine centimeters.

Finally, his expertise exhausted, he threw up his hands and accepted me as a little boy.

"*Frász* is what you have, Pisti. Put simply, the *frász*."

"What is that?"

"Well, it's exactly 'nothing.' The *frász*."

"What do you mean?"

"It could be anything. But probably it's nothing."

"But what's that?" my curiosity raced, wanting a cure for my puny stature.

"No one knows. *Frász* is 'what the heck.' Or 'something or other.' Just *frász*. Don't you know what *frász* means?"

I realized then and there that I could never be a doctor. There was just too much I didn't know and couldn't learn. Not only did I not know what *frász* meant, but I couldn't see how a doctor could responsibly give a diagnosis of "what the heck."

This upset me because I admired Apu and had recently come to think of him as truly my Apu, more so than Angi's. I wanted in every way to be like him. With Apu I belonged.

But even at the age of five I knew that such reasoning about my stunted growth would be as unfathomable as the resurrection of Christ, another mystery Apu held true. Of course, he explained that we needed faith for such understandings, but I never could believe that dead people would rise.

I quizzed him endlessly. Would they just dig their way out of their graves or float up, neat and intact? Would *all* the dead rise? And why shouldn't animals also return from the dead? This last point irritated him. After a season of eating the liver and the crackling, could the slaughtered goose ever revive?

Apu simply smiled down at me as I raised these many objections. "You will see when you gain faith."

But I never did. All I knew was that I was a tiny child, smaller than any peer, and thought myself puny. People kept commenting that my head had outgrown my body, wondering aloud, "Can it be?" They came over, taking hold of my face, and holding me up like a cantaloupe, looking me over. "It's hard to say," they mused. "He looks proportional." I grew glum in these memories, and Apu mistook my downcast expression for bewilderment.

"Don't be confused, Pisti. These are weighty matters. It's just *frász*," he continued to clarify. "It's for sure you have caught 'who knows what.' "

In fact, I soon learned, many people in the city understood the term well and simply accepted that *frász* could even be fatal, especially for illnesses with complications. And in certain of the medical specialties, it was the most common diagnosis given.

It had been soon after the Second Anti-Jewish Law, 4 május 1939, just before I was born, that Anyu began to prepare the Saturday meals "in secret." This meant that she kept Sabbath in mind and played her preparation game but rarely spoke about it directly. For her, as for me, Sabbath came before the flood. She read from *Népszava*, the People's Voice, the detailed definition of "the Jew." On that Saturday, when Apu's father ate with us, Anyu looked down at me as I sat on the kitchen floor with my wooden trucks and said, "Religion became race."

"What does 'race' mean, Anyu?" I asked, rolling the cars along.

"I still don't know."

"Does it have to do with the star?"

Having drained the fat from the pan for the pork and set it in the pantry to cool, she was scouring the burnt grizzle at the bottom. "I suppose so."

"Does that mean we are somehow different? That you and József are not the same sort of person?"

"Pisti, don't torment me."

"I want to know."

"Cut it out. Right now."

"No. No."

"Why do you put thorns into my heart even death cannot remove?"

As on that weekend following the star decree, we still had meat for Saturday lunch, but it was cold, usually tongue, beef salami, yellow pepper, and poultry and pork crackling with salt— traditional Magyar fare that Anyu ate also. I did not know that she had kept a kosher kitchen before my birth. All I knew was that we had an overabundance of dishes and silverware, many more than I saw while visiting neighbors with Anyu. I enjoyed visiting our neighbor, Kati Néni, on the floor above us, because I was just learning to skip stairs, my reach barely clearing two steps, and experienced the strenuous climb upstairs as an achievement.

"Imagine, in these lean times," Kati Néni once said to Mother. "Your kitchen is overflowing. Like you had double the rest of us." Anyu laughed nervously. "Had I only inherited money, even some pengö, dear Kati. But linens and silverware may bless me enough." At the time, I did not know that she was lying.

I also heard the story around our apartment about her younger brother, Miklós, who had disappeared one day a year earlier and could not be found. In the evenings, as I was falling asleep, I could usually hear my parents in the living room, as Anyu and Apu talked into the night. Mother's hopes for Miklós slowly faded. Then before Yom Kippur, she received an announcement from the temple near us, the Central Synagogue, asking the grieving for the names of their lost to be placed in the Book of Remembrance. "At *Yizkor* the names are memorialized," the sheet read.

She had run down the hall in her robe.

"Zsuzsi, Zsuzsikám," she yelled for her neighbor, rattling the old woman's door. "Did any of your relatives die this year?"

"What the hell?" The old lady stuck her head out of the door in amazement. "What do you think? You know I am alone. It's shocking."

Anyu rushed back down the hall, the old woman yelling after her, "And who helps me? Have you ever once taken my garbage down?"

Anyu had taken it as an omen. She fretted for days, pacing in the back. Finally she resolved that Miklós had really died.

And she had sat shivah, sometimes on the stool and sometimes even on the floor, wearing her embroidered slippers all day.

After the Second Anti-Jewish Law, after her sorrow lifted, she made commotions at the butcher's, where she ordered pork chops and spareribs in a loud voice. She attended mass with the rest of the family, confessed her sins with the appropriate Hail Marys, and together with József, her second cousin, took communion, the two of them kneeling side by side.

Although József was not Anyu's brother, he grew to be my favorite relative, partly because he was always around, a constant companion, and I thought of him as my fishing partner.

Years earlier, József had raised goats for milk and hide. One day, after returning from a spring herding, he had simply announced to Olga, his wife of twenty years, that he had chosen a new profession. Jewish leather merchants had been banned at the time, a result of the immediate Aryanizing of agriculture. The quotas on wholesale milk were extended to goats. This was when József became a writer.

According to Anyu, he told Olga of his decision calmly—as though he were commenting on the weather or wishing her good health after she sneezed without as much as glancing from his paper. "We have goats and little else, Olgi. And they won't last long," he began. "No children of our own to whom to tell old tales. Surely, we won't be poorer for it, Olgi." Olga liked her name said like that, with a little ring to it.

She was a most tolerant wife, Anyu repeated. She encouraged József to attend church after all their resources were lost in 1938 and they moved to the city. Nor did Olga fret after 2 augusztus 1941 when the Third Anti-Jewish Law was passed. "Mixed marriages destroy the national soul? Who ever heard such a thing?" Olga marveled. "We're in love for decades."

When Olga passed away soon after, Apu's favorite diagnosis could have applied, since X rays and lab tests showed nothing. But Apu remained silent and grieving. József studied the missal for her funeral service; soon after, he even instructed Anyu on the liturgy of the weekday mass. At first, the two of them took their cues from others in the congregation—when to stand, when to kneel, when to cross, when to strike one's chest. But József soon caught on to the Latin phrases of the priest and knew well the *mea culpa, mea maxima culpa* by the ringing bells. Anyu now kissed the rings of the priest, a common practice then. And on Fridays she religiously fried the fish I had caught the day before at Obuda.

When Anyu and Apu wed, Anyu wore her lace dress and

Angi led the procession, holding the jeweled cross in her open palms, trying to keep her eyes fixed on the altar in the distance. As they made their way down the aisle a low murmur went through the congregation. *Shabnda.* The word reverberated.

Mother's parents, Grandfather Leo and Grandmother Ilona—not quite "1848ers," the "true" Hungarians of the War of Independence, but surely from the days of 1867, the Jewish Emancipation—both converted the same afternoon.

József, who calmed Mother for the nuptial ceremony, lost his missal at the point they were to start rehearsing for the ceremony and memorizing her vows. Finally, József recalled that many doctors were saints, and he encouraged Anyu to simply offer a blessing to her new husband, who, after all, was also a physician. "At least it will be in good taste."

So when they stood at the altar and the priest, exclaiming in Latin, turned to Anyu and waited expectantly for her response, she blurted, "Release those bound unjustly." And here she stopped, having forgotten her lines. József, who stood near, coached her, "Break every yoke." Anyu went on, "Break every yoke, and shelter the oppressed." This surprised the priest greatly, who cleared his throat, and Apu began to shuffle anxiously. When the priest finally turned toward him, he repeated the one phrase: "I do. I do."

And that Saturday evening, when Boszor said he would spend a few more days with us, Anyu turned the lights low while it was still gloaming outside, and the living room became soft in pastel lights from the sunset. The building east of us, just across the street, lit up at the dentils like a crown glowing gold. Anyu lit a candle.

"A candle," Boszor commented.

"Yes, a candle." She lifted her hand toward the flame, her right hand, as I recall. "It is the time of division, Boszor." Her voice was steady and sure. "A wife to her husband clings more the more. And your son is my husband."

"What are you saying?"

"It is a time of separation between the sacred and the secular, the hallowed and the profane. Don't you think I know why all of the family is persecuted now?"

"Are you accusing me?" His voice grew sharp with indignation.

Anyu handed me the candle. The wax that had melted into a pool at the tip flowed over my hand, branding my skin with pain. But I said nothing. I was just watching Anyu and Boszor as they grew more heated.

"Blessed art Thou Who creates light, so that life may be separated from darkness."

Boszor wrapped a few slabs of salami in paper, tucked the package in his satchel, and left that very night.

Black Lady
The First Anti-Jewish Law
28 május 1938

Boszor was in the apartment one moment and gone the next. It struck me that his leaving was as sudden as Adám's. I even asked Angi about it. She said there was no comparison. Adám disappeared—Poof! she said—while Boszor slunk away. "That's a big difference." She did not shed light on my confusion. I only knew that he had left a chill in our home, that he had taken some of our family's warmth with him.

Apu and Anyu would not talk for stretches after the old man had left. Father was still loyal to the old man, having been raised in the peasant tradition: the father as *Ur*, or Lord, the mother as wife, or preferably, *háziasszony*, housewife.

It always took Apu time to adjust after Anyu had asserted herself. I recalled how she taunted and played with him, joking when he brought her his pay: "You are the Lord on Father's Day, payday, that is." She put the money aside and portioned his share as an allowance. He was happy to be earning for us, his wife and children.

New love comes slow. Even as a youngster, I began to realize what I can see clearly today, that love took to flight easily in those days, that it could readily be lost and grew back only with effort. It takes just a moment to cut down a tree, a generation for another to grow.

It was an early spring, and Anyu often took me for walks in the park in the warming breezes of late Sunday afternoons. The dogwood and crab apple were in bloom. She easily lifted me up among the petals. The memory is still vivid. The petals all red and white, the sky all red and gold, the petals coloring her face and the world. She let me run my fingers through the plushness.

She put me down. I looked up at the planes of her glowing face, her gently arching nose and full lips casting shadows from the low sun.

"Who is G–d?" I asked.

"G–d causes you to laugh, and I see G–d in your eyes."

"But what is that?"

"Like when you walk across the street with Apu, holding his big, soft hands."

"What does it mean that I crossed the street? What does G–d have to do with crossing the street?"

My child's mind formed the thought then that this was perhaps the reason we went to church regularly, not so much to pray as to cross the many streets along the way. Now I know. And I also know what it means to cross the street alone. It can never be done alone. The street streaming as a river, and the crossing so slow, slow as Abraham who crossed over to the other side. But he did not do it alone. Crossing from the other side, so slow, he was not alone.

"Yes, you can pray to G–d."

"And who do we pray to?"

"To the One G–d."

"Is that our religion?"

"Yes."

"What religion is that?"

A sudden gust raked the branches, and loose petals from the flowering trees colored the air as pink confetti would on May Day years later, during the giant parades after the war, when Hungary became a satellite of Russia. The religion then was selflessness, a sacrifice of the self for some sort of common good. The confetti would be loosed by workers of the Central Glass Factory, as seed cast to gust, and red and pink balloons would be sent aloft by the thousands, and thousands of white doves took to wing as one and bunched as a knot that seemed to be blown with a breeze over the river and up the cliffs of Buda, disappearing over the mountains.

"What religion are we?" I again asked as we trudged the cobblestone streets of Pest.

Anyu did not answer me. "Let's get some candy," she said. And again I persisted, "What religion are we?"

The man on the corner stood before his cotton candy machine. He spun the paper cone around the bin of whirling candy and collected a bunch. He smiled down at me, bowing. "For the young sir! Do taste it." My face sank into the sticky web, which covered most of my nose and part of my eyebrows.

The vendor and my mother laughed aloud, and then she led me along toward the zoo at the far side of the park.

The images of the stars had become a common fixture in daily life by then, but I became conscious of it only bit by bit because they were allowed out only from two to five in the afternoon, and then only exclusively for medical attention, cleaning, and shopping.

But that day, after Anyu had wiped my face, I saw a young boy, younger than myself, walking with his mother, both marked by stars, approach the vendor. Mother, who had knelt before me, her huge face hovering before me, licking the kerchief with which she wiped at my face, froze in place, staring at the stars.

The vendor, who had seemed so friendly just a moment before, laughing openly with Mother, suddenly grew cross.

Not only did he refuse the child wearing the star, but he swore at the child's mother. "Swines. What sort of medical reason is this to be out past the curfew? To feed the piglet cotton candy?" he spat out. "It's well past five o'clock."

I again yearned for some way to dispel my confusion. Yet I grew fearful and dared not ask anything, and I sheepishly followed Anyu as she led me away.

Still, once at the zoo, my thoughts persisted. "What religion are we?" I kept after her. The monkeys squealed and danced about as I threw pebbles into their cage.

"We are one religion," she repeated.

"Apu talks of the One-House," I said, trying to make some sense of one religion, One G–d, and One-House. They did not add up for me, even though I knew there should be three of something or other if they were to be added.

"That's right. One religion and One G–d." Her pace quickened abruptly, and her back hunched again.

"What religion is that?" I continued. Her eyes danced across the knoll near the museum. Her lips pursed. The furrows of the skin between her brows deepened to ravines.

Her mood soured suddenly.

"Let's go home, Pisti," she said. "I am tired."

"Why don't you ever tell me our religion?"

"I have. Countless times."

"Not once." I threw down the candy, and a breeze dragged it across the pavement. It lay in the street like soiled pink lace. "Never."

Again she did not answer. Instead, she pursed her lips, and then pressed them flat against each other, and then let them go flaccid and parted them slightly. But she could not relax. "We believe in the Messiah. The Messiah does not tarry. *We* are the ones who tarry."

I had no idea what she was talking about, some mumbo

jumbo from the middle of the jungle. I had not yet learned to assert myself and say, "I have no idea what you are talking about."

The rumor of the Dark Lady had spread quickly through the Seventh District like an infectious disease. As Anyu and I turned for home, we met up with my two older cousins from Uncle Oti's side. They were talking about the woman who had come to be called the Black Lady of Monday. Apparently she had been sighted only on the first day of the week. My cousins did not notice us, and I thought it funny that Anyu did not greet them, that we were almost eavesdropping. It took me a while to figure out what they were speaking of.

Zsóka, a brown-haired, blue-eyed student, was active with the Christian youth group. She also sang with the choir and played the timpani with the band at the Badacsony Inn on Lake Balaton during our summer vacations. In a shrill pitch, she was nearly shouting at her older brother, Pista. He had bushy black hair, unkempt and brushed to the side, and he towered above his sister. He was nearly triple my size, yet Pista's name was so nearly like mine that the two were often confused. He looked down at Zsóka, almost with contempt, although he was only a year older, in the second form of the Science Academy while she was in the first.

When we met the two of them on the divider of Vörösmarty Boulevard, lined with black oak, they were intent on their conversation. They were looking at an open van stopped across the street. Police and soldiers, dressed in colorful uniforms like the ornamental cavalry, with plumes in their hats, were grabbing people, running into the side streets and emerging with a star, and then running back and emerging with another star-sewn chest, like casting a net after fish when the river is bountiful. I suddenly saw the child whom I had seen in the park hoisted up over the guards of the van, his mother wailing below him as he was lifted over the side railing of the truck like a sack of sand, almost tossed over.

My distress grew. I asked Anyu, "Isn't that the little boy we left by the candy vendor?" I picked at my sticky brows. My hair grew moist from a cold sweat. I looked up at Anyu. Her forehead angled up, and her nostrils, holes in her face above her breasts, flared down. I asked again, "What are they doing with the little boy?" She looked down toward me, her face looming above. Her hair, collected in a bun, fell from her head like windswept autumn rain. She did not reply. Her hair unraveled and fell in layers, gray as October, streaked with silver strands I had never noticed before.

"I tell you, it was Shakespeare who first wrote about the Dark Lady," Pista was arguing.

"That's not what I'm saying. That form of poetry spread north from Italy. Edmund Spenser was the first who had the lovers actually talk to each other," Zsóka taunted him.

"I know that's how the teacher explained it, I know," Pista shouted back. "I remember the lectures, too, Zsóka. The sonnets started with the Italian Renaissance and moved through France, up to England."

I was bewildered and surprised. They could go on like that, talking High Hungarian in a way I had never heard. I wondered, is this what happens in the Academy?

"The lovers grew closer and more real with time," Zsóka continued. "But the woman always remained an ornament that could never be attained."

Lovers, ornament, attained? Sonnets? My bewilderment turned to fatigue.

"Shakespeare wrote about imperfection." Zsóka seemed to be finishing her point. "The tooth gone bad or the mole on a pale cheek."

"Yes, like this Black Lady of Monday," Pista said. Are they agreeing on something? I wondered.

"I bet if we pulled off her veil, we'd see something awful." Yes, they are agreeing on something or other, I concluded.

"What's unusual about that?" Anyu finally interrupted them. "There are plenty of widows to go around."

"Oh, look, it's Pisti and Auntie," Zsóka said, surprised by our sudden appearance.

Then they told us about the Lady in Black walking the streets in the early morning down toward the boulevard. She could be seen under the trees in the park by the Danube during the day. It was rumored that she was a war widow, as she wore on her mourner's band the bars of an officer, a major who died in the Ukraine.

Anyu laughed at them. "Along with nearly two hundred thousand."

Still they persisted. "She weeps endlessly," Oti's lanky son continued. "She keeps walking, turns into the Yellow Houses by Dob Street, and disappears. No one has seen her come out. And yet each Monday she appears again and enters the condemned houses with the stars."

"It is an omen," Zsóka said.

"Why are you worried, Zsóka?" Mother asked. "It seems more like a lament. Especially if the poor soul is crying all the time, as you say. It's a public lament. Maybe she is a practiced mourner, attending funerals when people are short."

The light changed. My cousins turned to cross the boulevard, and I heard their discussion continuing.

"Maybe she's a ghost," I joined in.

They laughed at me.

"Come, Pisti," Anyu interrupted. "The number twelve trolley's here."

We climbed up into the mustard-yellow trolley and sat in the back. "It was 1935 then," Anyu began one of her long tales. "Angi was still an infant, not yet two."

The action of the stories Anyu told of that time usually turned around some number or name that was always strange and often hard to recall, and her narratives often grew tedious. I had a sense that she was trying to tell me what I wanted to know. Though her language was simple, I still could not grasp much of her meaning, for much of what she spoke of was history that would be murky and perplexing to most people, whatever their age. I just stared dumbly at her broad face as she spoke in what seemed like a foreign language, and I chewed the strawberry taffy she kept for me in her bag.

I listened less intently and simply looked out the window, scanning the street for the Black Lady. Even though it was Sunday, I still hoped to catch a glimpse of her.

I heard mother drone on. "Take Bethlen, the premier way back then, before you were born," she began again. "You understand, Pisti, the whole thing was show. Law Twenty-five, for instance."

I did not know what I was to understand, but I liked the candy and focused my attention on the passing scene and the ample supply of treats she brought from the *trafik*, the tobacconist near our house on Damjanich Street.

She soon started in on the strange numbers and phrases as I had anticipated, as though I were a scholar or a historian at age five.

"Kún drove your aunt away, the crowds chanting before her window on the boulevard: *Zsidó, zsidó, gazember.* Jew swine."

At this point my chewing grew vigorous. "The crowds thronged before her window, their fists thrust up into the air. Poor Katalin, only eight at the time, never forgot her fear, let alone remembered any of her rage."

I knew her coming chant. "Law Number Twenty-five of 1920, the *Numerus Clausus* Act, was revised in 1928. That was to free the Hungarian Jew." Though I knew her incantations as if by heart, they still lacked meaning, were mere sticks of words.

"But aren't we free, Anyu?" I echoed a refrain. Of course, we weren't, it is easy to see now. But at the time, I had no idea, even if I had known what freedom was. Now, decades later, I often venture to the poet's corner in a local church and stand by the block carved for Emily Dickinson: Captivity is Consciousness . . . so is Liberty. Each time I visit her memorial, I ask the same questions about the homeless and the disenfranchised, G–d's variegated suffering: What is liberty? What is captivity? And are the homeless disenfranchised because they are not captives? Or because they are?

Such doubting thoughts did not eat at me then, as I walked the streets and rode the trolley with Anyu. If I grew troubled, I just reached into her jacket pocket and pulled out a caramel and chocolate toffee. Oh good, I thought to myself, more to chew. I reached into her handbag, swirled my hand about, greedily feeling the candies roll through my fingers. My troubled thoughts soon left me.

She raised a finger. "We were emancipated in 1868." Raising her finger higher, she asserted, "That's the point: why the need again fifty years later?"

"Anyu, you said 1866 yesterday," I recalled, without really understanding that I was talking about a time long, long ago.

"*Na, képzelje.* Just imagine, Talmudic at five."

"So we *are* Jewish," I said.

She did not answer me but continued her tale. I felt her press to repeat the stories, the press of one returning to the scene of a crime. "Bethlen was still known as a racialist. The law restricted Jewish admission for higher learning to 6 percent. I suffered for it. And my older brother, your Uncle Ervin, did, too."

Her press to repeat the stories was accompanied by my own urgency to remember them, to please her.

But was it only to please? It was also my need to remember, to hold on and not to lose her ever, not to lose love. As I gazed steadily at her, I felt myself sinking deep into the pool of her face. I was drinking her in with my eyes, I now realize, remembering the parched and thirsty feeling at the time. Yes, it was also that, a need to preserve, to retain, and to be a part, not apart from others.

She grew bitter. "I wanted to study biology, Pisti."

"You wanted to study how acacia would stop soil from washing away," I said. It had taken effort to remember the pronunciation for the name of the plant. At times like then I felt strangely responsible for her happiness; as a result, I had learned many ways to please her.

She looked surprised, then rubbed my hair. "That's right. That's it." She squeezed the back of my neck. "You even got acacia right."

"It *did* interest me," she continued. "Erosion is still a problem." She cheered noticeably when talking of her studies. "After all, if we say *anyaföld*, or motherland, it comes down more to land than to mothering."

The leaps in logic—from motherland to mothering to land—were incomprehensible to me.

I continued to console her. "You had a good job then." I believed it, too. Little else could beat running a candy shop, which is what Anyu had done.

She did not hear me, just kept on. "And *Numerus Nullus*, a given fact, will keep all Jews out of professions."

Hers was not a complaint, but rather an endless recounting, as though remembering helped her, too. "And businesses are restricted all the more."

I reached into her handbag again and grasped a licorice chew as we got off the trolley. Then I stood on the curb, next to the din of traffic and the drivers cursing their teams along the side of the road, which was fouled where the wagons ran.

And finally I demanded, "What is *Numorosz Nullusz?*"

She was shocked. "Why, you haven't heard a word I've said!"

"I have, Anyu," I defended myself. "I have."

"The 6 percent, you don't need to know. It's become nothing now. *Numerus* means 'number,' and *Nullus* means 'nothing.' Put together . . ."

"A nothing number," I anticipated her by rote.

"That's right. Eventually zero: zero dentists, zero internists, zero biologists. Even though many tried to assimilate, like your Uncle Ervin. Bless him, dear Ervin, a country doctor now. In the mountains of New York."

I wanted badly to talk of chocolates or halvah, but I also found myself listening to her complicated ramblings. I hoped to become a *valakivalami*, or "something or other," the most I could imagine of a profession. I did not want a zero thrown before me, to become a nothing, though even as a child, I could not imagine the occupation of a "something or other." Yet as a young boy I had little sense of who I was apart from the main streamings of history. And that is floundering, as one flounders on a sea of events. I have grown to understand that history is an impassive parent, as G–d is impassive and just. Parents smooth the bumpy road; G–d does not, nor does history. Impediments remain where they are, as they did with the Pharaoh of the Old Testament.

"Anyu, please forgive me, but what is assimilate?"

"It means you're like others, at least in daily life. At home, you're different."

"What difference is that?"

"A big difference."

"How can you be different at home and then not be different when you wake up for work?"

She laughed a good one. "It's hard."

"Aren't we Jewish?"

Her laughter stopped abruptly. The sun held still in the center of the sky, a blinding eye that cut my gaze up at Anyu's face. I held her hand as we walked, trying to understand her sudden silence. I lost interest. I looked across the street at the wet gutter, the cobblestones swelling like biscuits in a pan, glossy from the morning's rain. I scanned the street, up past the tethered horses and down the row of gas lamps, looking for the Black Lady of Monday.

We had ridden into the center of the city, the Belváros, past the furriers and clothiers and bookstores to the corner where Mother's own store once stood. Csokoládé Király, The Chocolate King, had once been a sweetshop, but it had been converted to a *trafik*, a tobacco shop that sold not just cigarettes but all sorts of common items: stamps, stationery, candies, newspapers and periodicals, and small toys. I wished Anyu owned her sweetshop again. Or at least a tobacconist's. I often got toys at the *trafik*, marbles and whistles, and once even a water pistol.

Before I was born and when Anyu still owned the franchise, Angi had often played in the Csokoládé Király. She spoke of it tantalizingly as a magic castle made of gingerbread. As my jealousy increased, so would her details about the store.

"Anyu was neatly dressed when she arrived the Easter when I had just turned three," Angi once told me. Angi had been playing in the aisles, driving a train across the black tiles that surrounded the marble table at the center of the store. Mother's white mink hat stood out against her long, dark hair, which lay in layers on the red fox collar of her coat. The skinned animal was largely intact. Its legs tapered. A molded snout and glass eyes were frozen on its flattened head. It looked as though it might swell into life at any moment and jump from her shoulders, yelping.

Angi and I both laughed at this. Angi had a great imagination.

"She told her clerk, Utci, all about the luncheon with the count of Nagytorony, and Utci also started laughing," Angi continued. " 'Better not tell my brother Ervin,' Mother warned Utci. 'He is still of the old school.' "

Utci, the charm of the store, a blue-eyed brunette, was Anyu's prized clerk, as Angi described her. Angi taunted me with tales of the store, knowing I had never had an experience like it.

"The count of Nagytorony once gave me a doll with a mink coat," Angi went on. I remember wondering then, for the first time, if she was lying.

She kept on. "I was just playing with the train, going 'Put, put, stop' and then 'Go, put, put.' He just placed the doll on the floor next to me." Yes, I remember that as the first time I thought Angi was making up her story.

Barons from the north and counts from as far as Pécs would come to this corner of Pest in order to buy a few grams of Odessa halvah or a single *télialma*, the store's famous rum balls. "They gazed into Utci's eyes, hoping for sweets only she possessed."

"What sweets?" I did not understand what this meant, to possess sweets. I only recall Angi continuing to mimic the nobles: "Sweet, sweet. Be mine."

I thought at the time that they had called Utci a sweetie because she worked in a candy store. I could very well imagine someone talking passionately like that to a bar of Toblers or a chunk of Turkish halvah. Had she worked in a dairy shop, I reasoned with my child's mind, they might have called her "creamie."

In 1931, I learned from Angi, Anyu had started as a clerk at the Csokoládé Király. At the time, a movie theatre, the Belvárosi Színház, or the Central City Movie, was just across Korona Herceg Street. In just a matter of a few years, she had worked her way up to managing the store. The Chocolate King was a chain known for quality chocolates from Switzerland and Holland, even fine cocoa from South Africa.

Along its mahogany shelves were displayed toffee from England, colorful hard candies in fruit flavors from Georgia, licorice, both red and black, and gumdrops, *gummi*, from America and Germany in exotic shapes: crescent moons, watermelons, and soccer balls. The crystal containers were of the best quality, and their colors danced in the noon light.

Every month after the laws of *Numerus Clausus*, Anyu sent Dutch chocolate to Ervin in Italy in seasonal wrappings, brightly colored and carefully packaged. Ervin had refused to become a *meshumed*, a willing convert, even though the dean of the university had spoken with him.

"You are fair-skinned, Ofner, just change your name," the dean had said. "You will thrive. Even your nose is chiseled."

Ervin showed *kuvits*, or respect, nodding his balding head in agreement. But even though he might not look like a Jew, his decision was out of principle. The dean said no more.

Ervin had gone to Padua to study.

I am only now able to piece together that soon after Ervin left, the anti-Semitic laws collapsed one after the other, like felled trees. The First Anti-Jewish Law, 28 május 1938, repealed emancipation outright. The proportion of Jews in professions and businesses was reduced to 20 percent. It affected fifty thousand families.

I recall that earlier in the week, soon after Boszor left, Anyu had dug out the old copy of *Népszava*, the People's Voice, that carried the text of the law and that she had hidden among unused linens in the closet. She had bent over the yellowing pages in our back room, and in a hushed tone had read with urgency. It was like she was telling secrets, even though we were in the back of the apartment at the time.

"I am not even in *elemi*," I protested. *Elemi* was grade school, and I had not yet attended even *ovoda*, or nursery. "Percents don't come until the fourth form."

Anyu kept on as though I were twice my age, rattling facts from the paper: private and public activities were restricted. The Jewish press had special chambers. Theater seats were confined.

"Are we Jewish?" It was after she read from the paper that my questions grew more frequent. She had stopped her reading as soon as I had become inquisitive, and she grew agitated, breathing heavily. Of course, this stirred my curiosity all the more.

But Anyu kept up business at her candy store as usual, Angi recounted, even while she was pregnant with me. This surprised people. A Jewish gentleman in his seventies, a retired podiatrist, frequented the store and claimed to speak good Yiddish. "Some people will say your mama the *shabnda*," he said to Angi one day, knowing well she knew no Yiddish. "But don't you believe it," he said. "There is danger in shame." He squatted to look my sister in the eye. "That will prove itself in all walks of life."

He took a huge bite of a rum ball. "And most will say of her, *meshumed*," he went on. "Of course never to her. That would be too cruel." He chewed the other half of the pastry. "But you know your mama is no devil. She is not a troublemaker. So you should say, why can't one be devilish?"

Angi was frightened and mystified by the man's veiled language, even as she retold the incident, trying to wash her memory clean.

He went on. "And a coarse man, mind you, but one trying hard to be polite, would say, *'Zie iz ah gehshmatter.'* To which you would say, 'Thank you for your politeness.' "

The pastry had soiled his lips and spread over his mustache. He was also enjoying the Yiddish.

"But a gentleman like me will say to her, *'Zie hot zikh mehgaiar gevein.'* " At which point he kissed Anyu's hand, closing his eyes as his lips touched her skin. Anyu grew flustered. Her hand was soiled with pastry from his lips. Nevertheless, she insisted he take home a few rum balls for his wife.

But he answered, "You know I am a widower."

"Then take for your kindness that you have given."

After the old doctor left, Angi had asked, "What was that word, *meshumed*, Anyu?"

"A convert."

"What's that?"

"Someone who has turned to a new faith."

"What did you turn to, Anyu?" Angi asked.

"You mean *toward whom*. . . . Your father."

As these memories of Angi's tales came back to me, I found Anyu and myself standing on the divider of Rákoczi Boulevard, named after the prince of Transylvania who had led the War of Independence against the Hapsburgs in 1703. Rákoczi's dream of universal charity clashed with the absolutism of the time, and the war failed. He spent the last twenty-five years of his life in exile.

The truck that had picked up the Jews as we stood by the fence outside of the zoo seemed to follow us like a spectre. It was just passing. I saw that the woman with the blue kerchief had climbed on and was clutching her child. But when it stopped across the street, an Arrow Cross jumped from the van.

"The youngster's crying is infernal, woman!" He climbed up into the van.

"Please, sir."

But the Arrow Cross was already on the truck. The grenadier

driver had also gotten out. He was relieving himself on the base of the oak tree that arched over the road. Then the youngster became a sack again, and I saw the Arrow Cross toss him down to the grenadier. The mother was screaming. I looked away but could hear her still.

A full eclipse drew across the sun and the land grew cold. I held onto Anyu's hand out of fright, even though we were not crossing the street.

The sky darkened. The lace and embroidery laid out by peasant women earlier before the Roch Chapel lost its purity in the muddy air. The old hospital on the corner vanished in the murkiness, and the marble statue out front, which had glowed white moments earlier, grew lackluster. Mother's smooth features disappeared, her brightly colored lips darkening to violet. The circular petals of her dress blackened at the edges, as flowers forgotten in a vase. Darkness covered the city, and an awful silence fell. No one moved, all traffic stopped, and people talked in a hush.

"Keep your eyes closed, Pisti," Anyu warned me. She covered my eyes with her cool palms, and the light was replaced suddenly by a pitch darkness.

As Anyu held my eyes, I imagined the shadow of the eclipse flowing toward the south, lapping at the avenues and into side streets with a dark tongue and sliding past the work yards. I imagined that it fell across Pécs and Mohács, cities to the south, and across the rows of poplars that lined the road where I played in summertime at Szigliget.

I still am not sure when the eclipse happened. I think of it as a half dream. But as we ducked into the shadows to avoid the blinding glare, Mother again told me the rest of the story, the part that I, only now, from the vantage of adulthood, understand as my first experience of past memory shaping the present. A real sense of history—its reality and potency. Prior to that, I only understood that the candy store had been destroyed somehow, not why it was looted.

The premier at the time, Béla Imrédy, had proclaimed that one drop of Jewish blood would infect a person's entire character. His statement was published on Christmas Eve, 1938. The mockery of this proclamation was compounded as it was soon learned that Imrédy had a German-Bohemian grandmother, fully Jewish. How Anyu did laugh then, when I first heard her tell this story, the first time I had heard her bellowing *röhög*. By the time she described Imrédy joining the Anti-Nazi party in great haste, she was crying from laughter.

Numerous decrees followed, calling up labor battalions wearing the yellow armbands and carrying the pay books with the thick marking in black, the brand, *Zs* for *zsidó*, Jew. The decrees all fell, and I saw Anyu's shoulders droop for the first time as she chanted names, muttering amid the thickening darkness: Waldman, Ofner, Schwitzer, cousin Berend, a historian, Kálmán, a lawyer, and his brother, Béla, a farmer. First, they worked in labor battalions, and then they were moved to the front as Hungary engaged the Russians. As auxiliary servicemen, they wore yellow armbands. But this perplexed the Germans, who associated yellow with the star. So white armbands were issued. But by then lineage hardly mattered; only the marking mattered.

After Imrédy's malignant Christmas greeting infected Italy, Anyu received word from Ervin.

> Wouldn't so much as spit on that ground. Or look at the sky above its soil. Or visit a cemetery, which is hard for me to say. It's *kaput*, all of it, my dear. But you and the children, I will think of you often and warmly. I just want to get far away. You, too. Leave, for God's sake, all of you, leave. Now. The soil is not just fallow; it swallows one.

> Ocsi

> P.S.: The chocolate was great support, even if not one Santa or Easter Bunny arrived intact. I was able to barter for salami and bread, bless you.

After the eclipse had passed, we walked across the square with the thick, yellow cobblestones, through the expansive boulevard, and turned up Hársfa Street. I kept an eye out for the Black Lady. As we were nearing our own street, Damjanich, Anyu went on with the story.

The day after Ervin's letter came, the Belvárosi Theater across from the candy shop showed a German propaganda film, *Jude Suss*, which incited the audience. Hitler's aggressions were praised, and the Jews were openly represented as leeches on the face of society, selfish and exploitive. United by rancor, the audience stormed from the theater as a mob—"Even the rabbi, a blackmailer and profiteer . . . Now I know who's keeping me down . . . One-fifth the people, four times the wealth."

The first sign of "Jude" was not a person but the gold-leaf lettering on Anyu's store less than a block from the theater, lit by the blue flames of the corner lamp. The name Waldman Cukrázda glowed in the blue light of the corner lamp: Waldman's Sweetshop. Stenciled at the corner of the window, it added quality to the display of chocolate candies with their bright bows and the variety of fat teddies stuffed with coated almonds. But to the mob it was "Jude" personified as wealth and profit, a store, the persona of a minority people.

"Utci, my dear, we had better get out back," Anyu said to her clerk as she looked through the diamond-shaped window of the oak door. She locked it quickly.

The throng was growing wild, Anyu continued, and Utci's crystal eyes lost their clarity. "They're a mad crew, ma'am," Utci said urgently. When she heard the shouting, closer now, her tenderness ebbed, and her cheeks became pale with fear.

"*Zsidó. Zsidó. Gazember.* Jew swine." They kicked at the door, banged and pressed.

Anyu and Utci made their way out and scurried up the side street, followed by the sound of shattering glass.

"Swine!"

"That's what they think, the bastards," Anyu cursed at them.

The gutted store with its burnt paneling and broken glass could only have been repaired at great cost. But Anyu ripped up the tiles, which were worth something, and a stonecutter leveled the break in the blue marble surface of the table. She bid business farewell and turned her back on the prized corner. With the little money she had salvaged she bought herself a lace wedding dress and a gold crucifix dotted with rubies.

At the corner of Damjanich Street we stopped at the *trafik*. I gazed blankly at the dried licorice and penny chews, which were called "metal" or *ón* chews, after the Hungarian penny, the fillér. This coin was made of a compound consisting largely of tin and had a hole so as to save additional expense on minting the precious alloy.

I saw the drabness of the *trafik* as if for the first time. It could not compare with the image I had of Anyu's candy shop. Dusty plastic clowns were heaped in the corner of a musty display case whose glass was cracked and held in place with yellowing tape. Crumpled balloons, all of army green, were heaped at the other side. Old cigars jutted from torn containers. A chipped cup contained rubber bands, another held paper clips. From the ceiling hung two strands of flypaper, pocked with dead flies. A few still buzzed helplessly, droning above our heads.

But the apartment was welcoming. The hall was scented with almonds from the cookies that slowly baked in the kitchen. The light above the stained-glass transom filtered in colors of pink and green, coloring Mother's hair.

The next day, just a week after the star decree, I was playing on the balcony of our fourth floor, which ran around the space overlooking the inner courtyard. The walkway was decorated with red marble inlay, part of the ornate decor from the Hapsburg era. The inlay still shone in the sun, but the gold-leaf ornaments on the side walls were flaking. I sorted my marbles and let the chipped clay ones slowly roll over the side and shatter on the ground below. Suddenly, a lady dressed in black came out from our neighbor Marinka's apartment. I knew that no one lived with Marinka, and I was surprised because I had not seen anyone enter. I grew frightened of the black figure as I realized it was Monday. It hit me at once that this must be the day, because Anyu and I had taken our walk yesterday, on Sunday. And on Mondays Anyu always prepared a grain breakfast, told me when Ibolya would come over to baby-sit, and disappeared till evening.

As she walked around the corner of the inner balcony toward the stairwell, this Lady of Monday, who had appeared as a ghost, did not stop to greet me. Rather I heard her lament, a soft sobbing as she walked by. She passed by me, her gown trailing along a section of rough cement, brushing under the railing and sweeping several marbles along. The veil was thick and I could not make out her face.

I was intent on her receding form and wanted badly to run after her and to lift the veil covering her face. Would I see something grotesque? Or only a tooth gone bad? But I did not act on my impulse. I did not need to.

I believed the Black Lady to be Mother. Her shoulders were hunched, weighed by the heavy satchels she carried that day. Her head bowed even as she walked, always looking down. The world was telling her to live life humbly, to look down. Guilt rounded her shoulders with great weight, much heavier than the satchels and bending her spine. Angi's spine would be molded as would mine, as though the world held us all in contempt and denied the dignity to look others in the eye with an even gaze.

It would be decades before she admitted that she had brought food to the houses marked with stars. She was never questioned, but seen as a hallowed widow. Once inside the marked buildings, she would distribute a whole chicken, or cheese, sometimes even slabs of bacon—whatever was available. She carried her mourner's clothes back out, stuffed in the empty satchel.

It is all a half dream. Even as she spoke the truth clearly in a letter when I turned twenty-one four years after my escape, when I was fully grown, finally telling openly of her Jewishness.

"Really, it was a matter of pragmatics," she said at the end of the first week of my visit in 1976. "I was only partly protected. And your young mouth, always open, would have led us all into trouble."

"But didn't it affect you?" I was amazed.

"What?"

"Your denial."

"Do you think that I ripped the stars from our relatives just to protect them? They were marked, sure. But I was a *Marrano*. Not Spanish, true, but equally unwilling. You and Angi were my fruit. How could I risk you?"

"So we *are* Jewish?" I was still not sure.

"The Island in Time will be yours forever," was all she said.

Back then, when I was five, I had stood mute in bewilderment. What island, and what time? I wondered. It was not that I was deaf to her words, but their veiled meanings escaped me. I imagine it as though I were crossing the street alone for the first time as a little boy, the street open and welcoming, with only some vehicle in the far distance, a truck or an ox-drawn wagon, indistinguishable in the haze of summer. No din of traffic. The street safe, as is the world. It is open. But it transforms to a challenge, to step out and to cross.

3

The Poker Party
Spring 1944

Dr. André Tóth, Apu's closest colleague, a pediatrician who had been his study partner in Debrecen for seven of his thirteen years in medical school, was rarely unpredictable, but he once surprised us with a visit. It was still morning, and Apu had not yet returned from attending to the ill among the forced labor at the Dreher Brewery. Rumor had it that they would soon be called up in the auxiliary service and sent to the front. What could not be foreseen was that in the fall they would all be "loaned" to Germany, along with the last of Hungarian Jewry, to build an "invincible defense" around Vienna against the approaching Allies. To lift the spirits of the men, Apu never visited them in military gear, but wore civilian clothes instead. The men understood this gesture and expressed their appreciation.

The day Tóth surprised us, I was out back in the playground, and Anyu asked him to fetch me from the playground for my ration of schmaltz, which she fed me twice a day. It consisted of a layer of reduced chicken fat on a thick slice of black bread, which she sprinkled with sugar. She hoped this would fatten me. She had held this hope for years, unwavering in her faith, but I remained thin and hardly grew.

My friends and I had been playing mumbletypeg on the flat area near the swings. A huge circle was drawn in the soil, which we divided by the throw of our knives from the center, where a small twig was stuck in the middle. When it came my turn, little territory remained. Furthermore, our throws had progressed from the straight toss and jerk at the hip to flipping the knife from our shoulders with a flick of the wrist. Sure enough, my blade did not hold, and hooting and hollering broke out at once. "Eat the peg, Pisti. Mumble, mumble. Eat it."

As I bent to my knees to lift the twig with my teeth, Tóth rounded the corner. My friends froze.

"Mumble the peg. Mumble the peg, eh? Is that how you spend your time?" he yelled at me. "Let's see what your mother thinks. You know of no decent games, is that it?"

And with that he grabbed me by an arm, jerking me to my feet. I burned with humiliation before my friends. To my horror he then yanked the knife from my hand, threw it on the ground, and crushed it with a heavy step. Picking up the shattered pieces, the large blade dangling from the shaft like a broken wing, he threw them over the brick wall behind the swings.

When we returned to the flat, the billowing aroma of stewing fruit from the kitchen could not ease my anxiety. Anyu agreed with Tóth that the neighborhood children were a bad influence and that I might well become a hooligan at this rate. She sided with Tóth in his announced conclusion that his home in the Buda hills would provide a better place for my afternoons. She stopped stirring the huge pot to consult with him.

"Don't you worry, I'll make a boy of him yet," Tóth consoled her. And then scowling at me he said, "A jackknife. And at your age, no less."

My discomfort forced a lie. "It was just a dinner knife."

"Shame on you. Do you think I am blind?"

"It may have been the butter knife, then," I went on. "I'm not sure."

"Keep digging your hole, Pisti. But remember what your mother said. From now on it's Kálmán Király Boulevard for your afternoons. The number five trolley will let you off by my office. We'll have no more of your games. At the rate you're going, you'd soon end up a *rablógyilkos.*"

I was shocked. "How can such a game make me a robber or murderer?"

He just scowled down at me. "I'll show you the way there only once," he said. "And once back."

After that I played in Tóth's courtyard alone, banging the soccer ball against his courtyard wall as the sun slowly slid behind Buda's hills. By the time I rode the mustard-colored number five trolley home, it would be growing dark. The building he lived in was like many in that district, with a huge stucco facade that was painted pastel yellow and glowed in the noon sun. Like most of the buildings in the city, it had a courtyard at its center, and the walls, or what remained of them, were also painted yellow. But they were cracked and pocked and huge slabs of the masonry had fallen away in places. Dust soon collected at the base of the walls as I kicked the ball vigorously. Tóth kept a watchful eye on me from his office window, observing me playing marbles or practicing shots into the corner.

He was a pediatrician with a natural love for children. He especially loved infants, and when a mother brought him a little one, he held it close and kissed it all over, lingering on the toes. The mothers liked this, were enamored of him, and his practice thrived. His vigilance over me soon eased, and he would bring me raspberry soda and milk crackers for treats. My grudge against him rapidly faded, and soon I found myself looking forward to my afternoon treks to his office.

Tóth looked like all the men I knew, with a high forehead and high cheekbones and a smile that was quick and free. He did not have black hair, nor was it long. He had brown hair, nut colored, light like an acorn, and he slicked down his curls in the fashion of the day.

He was dapper, quite a lady's man. Apu always teased him that he was the only man in the city whom women actually relished leaving, for they would then receive an endless stream of correspondence, sonorous poetry or lyrical prose. This did not bother Tóth. "I do all right," he said. "You're too settled to understand my design in writing. We all have to be loved somehow."

The covering on the soccer ball soon grew thin, and one day it blew. Then he bought me a hoop, really a bicycle rim from which the spokes had been removed, which I could roll by hitting it with a stick. "That's just for practice." His smile was mysterious.

At least this gave me good exercise. I raced round and round the courtyard hitting the wheel with a stick. "Flick a stick, not a knife." Tóth made his point.

One day he suddenly presented me with a brass hoop made by the ironsmith near his hospital. It glowed in the sun, and because it was thin and had no rims to hold it steady, it wobbled about as I tried to roll it. At first, it fell often. But after I got the hang of how to balance it with the rapid strokes that kept it rolling, the hoop reminded me of a halo, fallen from some saint onto the ground.

The hoop became my favorite toy, not because it glimmered and threw sparks as it rolled, but because it eventually gave me freedom.

Tóth soon let me roll the hoop up the winding paths of Eagle Hill and race back down again as he stood below waiting. The golden metal looked fiery as it rolled. At last, he let me venture as far as Budakészi Boulevard, which was far away and steep and thrilling as I raced, free at last, headlong after my magic ring.

Tóth had light gray eyes, I noticed one day as I ran down the hill and he caught me in his arms.

"Uncle Tóth," I said to him. "Your eyes look like one of my marbles." And I rummaged about in my bag to find the right one.

"But they see much better, don't they?" And he opened his eyes wide, and they became almost blue, sparkling like the Caribbean on Grandmother's old postcards, for which she had bartered dinner with a gypsy. Tóth's nose was also chiseled, an emphatic punctuation on an otherwise delicate face.

Perhaps that was it, Apu used to comment. "Tóth's trick. The real difference." This trait, of appearing delicate and vulnerable, was what Apu referred to as Tóth's "second trick with the ladies," the one after lyrical prose. "You're like a youngster, Tóth, innocent," Apu used to say. "You write to the ladies, and they take your innocent head to their bosoms."

The one who finally understood him best was a woman named Margit, eight years his senior, a brunette with full lips that she painted red. She always wore bright jewelry and a wide straw hat, a contrast to her tight black dresses. Even as she walked, she dominated the street. At first I thought she had a limp, but Apu set me straight. "Pretty women always walk like that. Think of the famous *amerikai* lady, Mae West." Of course, we often saw Mae West's pictures, but we could not understand the English, so all that came across was her throaty voice and her walk and the action that would periodically erupt into gunfights.

Margit looked nothing like a biologist specializing in the toothed carp of Lake Balaton. She and Tóth worked from the same lab and used to joke over lunch that they were in the same business—producing babies—she for export, he for domestic uses. They did not court long and wed on the steps of St. Steven's. In his reception toast, bursting, Tóth described his bride in one breath as a real beauty and a diligent housewife. Anyu laughed in a bellow: "The Magyar dream." Margit also mocked Tóth, "Thou Lord of the house hast spoken." Her formal tone highlighted her ridicule, and Anyu again guffawed.

It was Margit who took me to my first day of school. The decision for me to start first grade had been made by Apu. With a stamping of his feet, he exclaimed that it was high time I began my formal education, and any delays because of my small size could no longer be justified. But the situation was complex. My parents had kept me from school because of my size. Yet I was truly precocious. And so, even though I was a year behind, I ended up going directly into first grade, as if to make up for lost time. "It will keep you out of your mother's hair," Apu commented.

The evening before I went to school, Anyu had received word

that she was needed in the ghetto. I still gaped at her, puzzled, whenever she went out wearing her mourner's clothes with the black veil and the officer's pin on her black armband. At the time, all I knew was that she was able to bring food into the St. István Park territory, even after it had been cordoned.

So Margit was elected to take me to school, and she chided me as we ambled along the cobblestone street. "Now be a big boy, Pisti. You be brave. You're a big, brave boy, you hear."

As we turned the corner to the school, walking hand in hand, I suddenly burst into tears out of dread and longing for something I did not understand. To my alarm, she also began to sob long and hard, as though she were my mother and I her real child. She lingered with the other women on the corner as I walked the last block alone. "*Puszi, puszi, kicsikém,*" she cried after me. "Kisses, kisses, little one."

In the classroom, after we had learned the A, B, C, we began stringing the letters together into words and the words into sentences. And then there were numbers. Writing words and worrying about grammar or spelling seemed mere child's play compared to doing things with numbers in ink at the age of five. This was achieved by will power driven by a fear such that almost all class members outstripped the intellectual limitations of age. Mr. Molnár, the *tanár úr,* his formal title we understood not as "the teacher, Mr. Molnár," but as "my lord, the teacher," spotted our errors easily through what appeared to be divine powers.

Of course, this was not the case, because most papers were splotched where corrections had betrayed indecision, some even with holes where the erasing had been especially energetic. And Molnár inevitably spotted them.

One day he yelled at my friend Dezső, "Yes, you add, and then you carry. But what did you carry? Where did your ten go?" Dezső's erasing had left his page punctured with two holes each the thickness of a finger. "Find that ten. And carry it over!" The mess and the many errors, as well as the rebuke, eventually befell us all.

All, that is, except Tibor, who actually handed in his home-work typed. Everyone knew his father was doing his homework, but Molnár took his time and, as it later turned out, gave daily quizzes on only the items Tibor got correct on his homework, keeping careful records. At the end of a month, he snarled at the boy, "You got the lowest grade for the entire month. What do we make of that, eh, Tibor? Such neat homework, eh? What do we make of it?"

Then Molnár quieted and turned and walked a few paces toward the front, as if to continue his lesson, but this was a ruse, aimed at gaining sufficient distance to lunge back at the cowering youth. Charging, he shouted, "Bring your father before school. That's tomorrow. Tomorrow morning. Tell him to hell with work!"

Our lord would let nothing hide our sins of sloth or cheating in our duty as tiny soldiers building the nation. We had been prepared for this role from the first. "You are soldiers," my lord began the first day, "as surely as any of your fathers or uncles."

To prove his point, he then read to us from a treatise by Admiral Horthy, the ruler of Hungary since the 1920s: "Soldiers in the field, sailors manning the decks, and you, students bent over books . . . Horthy loves you."

Horthy's statue, placed prominently in every classroom, looked back at us, cheery and aristocratic. Cast in a rose-colored brass, the admiral was clean-cut and wore a well-fitting summer blazer and a naval officer's cap, more appropriate for yachting on balmy Lake Balaton than for manning a warship on the Baltic.

When we joked about an admiral ruling landlocked Hungary, it was never in the classroom, or in the corridors, but in secret, among the bushes of the park or under the overturned rain barrel of the courtyard. Even so, we did not understand many of the jokes. We had simply heard our elders laughing over them, and so we laughed, too.

Once, Apu elaborated on the joke and described battleships moored on the Danube, off the public beach where I made mud pies at the water's edge. Then in my own elaboration of Apu's tale,

I imagined myself stockpiling mud pies as missiles against the ships. In a flurry, I fired them at the war vessels. But the clay just squeezed between my fingers as I threw the pies, leaking down my arm and dribbling into the shallow waters by the shore, mud to scare the minnows, my Lilliputian revenge.

After the 15 március antiwar demonstration at Petőfi's statue, where over ten thousand members of the People's Front marched, demanding Hungary's withdrawal from the war, the government was paralyzed by Horthy. On 19 március, four days later, he permitted the occupation of Hungary not only by German military troops but also by the Gestapo. It was the bureaucrats who sought revenge on the left wing. Of these, some of the most influential were the educators, among them Molnár, my teacher, who was a supervisor in the district.

When I got my report card that spring, an armistice had been signed with the Russians, but no action had been taken toward withdrawing from the war, and more demonstrations by the communists were rumored in Budapest. So school ended early, and we got our report cards on a Wednesday, not on Friday as usual.

I ran home with my final grades for my first year and skipped up the steps two at a time, the long reach pulling at my thighs. I was happy because my first year of toil was over and I would soon be summering in the countryside with Angi.

But all around, as I rounded each stairwell, I heard weeping. From every floor came the wail of grieving women. I ran up to Anyu. "Why are they crying?"

She ignored me. "Where is your report card, Pisti?"

I handed it to her. "Why are they weeping?"

She took it quickly, adjusting her reading glasses and read it on the spot, carefully and long. Her smile soon broke into a laugh, transforming her intensity into release. Then she, too, started crying.

"Yes. Yes. You're going to the university for sure, my little one." She wiped her eyes. "Thank God, thank God. Sure as sure is sure." She hugged me and kissed me. "Look here, Pisti, it says right here: 'doctor, lawyer, head administrator.' It's the school's edict. Mr. Molnár even signed his name. It also has the school's seal. You've made your mama so happy."

I did not know what to say. I did not really know what a university was, let alone a head administrator.

"What does that mean, Anyu? What's a head administrator?"

She rattled on. "It hardly matters. The world is yours with the new decree. The nation must plan for its workers, just as it planned for you. By God, you'll work as a doctor, like Apu. Or as a head administrator in the Assembly." Her eyes gazed far into the future.

"But why is Varga's mother crying, and Dezső's, too?"

"Didn't they show you their cards?" She seemed amazed. "Varga will be attending trade school in Obuda after third grade. His card read, 'cobbler, tinker, or floorscraper.'" Anyu laughed. "That's poor Varga's edict. But nothing's wrong with that, Pisti. You will be his friend, mind. They're honorable crafts of the people." Her brow reddened at this point and her nose flared.

I heard shouting from the third floor through Varga's kitchen window. "Son of mine, eh? No son of mine!" The rhythmic blows sounded like the chopping of wood. "For this we've slaved? Me, your honorable father, a tailor," the voice continued. "The shame."

I imagined Varga absorbing the beating with stubborn pride, holding back tears, and then I heard him burst into loud wailing.

I counted my blessings. I had been fortunate, I knew. And lucky, because the previous Monday, Molnár had gone to deliver his observations on two classes in a nearby school, having abruptly announced that he would be leaving. The room broke into tumult soon after he left. It was spring and to be expected. The staff was unusually short and there was no supervision. Only Old Lady Népdal stuck her head in the door now and then, rolled her eyes, and left.

We had a free-for-all most of the morning. Some students

actually fell to the floor in mock combat, crawling under the tables between the legs of the chairs. Others, the parachutists, jumped from desk top to desk top.

I grew increasingly anxious as I imagined the door suddenly opening and the scowling face of our Lord Molnár peering over his spectacles with the biting eyes that would tear at our fearful lot. In a fit, I ran to the front of the class and stood beside the statue of Horthy, rubbed his cap as a charm, and shouted loudly, "Stop it. In the name of our Admiral Molnár!" I did not recognize my slip of the tongue until later when Dezső pointed it out at recess.

I shouted "Admiral Molnár!" in that awful moment. And as I did so, I realized that I hardly cared about the uproar, that I merely wanted to quell my fear of Molnár's retribution. But to my amazement, an immediate silence fell, part timid, part dumb, and also confused.

"You said our lord's name for Horthy's statue. Why did you do that?" Dezső asked later. I could not answer him but only recalled, with a twisting in my chest, the dread of standing up front and addressing the class.

Then to my greater amazement, our lord, who must have been approaching down the hall, entered just then, and without pausing to rebuke those frozen on top of desks or sprawled in the back corners, stroked my hair and merely said, "Good work, Pisti. You will be commended."

When I looked at him, Molnár seemed transformed, as from a quick character change in a one-man play. This day he no longer wore his loosely knotted tie and beige jacket. He was now dressed in a tight brown shirt with black straps crossing his torso. His black military trousers were covered by knee-length boots, so that the pants billowed at the knees. Two brass arrows, crossed, were pinned to the epaulet on each of his shoulders.

How striking he looked. Crisp as autumn foliage, the leaf of black oak. I imagined him the *huszar* from the ornamental cavalry of days past, his nut-colored horse rearing and foaming at the mouth. His brown boots snapped at the wooden floor as he walked past me. They were the shade of his tight shirt.

He turned. "Yes, Pisti, you will be commended."

The night of the report cards, while Anyu diced onions for stew and salted the cubes of beef, I collected all the matches from her dresser, the cupboard, and those for the kitchen stove when she went to the pantry. I then went out on the balcony and flicked lit matches into the street six stories below.

Fire, fire, I thought. Light the fire. See the fire. Feel the fire.

The matches scraped against my zipper, and I also lit them against my fingernails and my teeth. But the rough surface of the matchbox's edge produced the brightest flare, blue and yellow, that burnt longest. I backed into the hallway, challenging myself to clear the railing.

Hear it. Smell it. Guard the fire. Fear the fire.

As I chanted to myself, the thick wooden matches flew between the railings, arching in the air and spinning slowly, like fiery logs catapulting in a medieval battle.

I heard Anyu rummaging about. She opened the cupboards, looked in the drawer. "Pisti, I can't find any matches." She came onto the balcony holding three large empty matchboxes.

I let her look a while. "I swear, we had a dozen boxes."

I emptied the pockets of my pants and two jackets into the umbrella stand, then ran to her with only a handful. "Here, Anyu," I said. "I found some in the couch."

"Aren't you a dear." She stroked my head, bending to kiss me, and lit her cigarette.

We ate before Apu returned. The rectangle of hazy light from the kitchen window quickly darkened, and the brown sky took on the texture of wool and the shape of a comforter.

I again heard blows from the neighboring apartment, and I again heard Varga wailing.

4

The Poker Party
Autumn 1944

Wednesdays were the days when father came home late and I went to bed early. An empty evening. Wednesday nights were saved for Apu's poker parties. When the party was at our house, Anyu could not be present but had to stay in the bedroom chatting on the phone or knitting. Even so, she spent the entire day before the game preparing snacks of tiny pieces of toasted bread, cheese, and cold cuts, as well as a dip from chicken livers.

Most days Apu came home by six. But on Wednesdays, when the party was elsewhere, I would be asleep by the time he returned from Uncle Oti's apartment by the boulevard or from Dr. Tóth's in the Buda hills. I would not hear him lightly scuffing the mat of the front door. Familiar with the keys, he made no noise unlocking the door, and he eased the warp in the frame so it made no noise. I never woke at night and was happy to be roused to his call in the morning: "The rooster crows. The rooster crows. Breakfast is ready."

Today the party would be at my house, I recalled, excited.

Apu would have time to play with me before the group arrived, perhaps with my race cars or roughhousing. I would have him hold me in the air with his arms and legs, and I would hover above him, pretending to fly.

I had never actually seen the poker party, but I tossed long in my bed when it was at our house, bothered by the rough laughter and sudden outbursts of cheers. Several yells kept repeating. "Good bluff, old warrior." And "It's only a penny ante . . . Any changes must get our unanimous vote . . . I veto." Sometimes they even got wild, as toward the end of the game when they played Showdown for a full ten-pengö note.

One story had it that on a summer's evening while at the apartment of István Boszormenyi, a jewelry setter who lived in the fashionable Váci Street district, they actually threw an entire cheesecake out the window to get the attention of a shapely brunette passing in the street under the blue lights of the gas lamps.

Anyu was quite upset the next morning when she heard of it. "Why don't you just hang a sheet out the window next time?" she snapped. "A cheesecake is more than cheese during these times."

Apu doubled over laughing. "It was a record. You should have seen when the trolley hit the cake. Left a streak of filling all the way to the square, following that little good-looker as she walked along like it was her poodle."

Anyu was still upset. "God bless grown men. Where did you get the cheesecake anyway?"

It was a Wednesday. This day I will be sent to bed very early, I realized.

And then a bold thought occurred: But I can get up. Yes, I can.

When Apu arrived, I roughhoused with him and tore off his shoes and hid them and then tried to rip off his socks. He laughed, "Pretty soon I'll be naked." The idea intrigued me, and I went to undo his belt then, but he picked me off the floor, raising me high.

When we played hide-and-seek, I dashed into the bedroom and slid under the bed. He knew I was there because that was where I always hid. But he walked about in the darkness wondering out loud, "Where oh where can Pisti be?"

And then I heard his voice closer, saw the outline of his

trousers by the bed before my face, and heard his voice above me grow playful, growling and terrifying, "Fee, fi, fo, fum. Under the bed I come."

I scurried to the back of the bed, against the wall, and he reached in with his hands, growling and snarling, sweeping close to my face with his arm. I shuddered next to the wall, crouching into a ball, my heart thumping so I could feel it. Then he reached in deep, hooked a leg, and pulled me out. He snorted, "*Eszlek. Meg eszlek.* Eat-cha, eat-cha. I'm gonna eat-cha all up." I squealed both in joy and in terror: "No, no. Please, Apu. Don't do that."

Later, exhausted and near sleep, I nestled over his shoulder as he carried me to bed, my head cupped in his neck. I was too worn to refuse or to protest, and I fell asleep at once even as he carried me.

After I had begun to doze, the men arrived. I knew they had come because the scuffing at the mat and the creaking of the door woke me. Once awake, I lay still, plotting my entrance to the group. I listened to their greetings.

"*Jó estét. Mi újság?*" they were saying. "Good evening, good friend. What's new?" István slammed the door.

"You must be joking. New?"

"How does the little woman fare?"

"Tóth, you look glum," István noted.

"The wife any better?" Oti asked.

But Tóth said nothing.

"I've my own woes today, let me tell you," István said.

"We'll get to it. We'll get to it all," Apu said, and they went into the parlor.

"Don't wake the boy. He's fast asleep," Apu said, and they tiptoed by my door.

It always struck me how much Apu's friends talked, discoursing endlessly into the evening. At times I hardly heard the jangle of chips or the snap of shuffled cards. It often occurred to me that they were not really a poker group but a talking and eating group. Nowadays we would call it a men's support group, but such things were unheard of at the time.

Besides the treats Mother prepared, István always brought a bag of olives, most of which he ate himself, Apu complained each morning after the games. And Oti, who was forever trying to lose weight, often by health diets, brought rennetless cheese. Of course he was the only one to eat that.

Dr. Tóth, however, who bartered with a baker for his professional services, sometimes brought pastries, *Rigo Jancsi*, named after the famous chef, Johnathan Rigo, or *dobos torta*, a creamy layered cake.

"Think of the children," Apu protested as his friends ate heartily.

"Bread is better for them," came the predictable laughing reply.

This night, István started in about the loss of a costly diamond, rare during these times, which he had chipped. Besides piecing necklaces, he had become a master setter in his youth. From time to time, he proudly showed off the overgrown calluses of his left hand, one near the knuckle of his forefinger and one by the crook of his thumb, the marks of his trade. I could never understand how they had grown so huge, the size of my snake-eyed marbles, until he took me to his shop and actually showed me his work.

"First I use a bead raiser, like this number fifteen," he started, sitting by his bench, which contained the peg that held the ring. "It pushes a little gold against the side of the diamond," he went on.

Then with a firmer hand, he raised a bead against the opposite side. He did this again and again on all four sides of each diamond. I noticed that his hand was continually moving against the bench peg that held the ring clamp firm. And all the time, the crook of his thumb rubbed the clamp holding the ring and the knuckle of his forefinger ground under the bench peg. He removed the clamp and rubbed his sore calluses, grown red from the friction.

That day, István had lost over five hundred pengö when a two-carat diamond chipped.

"Of course, it was the caster's fault. Who knows what sort of junk he put into the alloy. I never did believe in any such a thing as rose gold, only gold with copper alloy. And that's when you get those damned bubbles that make the cutting tools slip," István said. "I had to give the jeweler something for his loss."

"Well, two carats are worth far more than the five-hundred note," Oti observed.

"Of course. Don't you think I know that? But the caster's the one responsible. I told the jeweler the money was just a little something for him. I'm not responsible, I told him. And he understood."

"The caster tried to cut corners," Apu said.

"You're a master sure," Oti added. "Tóth, what say you?"

But Tóth said nothing. An awkward silence fell over the room.

Apu spoke then. "There's serious trouble in the ghetto. For the first time, my satchel was searched, even though I was in uniform. It was my luck I was not carrying food or identifications."

"They searched a major?"

"That's the least of it. I also diagnosed two of the condemned with tuberculosis, an old man named Bórisz and his daughter, and rushed them to St. Steven's Hospital. The ploy has never failed before, although there were complications. At least they could get papers to leave the ghetto. This time I coached them on their symptoms for nearly an hour. But the next day, the Gestapo actually entered the hospital, a private hospital at that, and took them from their beds."

"It must be getting dangerous for you, too."

"Once the Gestapo shunned the contagious," István said. "An illness like TB ruined all pretense of good intention."

"But now they'll take any Jew," Apu said. "As long as they're Jewish, and often even if not."

"You must be worried for the little woman."

"I'm afraid I can't even protect her," I heard Father say. "They came just yesterday. She wasn't in, thank God. You know the ruse.

To start shouting in outrage. I told them that she wasn't Jewish and then started yelling that I knew Szálasi, which really set them back. That I had even treated Szálasi's wife. They left soon enough."

In the dark of my nearby room, I worried about his words. Why should Anyu be in danger? And why couldn't Apu protect her except with lies?

Then in my dark tomb materialized the spectre of Molnár as an ancient warrior, with jutting jaws as sharp as his open sword. His stallion reared above my bed as though to crush me. I remembered Major Király in the hospital near Uncle Kálmán's, lying lame under the Arrow Cross commander who hovered above him. Pinned and wriggling, I cowered under the sheets and prayed that the vision would vanish.

As I recall, a light spirit never did come over the group that night. I lay still under the sheets listening to them talk, and I only occasionally heard the jangling of the chips, the tinkling of coins. But even these meek sounds soon subsided, and Dr. Tóth, Apu's closest colleague, finally spoke.

He spoke softly, and across the darkness of my room, he seemed to be whispering. I heard his muffled words describe the condition of his wife, Margit. She has cancer, as you all know, but her condition is rapidly deteriorating, he said. She is hard to recognize, having lost much weight.

I felt badly for Margit and could not imagine her big-boned frame shriveled.

"Is there nothing that can be done?" Oti asked.

Tóth remained silent. But Apu, who was an internist, replied, "It has spread. Probably to her liver by now. She will have to be hospitalized."

"Will that be of any help?" István asked.

Silence filled the room and, like a tattered fishing net drawn onto shore, drew empty into my dark chamber.

"So very sad, good André," I heard Apu say. "Especially as

the war's nearing an end. I mean, to be spared the bullet, and then to have it this way."

I heard sobbing then. And the broken voice of Dr. Tóth: "It seems unfair, I know. But that's not why I brought it up. She needs to be hospitalized. But she refuses."

István, a good friend of both my father and Dr. Tóth, said, "Not meaning to insult the physicians here, but what could a hospital do anyway?"

"That's just it, István. Margit knows that. She still has her wits. She wants to do away with herself."

Then a long silence fell, and in the silence I imagined them still talking, perhaps more softly now, and I peered into the blackness of my bedroom, trying to listen more intently.

Finally, a phrase was spoken. "What will you do?"

"She refuses any pills I could give her. Fears they will be traced back to me. Asked about some way, the quickest and surest. So as not to implicate me. She wants to hang herself. Actually asked my advice about binding her jaws."

"When would she do it?"

"Some day, any day, just so it looks unplanned and I can't be implicated."

I crept out of bed then, not because I really wanted to, but because it had been my plan earlier and I felt the need. I shivered as my feet crossed the cold floor. I stood in the doorway watching Uncle Oti blow on his pipe as the rest of the group sat motionless, the many-colored cards scattered on the table. The smoke from his pipe rose into the solitary lamp over the table and filled the room with a sweet odor. They looked wooden, rough-hewn, like life-sized carvings by some country craftsman.

Light angled dimly from the single lamp above the table. Rustic foods, gathered with hardship during these lean times—crackling, goose liver, yellow peppers, and raspberry syrup for the seltzer from scuffed bottles—rested on a side table. Yellow Badacsony wine used in church services, which Apu had procured from a priest, a longtime patient, sat in the middle of the dining table.

The red-striped tablecloth had turned brown in the dim light, sullied. The men had stopped playing. Even stopped talking. They did not look toward me, but gazed at the surface of the table, dumb. The food went untouched.

I returned to my room unnoticed and fell asleep quickly, but at two in the morning by our chiming clock, I woke to shouts from the street. And pelting gunfire. In my state of stupor and twilight consciousness I thought I was dreaming. Lulled again by sleep, I dozed, then faded to slumber.

But the shots had been real, and the rampaging of the Arrow Cross, the Hungarian fascists, Szálasi's men, had lasted all night.

The phone rang early.

"What? What was that?" Apu kept shouting into the speaker. "Speak a little louder, my dear Margit. It's about what? What about André? He didn't have his papers. Is that what you said? What's that? I can't hear you. His papers were in the dresser?"

When he finally understood, he put down the receiver, almost dropping it from his fingers.

Then he turned to Mother. "André is lost. He didn't arrive last night."

"They'll be back after us for sure." Mother spoke as if she knew.

"Take Angi and get our gold from István, and I'll take the boy. We'll meet back here."

"István left the gold last night. He spoke only to me about it, after the rest of you had gone to the lounge. It's in the pantry with the walnuts."

"Good. Good. We'll get it later. But first stop by at Margit's for a minute. See that she's all right."

My father grabbed my hand and took me with him. I do not know why. But he took me with him, and I clasped his hand and went.

Father and I walked by the Danube, by the stone embankments that lined the shore, past the rippling green water, and under the Chain Bridge, which arched delicately toward Buda's cliffs. He held my hand gently with his big, soft hands, as he usually did, but he looked pensive.

His grip tightened, and I saw a bloated form in the water, turning slowly near the shore and away from the main current, a naked body.

I looked at the chipping green paint of the bridge then, bubbles of paint big as fists rising from the metal surface. I saw the two lions guarding the entrance to the Chain Bridge on the Pest side, wounded and pocked with bullet holes like animals that had been hunted. The purple eye of the sun hung in a haze of clouds. We came upon a tangled pile under the Chain Bridge. At first I did not recognize it. And then I saw that the pile was not tangled but stacked neatly. As neat as a cord of wood stored for winter. Only the top layers had fallen, like a stack with the top collapsed.

"A little farther, my little one. Just a little farther," Apu repeated. He kept pulling me along.

The stones of the embankment were as huge as cannonballs. How heavy they must be, I thought. Who could have moved them there, right next to the water?

Only when I saw a small mound of clothes nearby, flowered skirts and flannel trousers, and farther down a heap of shoes, did I know we had passed a stack of bodies, stiff and stacked like wood.

"This way, this way, my little one." Apu led me toward the shoes. He picked up several strays. A workman's boot and fine shoes, a lady's shoes, turning them in his hands, unbelieving. Then he started shoveling with his feet and kicking them about, as though desperately searching for something. Only after a time did he stop.

I looked at the water, still rippling. Two withered women in black shawls had begun to sift through the clothing, also seeking kin. I only presumed this because they were weeping. The clouds having passed, the sun's eye glared blinding, canary yellow. A carp jumped near the shore. The bloated form we had seen earlier still swam in circles, but nearing the main current had moved downstream.

Again, the paint of the bridge. Fists rising from the metal surface. The wounded lions, lying still.

We retraced our steps, seeing all of the horror over again, and then, as we passed from under the bridge, Apu looked at the supporting beams. He froze, stiff as the lions. Tied together, a pair of shoes dangled from a nail, a neat pair of two-tone leathers.

Dr. Tóth's fine shoes swung in the biting wind like the loose ears on the pelt of a rabbit.

5

Corners
1944

On the way home from the Danube, it was clear that Béni, our neighbor, had been waiting, for as soon as we rounded the corner of Dob Street, he darted from the doorway of our apartment building and ran up to us, carrying a bundle. He tried hard not to appear to be rushing, but he was panting by the time he reached us. "How should I say such an awful thing, kind sir?" He looked awkward and urgent but could not spit out his words.

"Well, spit it out, Béni." Father chided him. "What's up?"

Béni wrung his hands. "They've knocked in your door, sir."

"Are they still up there?"

"Yes, Doctor. Four of them. With machine guns." Old Béni's face twisted.

Father suddenly grew angry at Mother, and this confused me. "What a damned thing! Now, of all times," he yelled. He quizzed me, as though I should know the answer. "Where is that mother of yours?"

I grew frightened by his outburst.

Béni was also taken aback by his reaction.

"Sir, how can I help?"

Just then Father spotted Mother and Angi nearing the apartment building from Szófia Street to the north, and pointed wildly for Béni. "Run now! Back to the house," he was flailing at the air. "Tell her to meet us at the intersection of Szófia and Hársfa streets at once. That way she'll just have to turn the corner."

There was no need to worry, because as soon as Anyu saw our neighbor limping urgently toward her, she pulled Angi aside and stood by the building, vigilant as the red-tailed roebuck downwind from the hunter. We watched until they had turned the corner of Szófia, and we went down Király Street, directly parallel. Apu hurried to the corner of Vörösmarty Boulevard, the next block, and looked over to see if he could get a glimpse of Anyu. But they were nowhere to be seen. "For crying out loud, they must have run. We must walk slowly. A regular Sunday stroll."

Anyu and Angi met us at the next corner. Anyu was panting. "The super told me everything, how they broke in. We have to leave."

"Don't you think I know that?" Apu was still irritated. "But how?"

"Just by leaving." Anyu glowered at him, grinding her teeth.

"Well, surely we can't run around the city." He tried to recover. "We must walk like nothing's happening."

We walked on the narrower streets, slowly, as Apu insisted, all the way down Hársfa Street, shaded by sumac. We trudged past Dob Street, where the Orthodox church had been newly painted, until we reached Wesselényi, where roasted-chestnut vendors stood at all four corners, modern angels guarding the four corners of the earth. We turned north on Dohány, and the low-hanging branches of willows brushed against my hair.

My parents were numb. They were not walking casually at all, I noticed, but staggering from exhaustion.

"How was Margit?" Father panted.

"The door was bolted."

"Did you try the super?"

"We couldn't find him."

I finally dared to speak. "Where are we going?"

But they did not answer me.

"They're probably both lost," my father said.

"You found André?"

My father did not say anything. He nodded.

"Why are we walking so fast?" I asked, noticing that our pace had picked up.

"We are *not* going fast!" Apu yelled.

"We are going to the station," Anyu snapped, pulling Angi by an arm.

Angi started to scream at the abuse and actually swore at Mother, actually using the "zs" word. I was infected by her anger and suddenly sat down on the sidewalk, even though I was too old for such behavior.

Apu grew frantic. "Dearest God, what are we going to do?" he fretted. "Shall we just have a picnic? Shall I get cheese and soda?" He became wry. "Get black bread? Pumpernickel? What gives here?"

He picked me up. "Now, now," he finally soothed. "You go with Angi," he instructed Mother after I got up.

"The gold that István left us—didn't you mix it with the walnuts?" Anyu asked.

At this Apu stopped short and laughed. He had to put me down. It was a laugh, not at all pure, but filled with anxiety, fending off irrevocable defeat.

We finally turned the corner of Szabó József Street.

"Is this the last corner?" I asked.

"The nearest corner."

"To the railroad station?" Angi was panting from the forced march.

The last corner of the nearest street, I thought. With only what we had on us. No gold. Just what we possessed that very afternoon, on the way home.

We turned, walking slower now, like marchers at a dirge, toward the nearest train. A train that ran. Any train. That simply ran. South. Let it be south. Toward the Russian-Romanian front.

"Is the train running?"

"In ten minutes, sure." The porter had one short leg.

"Sure?"

"Sure as sure and as surely as sure can be sure, sir." The porter rubbed his palm.

The infected rays of a green sun leaked through the soot of the glass dome covering the station.

"Where to?"

The man in the conical blue cap snapped. "What the hell! It's running south."

"How far?"

"Far enough, damn it."

Apu handed him his watch.

"The lady's bracelet is very delicate," the porter said.

With a limping gait that jerked his cap and swung his shoulders in rhythmic loops, and with the watch and bracelet jangling in his overstuffed pockets, he led us to the rear boxcar, where four other families huddled in the darkness.

He put a hand on my head, muttered again, "Sure as sure as anything."

The train suddenly lurched and rolled slowly. It did not gain speed.

"Nah, when will we move along?" Apu asked.

"It'll take a month to near the border. Worse than a local," a man's voice from the far corner laughed.

The train did not gain speed for some time.

The parcel left by Béni contained Father's uniform. He changed hastily, in a dark corner, then exclaimed, "There's no belt, for crying out loud."

Apu looked out the corner opening. I could see his pants sagging. "At least we're crossing a bridge," he said, holding his pants with one hand. "We're out of Pest, at least."

He kept looking out the window, seeming puzzled, the pants continuing to droop. "I think we're heading north." And as he said this, the train picked up speed. "We're heading north. Jézus Mária, we're heading in the wrong direction."

He grew agitated and paced the little cubicle of the car. "This is really something. The damned fools." Anyu kept telling him we were better off than at the apartment. "God bless we're still of this world," she repeated. But he paced the car. He looked quite pathetic in the dim light, his pants drooping, and he walked all over his pant legs, nearly tripping.

"Look, dear," Mother told him. "You've your uniform. That will help."

"As we crawl out of a cattle car? How does it look, a major, a medical officer, hopping from a cattle car, in my condition."

Anyu laughed. "You'll shock them, and that will be that."

As she spoke, the train suddenly did stop, and Apu yanked open the door and saw the sign in the distance: Szentendre.

The conductor ran up and down the train, hitting the cars with a stick.

"This is it. Get off. Get off."

"*Micsoda!* This is some craziness," Apu yelled at him.

"Get off, sir."

"We're less than thirty kilometers from the city, you fool." Apu was furious. "Hardly a spit or a stone's throw!" he yelled. "You said we were headed south."

Anyu tried to calm him. "This is fine, I tell you. We're in luck. Get the children off."

Apu did not understand her but did as she wished. He hopped off and, holding his pants with one hand, eased Angi's jump with the other. Anyu quickly followed.

"Gyula lives here, and with some luck, if you hold together, the uniform will get us there safely."

"Don't I have a role?" Father was delighted at her discovery.

"The uniform does," she mocked. "Especially your pants."

They were happy about something, but I did not know what.

6

Dawn on the Danube 1945

After Apu had helped us down from the train, he began to walk toward the village, still clutching his trousers. Stumbling, he caught his foot and fell, rolling down the steep embankment. He did not break his fall, for he was still self-consciously holding his trousers, and he rolled all the way to the bottom, where a puddle had formed. He sat up. Mother looked at him from the embankment in disbelief and began to guffaw. "Some officer you are."

Apu stood, dazed. As he tried to focus his eyes in the direction of the laughter, he let go of his pants, and they slowly slid down his legs and collected in a heap around his ankles in the puddle. Mother continued to laugh as she helped me down the slope, "A leader of soldiers and a savior of souls." Her laughter was full and deep, the *röbög*.

While walking into the village, I recalled an earlier experience at the train station with Anyu, a painful experience that had also ended with the cleansing laugh. This was when the soldiers were returning from the Don in 1943. Anyu and I had crossed the city to the beautiful old station while Apu stayed home with Angi to tend the garden, raking away the autumn-dry leaves. We waited from noon, when the blue sun glowed pitilessly through the glass roof above the train yard and lobby. The crates and dust of the platform, silent and in wait, blanched in the hot sun. We sat with the soldiers and the nuns and paced among the many women who brimmed with desire and fear. Limping and maimed, the porters who had returned to civilian life still wore regimental caps. They adjusted them now and again and engaged in discussions of where they had served, talking loudly of their wounds received in action. This day they also waged a hopeless war against the crush on the platform.

We waited for the trains from the River Don till night, when the moon shone into the station, radiant. The crisscrossing tracks glowed in the bowels of the terminal like makeshift stitching on a stomach wound. We paced the worn tiles of the lobby, past the cement platform and beyond the oiled beams.

There was nowhere to sit. My head rolled about, and I leaned against Mother. "Just a little while, Pisti." She put her arm around me, holding me firm.

When I woke, the train was already in the station. The three black engines had the Hungarian and Nazi flags joined on the front. The enormous engines appeared like bulls edging into a stall.

The first to be removed were the *kosáratok*, the basket people, without legs, carried in wide, wicker baskets like wilted produce to market. Anyu was beside herself. "Dear God, let them have legs," she repeated. "Let them have legs."

Overcome by doubt and fear, I started crying at once, loudly. I was swept up by the sudden swirl of people pushing and calling: "Get out. . . . Move, I say." A soldier barked at the limping porter: "You, the slowest . . ." An officer noticed me. "For Christ's sake, what's a child doing . . ." He rushed past.

Conductors of our suffering and hope, the porters maneuvered the crowds: "Last names P, R, S, Sz, by the south wall."

They grew frantic, their voices shrill. "Please, form a line. A line, please." They motioned with their hands. "Last names starting with P, R, S, Sz by the wall." They drew imaginary rows. "Earlier letters to the entrance." They again gestured with their hands.

Ceaselessly, the porters yelled the schedule for the next train. "Three A.M. Surely. Three-thirty, sure. Latest report. Form a line. A line, please. You need to be out by two-thirty." In the confusion and din, and swept up by her own thoughts, Anyu did not notice me weeping until I buried my head in the folds of her skirt. She carried me to the end of the platform, past the oiled beams, where there was quiet.

A small black pine thrown from the doorway of the last car landed at Mother's feet. "It was meant for Christmas," a voice said from the darkness.

The man, worn and thin, had a splint on his leg. A ragged beard covered his face. This much I could see. "I cut it in the mountains," he said to Mother. "It's been in a bucket for weeks," he complained. "Probably dry."

So what, so what. Anyu ran to him. He was alive. He was whole. "It's Balázs, your uncle," she cried to me. I did not recognize him. She embraced the soldier. He held her. Then, startled, she drew back. She looked at him in the darkness and suddenly realized that she had been mistaken. It was not her cousin, my uncle Balázs. It was not her cousin. But the soldier would not let her go. He clung to her. She struggled. Finally breaking from the stranger's embrace, panting and shaken, she cried to me, "Come. Run. We must go."

In the end we found no one.

Her deep disappointment when none of her relatives returned from the bend of the River Don began to fester that very evening on the way home from Keleti Station. It took several months of crying and after that several more months of cleansing laughter to heal her wounds. But I could understand her sorrow only in the abstract. I never did understand the depth of her losses, even as an adult, even when I could clearly remember her talking about her family tree bereft of leaves.

"Our family? A tree cast in doubt," she was wont to say even into old age. "But doubting always carries with it the kernel of hope." She would begin to laugh again.

Although her family tree was bare, she perpetually hoped that it would revive, perhaps after a heavy rain, sprouting a new shoot up through the cracked trunk or awakening an old root from dormancy. She hoped her family tree would grow anew, becoming rich with the buds of pregnant life, just as she hoped this or that distant cousin would return.

"Australia, New Zealand, Canada," she chanted. "Far away, true, and on the other side of the world," she repeated, stewing the chunks of beef and pouring thick sweet paprika from Szeged into the broth. "And hope still so near, and my life, you, my dear." She turned toward me and smiled. Rózsi noticed her, too. "Good to see you smiling."

But the last of Anyu's remaining relatives were "loaned" to Germany beginning in October 1944. Her losses continued unending until Decree 975/M of late October swallowed the northern tribe of Israel, the Ashkenazim.

After the pain, she cleansed her sorrow and rage. With her guffaws and belly laughs, the Hungarian *röhög* resounding like the bass of a church organ, she simply washed it out. She cleansed herself of rancor as well as sorrow almost self-consciously, like a cat licking its paws.

The cottage in Szentendre, owned by Gyula Ofner, Mother's square-faced and bearded cousin, was at the base of Northwest Mountain, amid cragged terrain. Anyu laughed again when she saw the rocks jutting through the soil, washed away at the base of the boulders by years of erosion. All the houses near the cliffs, like Gyula's, were low lying. Many still had thatched roofs.

That last winter of the war, the winter of 1944, the Russians had crossed Hatvan seventy kilometers to the east of Pest, and everyone knew liberation was surely at hand. The Germans and the Arrow Cross had dug in all over the city and had assembled heavy artillery on Gellért Hill. Szentendre was less than 30 kilometers from the city, and it was clear to Apu that our district would be bombarded by both sides. It was also clear that, lacking a cellar, we were in danger.

In the middle of our garden stood two mulberry trees that were a joy to Gyula. They had been planted before the war by the previous owner and were tended lovingly by my uncle. The trees were bountiful in the extreme, producing mulberries the size of a thumb. The berries glowed with firm sweetness, each bunched by the hundred, bloated with juice and corked at center by a tiny gold navel from which minute silver filaments grew. Gyula's geese waddled a kilometer from near the shores every Friday to peck ravenously at fallen fruit, their necks quickly sweeping the surface of the ground under the trees.

Gyula, "the Lord of the Manor," as Anyu called him, told us it took stealth and luck to get the trees. He actually pretended to have planted the trees himself. He and his wife, Bórika, had a regular routine about it.

Protekció, the traditional bribe, had been given to the gardener with a bottle of wine and a crumpled hundred-pengő note. Fruit trees were in short supply that season, yet when the nursery opened and the crush of people moved into the yard, Gyula's mulberry trees stood leaning by the fence of the nursery. Gyula told and retold the story with fresh enthusiasm each time, as though he were reciting a wise allegory whose many levels of meaning appeared only on retelling.

He hardly had time to start his tale when his wife, Bórika, her full cheeks bundled in a kerchief, broke into lively prattle and told of Gyula standing over the trees for three days straight, enthralled like a parent over a newborn and stroking the bark as though it were tender flesh. Bórika disclosed that Gyula had even muttered all the while: "You will be good trees. You will take root."

As Bórika spoke, Gyula grew increasingly uncomfortable, glowing poppy pink and meekly interjecting objections. "That's *just* how a woman would see it," he said, his voice trailing off. And later, "How could you hear me muttering? I was out in the garden. You were on the porch." Here, his voice broke.

But Bórika ignored his protests and continued to divulge Gyula's passion for the trees. She recalled how by nightfall he would be mumbling, "Dear trees, be kind, be abundant."

This routine could go on forever, with dozens of variations. An embrace, I learned, was the way it usually ended. When Gyula kissed Bórika's full lips, she could say nothing. "I kiss your eyes, my dear," Gyula muttered in her ear. And then he kissed her eyes. They were two stocky and solid frames embracing, short and squat, like two cans rubbing together. It cheered me to see them like that, two institutional-sized cans of pea soup or tomato paste rubbing against each other.

"Have no cares," Gyula said. "Have no cares."

It was true. Gyula seemed to have no cares, as though the war were on another continent, the synagogues intact. Anyu had started mocking him as the Lord of the Manor when he had refused help in leaving after the mobilization laws of 1941, but insisted he had rights like any other Magyar. He had remained pigheaded even after the ten-centimeter six-pointed canary yellow stars were decreed on 5 április 1944, stating, as Anyu had also, that shame was dangerous.

In fact, Apu had helped him gain first one, then another Aryan identity through the Keleti offices. He had accompanied Gyula to the station dressed in his uniform. There he was able to obtain identity papers for refugees from Transylvania, and Gyula's family got the well-fitting Transylvanian name Meszáros.

Yet now, despite Apu's having diagnosed Gyula's yellowish complexion as jaundice and having sent the forms to central headquarters, Gyula was still threatened by conscription as a laborer with the likelihood of being sent to Germany. "If the ratio is four soldiers to one Jewish serviceman and a hundred Magyar die, you can bet sixty of them will have been Jews," Apu told him. Gyula did not need convincing. "And as far as being sent to Germany on loan, it is a debt that will never be repaid."

"Believe me, Gyula," said Father, continuing to press him, poking at Gyula's nose now. "The end won't be long now. You and the family are doing the right thing by leaving."

The next day, we watched this sprig from the family tree that would be saved by prudent transplanting assemble in front of the house. They were dressed in plain clothes, like workers, except that Gyula had an American fifty-dollar bill nailed under his heel. None wore the star. They were no longer the Meszáros family, but the Molnárs, the simple surname for mason. Anyu gave Bórika a kerchief full of sunflower seeds, citing the aphorism "Rich seed take root."

Anyu handed each of the children a crackling scone and a coin. We gathered in the front garden and the sun showered a white light, sparkling in the clarity of the cool morning air. Blazing, it fired the lower sky. But no warmth reached us. We shuddered, like children craving the lap.

Then the newly named Molnár family trudged up the lane. They rounded the whitewashed church on the corner, stark silhouettes cast against the brightness of the facade, and disappeared forever that morning of 5 július 1944.

The trees, the gardens, both front and back, the short walk to the Duna's shore, where Angi and I could swim or our family could picnic, the closeness of the hills where I anticipated many adventures, all this had been left behind for me and my family. We were the ones to benefit from their misfortune. As I gazed out the window at the spot where Gyula had rounded the church, I thought of the sunflower seeds.

But my melancholy over the unnatural inheritance soon faded as I took increasing delight in the garden. Gyula's garden provided much of the produce that we could no longer get at the market— yellow peppers, white beans, and onions. The potatoes were as big as my shoes. And though it was a small plot of land, hardly bigger than the L-shaped path that ran along its edge, there were rows of raspberries, white currants, and gooseberries, which Anyu boiled down into preserves for winter. I could appreciate bounty. Already in my young life there had been times when I relished our meager fare of lard and black bread.

It was on a crisp, ice-clear winter day that Apu started to tell stories of how the garden reminded him of his boyhood in Zalavég. He tended to do this after meals, while he chewed on stewed apricots and placed the pits in a pile on the side of his dish.

"Oti, Sándor, and I trudged out daily to the plot at the outskirts of the village. In the fields, I used to call your grandfather *édes apám*, my dear one and only father. Sándor, the oldest and the only one of us to use a full-weight scythe, was more familiar with him, the only one who could speak freely with this man I eventually came to know as Boszor. He actually ribbed your grandfather as *öreg harcos*, the old warrior."

Angi and I gathered around him and, still small framed and light, I crawled up on his knees. I eyed the growing pile of pits in the bowl, which I would later inherit and crack for the seed, pretending they were almonds.

"It was grueling work," he continued.

Anyu listened to his stories intently, huddled by the door, staring at him with penetrating closeness. Her eyes narrowed, so that she seemed forceful in her intensity, like the osprey with the yellow eyes I had once seen in a field near Szigliget. Her gray-streaked hair, which had been clear black years earlier, was unkempt and fell across her forehead like autumn rain. She finally spoke her mind, confronting Apu with a harshness in her tone I had never heard before. "God spared you from the Don. You were spared. Your children are a blessing of life," she spat. "It's as simple as that."

And so it was that Apu resolved to dig up the garden, and he divided up the labor of building the bunker. Angi was ten by then, still growing, and always dressed in the same cotton dress that billowed as she ran after Anyu toward Szentendre Road. We would need matting to protect us from the cold ground, and they could still get hay there among the abandoned barns that lined the road. Day after day they collected meager bundles from the leavings of the bone-bare horses that ranged free and untended along the empty streets of the city, not worth the butchering.

Apu and I set to dismembering the garden. I was only five, slight, and of little help. It took two days to unearth the trees, and then Apu felled the bigger white mulberry tree with an ax. He asked me to brace his bad leg as he chopped. Only a two-foot stump remained. He spent far more time chopping at its many unyielding roots. Massive clods of red soil clung to the fibers. We dragged the stump to the side of the house with the rest of the tree, heavy with buds that would soon shrivel.

The smaller mulberry tree was easier work. Many of its buds had already opened, and as I lugged its branches across the yard, their thick nectar stained my shirt. By week's end, we had uprooted all of the gooseberries and raspberries. That Sunday, with no respite, we started digging downward.

We dug for days into the cold soil. As the trench deepened, the history of Hungary opened up to us. At one meter we found a Turkish shard, which Apu recognized by the indentation of a single letter that curled and slanted and looked like a wave on Balaton during a windy storm, with markings on the top that could have been spray. Later Angi found a tiny silver coin with a hole.

From the outside, rising from the backyard, our shelter looked like a mass grave, but once through the tiny opening there was enough room to stand up. We had some ventilation, even a flue for a lantern, and straw to lie on. It struck me as an adventure to live underground. It was quite comfortable to my child's playful mind. What was more, the trench was L-shaped, following the form of the path; if necessary, we could hide or sleep safely in the far side.

Angi and Anyu had gathered enough straw for a thin mat, and we all went to pull home long half-burnt beams from the collapsed synagogue on Futó Street by the river. These we laid crisscrossed over the trench, then scattered pages of *Népszava* across the beams. Over these we heaped the red soil that had nourished our garden.

* * *

It took twice as long to liberate the few hills surrounding Buda as all of the plain. Fighting moved from knoll to knoll, bunker to bunker, and house to house. We could not be certain of this, but Apu told us tales about the street fighting as though he went out to inspect each day. "It's all rocks and hills here. Tanks can't get through," he said. "It's hand to hand, dashing around the corner or diving behind a wall." The big guns in the distance rumbled deep, and those placed by the Germans in the hills bellowed and boomed.

We spent nearly all of our time in the trench. We ate gruel or bread spread with fat and chewed sweet acacia blossoms that Anyu had dried. When she was able to trade for sugar, Anyu would carefully sprinkle the crystals evenly over our bread.

She also read aloud from Job for countless cousins and relatives of all degrees. Apu, too, turned to his faith. His staunch beliefs always struck me with surprise and awe, especially since few of his ardent prayers were answered. Though his faith did not waver during the war, he did develop a peculiar habit in the bunker. He bundled his pleadings to God, as if in a blanket, by countless layers of Hail Marys and several Our Fathers. Amid the distant shelling, I could hear him praying softly, the way I imagined Gyula speaking to his young trees. "Our Father and our Mother who art in heaven . . . You loved Your own child dearly," Apu prayed. "He is by Your side forever. Let mine live and prosper, dear Father. . . . Dear Mary, Mother of God . . ."

In the early hours one night during our third week in the bunker, we heard the rumbling of armored vehicles, then rapid fire, and finally two grenades exploding in our house. Apu peeked out of the entrance as soon as silence fell. In the darkness he made out the dim outline of our house. The roof had collapsed, he said. Three Russian soldiers were marching toward the bunker. He waved to the Russians. An officer who spoke Hungarian approached him and asked if any Germans were with us. Apu replied to him in Russian. But the officer ordered us out in mixed Russian and Hungarian.

We could hardly make out one another in the darkness, and, as the officer descended into the trench, his pistol drawn, I suddenly missed Angi. She had been left behind sleeping in the space at the far end. She had slept through it all. But what if she stirred? What would the Russian think in the dark of the bunker? I tried to find words to respond to the crisis. I wanted to scream, but I stood paralyzed. As in a dream, I heard Anyu saying my sister's name over and over: "Angi, my flower. Angi."

Then I heard Anyu scream out my sister's name, and the realization that Angi was still in the bunker sent Apu running to the trench. "A girl's in there!" he shouted in Russian. "Don't shoot!" At once we heard the officer shouting, *"Stoy! Stoy!"* Angi's high-pitched cry soon followed. A faint glow from a lighted match filtered through the opening. Finally, a deep wail joined Angi's rhythmic cries from below.

"My dear. My dear. I have found you," the officer repeated in broken Hungarian.

When they emerged, the Russian held Angi in an embrace. Against his mountainous frame, Angi looked smaller, like a young girl. And her face looked it, too, as though she had shed eight years in the bunker and had emerged as a toddler. Her lips and cheeks were covered with chocolate. The Russian wept as he staggered out into the street with my sister, carrying her much as she used to carry me, cupped in an arm. The rest of us ran along behind.

"Dear God, no. Where is he taking her?" Anyu was beside herself with fear.

The Russian trudged toward the landing where the Esztergom ferries docked.

Anyu continued to agonize. "Please, please, she's just a tiny girl."

But she had mistaken the Russian, for though Angi was ten, he held her close and tender against his breast as though she were a baby, one hand cradling her head. With no sense of fear, as though swaddled, Angi looked tinier than I had ever seen and nestled easily against his enormous chest and sucked at her stained fingers. The Russian plodded toward the Duna, his huge strides interrupted by sobbing.

In the gray light I could see a thin mist rising from the surface of the river, luminous above the water's surface.

The Russian did not stop sobbing till he reached the bank, where he finally released my sister from his massive embrace. Crouching and pointing at the river, he said at last, "The Duna is like the Don."

Bright now, the mist, like a fragile blue ribbon, wavered in the air above the water in the dawning light and dispersed with a breeze. It was an early spring, and the Duna, abundant with life, sang many songs that morning. Its waters splashed and bubbled, and from its banks came a chorus of buzzing and cawing. Reedlings flew at sharp angles over the surface of the river, and the twilight sun slowly stained the quick-flowing waters ever-lighter hues— violet and pink and beige.

"I have a daughter." The Russian stroked Angi's face. "I do not know the color of her hair, the glint of her eyes. I have never seen her smile. All I know for the last five years is war. The thunder of shelling. Men frozen in place as they march at night. Not just German, mostly Magyar. Your people. At dawn, when we traversed the river, the fields across the Don were pocked with the lost, like tree stumps shrouded with snow. Men frozen in place. A forest of loss."

With a burst of light, the sun rose over the horizon of the opposite shore. The distant shelling started up again. The Russian looked across the river, this river, our Duna, toward the morning sun.

"What is the name of your daughter?" Angi asked. She gripped her side with one hand and with the other picked meekly at the chocolate caught in her hair.

The Russian did not answer. He kept looking at Angi, then looking far east, then at Angi, and back again east, as though he could see to Asia.

Explosions broke softly in the distance. I felt a sudden chill and began to shiver like Angi. I was chilled by a biting cold, and although I had my heavy coat on, I felt as if I stood naked to the wail of winter winds.

Crouched beside Angi, the Russian now seemed small and frightened. He again clutched her close, as though fearing she might leave his side. "Dearest God," he prayed aloud, "is my Lyuba alive?"

7

Kindness
1948

Although the death march to Hegyeshalom was a key to Anyu's sorrow and guilt, the losses at Voronezh were a source of guilt for Apu. He had saved his own life so as to save others, true. But the mind is not nearly as forgiving as all that, and as he walked the streets of Pest, where there were hardly any men his age visible on the sidewalks and in bars or in the espresso shops, he kept commenting on it. "A whole generation lost," he would remind me.

And the defeat at Voronezh kept coming up, more so than the Holocaust, and well after the war. It would have been easy to blame the Russians, easy to hate Stalin. But that is not how I was raised. Although I eventually learned to despise Stalin, even today I cannot make myself hate the Russians. Especially today. . . . The Christian road to the soul is through the eyes, and the Russians have the saying "I kiss your eyes." But for the Jew, the way to the soul is through the face. Few people have faces as open as Gorbachev's, one so soft, a hard-chested man living from his wounds. He reflects the Russian people, and his open yearning makes him pragmatic—able to acknowledge and respond to need and to shun lofty bombast, the ideals of this or that empty credo.

I fear the Germans, not the Russians. Hitler had been the one to refuse the Hungarian retreat at the Don. He had been the maniac, and the Russians had suffered greatly against him. They crushed Hitler at the Don, the Hungarians being merely unlucky bystanders.

I feared the Germans, and perhaps that is why I hated them. I hated them even as a teenager when I lay with friends on the beaches of the tourist areas of Lake Balaton where the Germans summered. Pista, my cousin, would spit on the West Germans' Mercedeses, wiping the saliva from the windshield with a sleeve, and demand loudly, *"Deutsche mark! Deutsche mark, Herr Kapitän."* The Germans were fools enough to be taken in by the gesture. How my friends laughed the cleansing laugh then.

I blame the Germans, even though I have only shadows by which to weigh their true hurtfulness. Katalin, the aunt who raised me, hugged me only once. She had been hardened by the White Terror of 1919 when the throngs marched in front of her window and chanted with fists pummeling the air, *"Zsidó, zsidó, gazember."* Jew, swine. But was that it? Merely that? The crowds thronging and cries from the street?

Or was it the Nazi and Arrow Cross that hardened her? And the details with which she recalled Néomi, her own aunt, recounting the burial of her mother. Stacked like wood, the bodies heaped two meters high, as I had once witnessed at the river's edge. Néomi had pulled her mother out from somewhere in the middle, having recognized the pattern of her dress. And the story was passed in hushed tones from generation to generation.

What did the dress look like? I wondered after having heard the story twice. How should I know? Katalin said, but Néomi recognized the dress, that's all, and her mother was somewhere near the middle, close to a meter from the bottom. Katalin's face screws up and her nose seems to snarl, the skin folding. But my mind turns: Did the stack fall when Néomi pulled her mother out? How did she pull the woman out anyway, with nearly a ton of frozen bodies heaped on her? Did she restack the bodies or leave them scattered? The mind turns, but these are questions that it cannot ask. The questions are too morbid, and one is too fearful, or perhaps too human.

Néomi buried her mother in a shallow grave of hard-cold earth next to the heap.

And there were other twice-told tales, of how Néomi told of Jenő, Katalin's oldest nephew, dying the day Auschwitz was liberated. Apu and Anyu had failed to help this rising opera star. And when Katalin recalled him, she wept openly but in a way I had never seen anyone cry, her face twisting in excruciating agony and her lips distending with a yell. Then just as suddenly, a hard swallow and a grimace, and silence again. I cannot tell you what I mean, she punctuated her repressed outburst. If I let my feelings out . . . Her voice faded as she raced from the room.

There was largely silence, a pallor, about most of it. Sticks and stones do break our bones, but silence still breaks hearts. Except now and again, when there's a massive breaking forth, a burst of memory and discharge and then silence, the way a dam bursts with the torrent washing downstream, memory imprinting the future with a roar, and then silence upstream, quiet again, placid waters and only spillage and mud, while nearing the valleys the onrushing torrent surges to the sea in a new apocalypse of our own making among homes and lives that would be our own.

Only now, years later, am I fully aware of the German sitting on my back, riding roughshod and bending my back with an anger I fear too dangerous to vent, lest the world be destroyed in the venting, lest apocalypse come back once again, of *my* making now, perhaps again of my making. . . . How can something so total and destructive as the Nazi have been met passively? There must have been action, a bigger meaning than no meaning, the nihil of nihilism, some sort of hope and light to recover from the utter pitch, something much more than "all we as sheep." But if anger is vented, perhaps the darkness will return, simply because one is alive, as I am alive, alive now, and had not experienced the horror in the flesh. Better to slink through life? As pariah? Never to ask but to yearn silently, and to feel perpetually cheated by one's own passive stance toward history. Can one be the history maker when history has undone one's people? Say *I* do this, or *I* want that, instead of This was done to *me*, or *I was cheated* of that.

And still, there endures the will to persist, and the persistence of will. A desire for joy and pleasure and success and rest.

I met Mari, a widow of Voronezh, the Battle at the Don, in 1947. She was one who revived. Born and raised Catholic, I would witness her conversion to Judaism many years after her husband's death. Actually, her turning wasn't so much to Judaism. She believed in one G–d and in the One-House, a garden called earth, was how she put it. I spent the summer of 1947 with her in Szigliget. That summer, the sun was painful and brilliant, scorching the earth. The red soil was scarred with cracks, and the dust pounded by the herds returning from grazing hovered in the evening air above the paths. Like the tiny flies common to the region in August, the dust did not settle until weighed by the wetness of early morning.

There was no wind that summer, and Lake Balaton, the hand mirror for a duchess, smooth and ornate, reflected the blinding light. The peasants working the vinery for the Szigliget commune could not look down at its surface. They diverted their gaze from sky and water, intent only on breaking the hardened clods that sustained the vineyards lining the conical hills around the lake like circus tents with green stripes.

Mari Néni was a middle-aged woman, already graying. Uncle Kálmán, with whom I usually stayed when in the country, had fled. Or so it was hoped. Mari was a distant cousin of Apu, but while Apu tended to stay on an even keel, Mari had the temper of a goat from the start. I instantly understood my parents' ambivalent discussions about my summering with her. Father had prevailed for once: "Nowhere is the air so clear as by the lake. He can go fishing and swimming, and the world-famous row of poplars is right by Mari's cottage. Plus, without Izsák, her husband, she'll probably welcome a young boy for a guest."

But hardly had she greeted us when Mari started complaining, as though I were not welcome.

"I'll have no yelling or messing," she bleated. "And the

washbasin, you mind, is emptied by sunset." A gnarled finger bobbed in my direction.

Apu grew restless as he tried to counter her. "Just wait till you taste her strudel, Pisti. Poppy seeds with raisins no less."

"And when the rooster crows, we're up. Your bed made," she went on.

"And you be sure to wash the sheets and hang them billowing," Apu laughed at her. "But first, slaughter the he-goat." His mocking brought a smile to Mari's lips.

"There's a smile. There's a smile," Apu prattled, not letting go, and danced around her like a fool. Then she stroked my face with callused fingers, her thin smile exposing a missing tooth. Mirth left me at once. Here I was to stay for two months, with this overgrown woman, broad shouldered and muscular, so like a workman that hair even grew on her face.

I watched Apu drive off in our three-cylinder Trabant, the engine coughing into the distance, and grew tense. He had said only nice things about this woman.

Then I heard behind me, "Here, little one." Mari came out with a plateful of strudel. Would she prove unexpectedly trustworthy as Dr. Tóth, who had at first seemed cruel? I thought back with a shudder to the walk by the Danube. Thinking that I was chilled, Mari put her arms around me, huge and uncomfortable as sackcloth.

It was the custom in Szigliget to whitewash the cottages every five years. They were transformed from a dust gray into a brightness that could be seen from across the four-kilometer distance to the opposite shore. The thatched roofs were removed, the houses crowned with fresh reeds from the lake, and the whole village took on the air of a well-scrubbed child—self-content, yet eager again for dirty play. People on the other side of the lake would see the dotting of cottages in bright rows and say, "Szigliget has bathed again." The proud villagers would make many unnecessary excursions to the opposite shore.

But this was the end of the fourth year, and the dust of four summers had tainted the white walls. The rain and snow of a half decade had discolored the thatched roofs. A dreary haze, like a soiled blanket, covered the village and the countryside.

I often walked up the hill called the Queen's Skirt. I thought it a peculiar name—a skirt, of all things. Surely it was more like a circus tent. Anyway, how could one walk *up* a skirt? I could well imagine going *under* a skirt, as when I would hide under Anyu's skirt when I was a toddler. It was still like a tent, even back then, as I hugged her stockinged legs.

Now I played among the ruins of the castle at the top of the skirt, mere debris from King Arpád's reign, worn nearly flat. From there I could see all of the district of Veszprém to the west. The rows of poplars lining the road in the distance below looked like troops of toy soldiers, and the square plots of land planted with cabbage, rye, and wheat formed my chessboard. The fields of sunflowers, miles away, faded in the rising dust.

Mari Néni, the odd one, as I soon heard the villagers calling her, did not care.

"They talk about me less now," she told me in muttering tones. "Less talk about coal among eggs."

She busied herself slicing a black loaf and buttering it for our dinner.

"Just as well. Just as well," she kept on, not even noticing me, pouring the bean soup into a bowl. "Next month they'll have more to talk about."

Then turning suddenly, she looked into my eyes. "And you'll be here for that. You'll be here, won't you?"

It was only then that I realized she wasn't looking at my eyes at all, but somehow off-center, at my cheeks or my forehead. It frightened me, like her language did, which seemed full of hidden meaning.

As I played with other children in the lower field and spoke to adults on errands at the market, I made more sense of her veiled words. I pieced together that Mari was being scrutinized, now that the 1947 autumn cleaning was only a month away. When I was fetching water or herding her single Palodian longhorn to pasture, the many questions about her intentions surprised me at first. The manager of the co-op, where I was sometimes sent for sugar or salt, actually glowered down at me through bushy brows: "Well, what have we, my lad? Yea or nay?"

I did not know what he wanted.

"Yea or nay?" he repeated, bending low, insisting with a foul breath. "Sale or no sale, my lad?" he continued. "Shall she buy the paint? Speak up, speak up, what have we?"

On Saturdays, Mari and I walked the six kilometers on the rise between the ruts carved by wagons to the synagogue in Badacsony. The first time we went, the road stung my feet, as it pricked hers. She lifted the broad, archless soles of her feet now and then, rubbing away the dust from the thickly callused bottoms. Mine blistered by the time we arrived at the four-kilometer marker.

"Your soles are so thick," I marveled, sitting by the road.

"I never wore shoes," she laughed. "Out here there is no need."

As we neared Badacsony, my blisters broke and my feet bled.

"It's not far, little one," Mari said, looking at me sadly. *"Upla, upla,"* and she lifted me onto her back. This was a treat.

Soon she began to pant. "Look here. From now on, you'll wear your shoes, you hear. No need to be a country boy all at once." And when we arrived at the white stucco building, she placed me on a step and stretched her back. She grumbled, "We'll have to get home, no less."

In the one synagogue in the entire district that had remained intact after the war, her secret as well as her silence was allowed to rest. Neither the small sprinkling of the community, nor the eldest surviving male, the *Gabbi*, who collected a few forint each week, marking them in a ledger so all could see, tried to force on her any sense of duty to her village.

"A locked heart is a sin only when the Great Temple's gates are open," Annus, the reader for the group, assured her. That

Annus was a woman and also the reader was not out of the ordinary for this small group of Jews, which consisted of only three men and twelve women. This included Mari, who was Catholic. But neither was this seen as odd. They remembered well Izsák, Mari's Ashkenazi husband, a shepherd in the area since boyhood, and they welcomed her, knowing why she came.

The community worship went on, even without the ten men, for the ten scouts of Moses, required for a *minyan*, because Annus had come to understand the word *minyan* as meaning "a few" or, in her opinion, "perhaps just a very few," having researched it in Leviticus and interpreted the scripture according to the needs of the assembly.

After all, they were mostly women. By placing little emphasis on numbers and more on the role of Jewish women in creating the Jewish community, she argued that their role was important and not of a lesser obligation.

"We are public, certainly in the eye of the district we are visible, the fifteen of us, and God has asked us to perform a public act," Annus often repeated.

The fact that a quorum could not be achieved made their own version of the *minyan* a matter of practical necessity. Annus, a ruddy woman in her forties, was seen by most of the others as a teacher, as well as the reader. They listened intently when she argued on their behalf: "Either there is a public act in the worship of God, or here, in the district of Veszprém, there will be silence."

And in this way, bit by bit, the community went on to read from a grease-stained Torah that old man Babel had preserved; after some debate, they even dared to sanctify God. Soon I learned a few words that kept repeating: *"Baruch ata Adonai. Blessed be our Lord."*

Annus seemed so pleased when I muttered these few words. To make her happy, I said them over and over, going out of my way to let her hear it.

"Are you a priest?" I once asked her.

"A reader," she said.

But I did not believe her, because I knew everybody could read.

"You're a lady priest," I said. "How can that be?"

"I am the reader," she insisted.

"But I can read, too. Why can't *I* be the reader?"

"Just come, and next week I'll read to you."

And when that Saturday came, I wore my shoes and long pants, and after the service she held me on her lap and read me the story of the canary and the black fox, her lips pursed and her brows raised as her voice sang up and down, just like the canary's song in the story. She told me how the canary's song lulled the angry fox, until the bird could fly away far across the meadow. This was not in the book. She just liked to tell it. As she read, she pointed to the sharp teeth of the fox and the bright wings of the canary.

"Annus," Mari asked, after one Sabbath reading, "canst thou tell me how long the gate has been closed?" She spoke in the formal voice out of respect.

"More important is when you will take the yoke," Annus replied. "You were Izsák's wife. You are always welcome here."

At that time, I only knew one meaning for the word *yoke* and started laughing at once. I did not know it to mean the conscious cultivation of a life according to the laws, the Torah.

Annus laughed with me. "You think I'll turn her into an ox, a mean witch like me. Maybe set her to plough."

Then turning toward Mari, she grew more serious. "The little one knows more of the prayer than you do." Annus mussed my hair.

"It is a matter of time, Annus," Mari replied. "What I ask is how long the gate will be closed."

"Your questions, like you, jump about, future to past. But you've answered yourself: it is only a matter of time." Annus suddenly smiled. "The sun will surely rise in the south. Just read the city paper. It's sure to be. Probably in a few months."

By now, I was stifling my laughter again, my child's firmly held knowledge of how the world functioned shaken.

"And will the gate be open for us to go to the sun?"

"In a matter of time," Annus repeated. "But it doesn't matter. It does not mean what we think it does. There will be a homeland. That is what matters. To *know* of a home, just knowing of it, can bring belonging and hope."

The long arid weeks of July had given way to the sudden torrents of August, which churned the lake into peaks. One Sunday, Mari sat in the back pews for the morning mass at the Lady of Mercy, the Catholic church at the far side of Szigliget, where she had been baptized and confirmed as a child. The church, built in the 1500s, was marked by two bulbous spires, remnants of Turkish reconstruction. Throughout the service, Mari muttered the rosary as though at the confessional: "Mother of God, Mary, Mother of God, Mother Mary."

The priest chanted in Latin, and the congregation all around us stood and knelt and sat and stood again in unison to my amazement, as though they all understood some Latin cue. I scrambled to keep up, but my anticipation was awkward, even though I knew the service. For some reason I could not understand, I felt uncomfortable. I clumsily stood when others knelt and remained seated as others stood. Mari, kneeling throughout the service, continued her chant.

I felt even more uneasy seated next to her. A woman in a red kerchief cast a glance toward us, then turned away. The lace-headed peasant turned, while the spectacles with the wizened face looked at length. As we finally knelt side by side, I dared to whisper, "Why are you just kneeling, Mari? Why don't you also stand and sit?"

"It's the act. I'm praying." She went on chanting the rosary, the beads racing through her fingers. And still, many heads continued to turn, even though, as I noticed, several other women also chanted to themselves.

After the service, when Mari had lighted a votive candle for her offering, the priest in his embroidered vestments, green silk for summer's bounty, quietly approached her. "It's not right, Mari. Why dost thou hurt thyself with thine brethren?"

She did not answer.

The priest's voice grew stern. "I asketh of thee."

She did not answer.

Having taken her earlier statement literally, and being frightened by the priest's tone, I blurted, "It is just an act."

"Shush, Pisti," she snapped, and she smacked my head. Then turning to the priest, she said, "He knows not what he's saying, Father."

She scooted me out, firmly gripping my neck. "Perhaps he does know," the priest called after us as we scurried from the church.

To my surprise and fear, the priest followed us out.

"It is not right," he repeated. "This is a community. You're part of it."

Mari quickened her pace, yanking at my arm. Alarmed that she should be snubbing such a hallowed figure, all I could focus on was the change in the priest's language. He had dropped the formal voice once outside the church.

The priest kept up with us, his vestments billowing. "Are you a part of us, or are you apart?" His face was red now, from exerting himself in the noon sun while bundled in his heavy vestments, I thought. I did not want to think he was angry.

He stopped short. "Look at you, Mari. Running. Never will I run after you." And for the first time it hit me: this is the way Mari was. Always running, running to the well, running about the house, even scurrying to church on her day of rest.

The priest did not keep his word, for he continued running after her. And we, too, started up again. "You are apart, aren't you? Apart from the rest of us and from the House," he shouted, part of his vestments dark green with perspiration. He was angry, I finally saw, my denial broken.

But by that time, we had caught up with some of the congregation who had left earlier, and the priest finally turned back.

We returned to Mari's cottage at the outskirts of the village as we always did, alone. But that day we were shaken. We did not speak and walked on opposite sides of the road. We passed several families. I was not part of the riotous gangs playing loudly with their many cousins, their laughter pealing, alongside parents and relatives. With each of her plodding steps, Mari pounded dust that rose and clung to the moisture of her ankles. I straggled behind her, smacking at the road with a stick, not really knowing why, playing, perhaps to keep my mind off the priest. "Are you punishing the road for the biting heat?" She came to my side and took my hand for the first time.

Mari Néni had not whitewashed her cottage for nine years, having ignored the 1942 traditional cleaning to the bewilderment and outrage of the villagers. I learned of this for the first time after being excluded from a soccer match in the lower field during a heavy rain. The field was muddy, with poor footing, and the boys were slipping about when I got there. A tall, thin boy told me to go away.

"The stitch! Stitch of bad blood!" the kids yelled. "When it reaches her brain, the devil dances in her."

I was near tears. "You always let me play before."

"You live with a witch. Filth and slime, before your time."

"What do you mean?" I clenched my fist to keep from sobbing.

"She hasn't been a part of the village since before the last cleaning," a boy taunted.

Then the others, equally eager, quickly backed up the boy who had first confronted me. "Really, it's like not bathing for years, her skin pocked and reeking."

With that, my hurt gave way to anger. "And look at all of you. Every one of you. Are you clean? Caked in mud and more, *you* are the filth of the village." And I turned and took my leather ball, which I had brought from the city. I knew it would be missed, even if I wasn't, as all they had were rag bundles that had become soaked. When I turned from the field, I could not keep back my tears. Enraged at having been so demeaned, I turned and shouted back at them, *"Disznók!* Pigs! Swine!"

They remained unperturbed and grunted back at me as a group, then laughed aloud.

As the end of August neared and autumn crept closer, the community's disdain toward Mari grew more open. Her obstinate ways, even with the priest, fueled rancor among most of the villagers, and her solitude became a lesson in divine retribution for the children. When she walked to the village well, the children on the path hid their heads in the softness of their mothers' aprons, and the women simply nodded at her in greeting and walked past. There was no talk of watered-down milk or the failure of the potato crop. I was again outraged, and as the women nodded, I mocked them with a bobbing head, loose about my shoulders, that took them by surprise. I looked just like a puppet.

The priest, whose name was Torda, actually gave a sermon on the autumn ceremony as an act of purification in which all should partake. *"Az ami rendes, az rendes,"* he asserted. "What is proper and good is just that. A house in order."

That day, Mari was kneeling in a side corner. The priest spoke louder than I had ever heard him.

"Our community is as a body. The body of Christ, Our Lord, Himself. The body of Christ will not be tarnished. *Ez az Isten akarata."*

He turned dramatically then, completely around, and faced Mari, repeating, *"Ez az Isten akarata."*

I grew excited at that moment because I did not understand him and feared he was talking to me, perhaps angry at what I had said to him weeks earlier.

I whispered anxiously into Mari's ear, "What's that, Mari? What's *Isten akarata?"*

"Shush."

"But he keeps using it over and over. *Isten akarata."*

" 'God's will be done,' " she snapped, interrupting her chant, and stared back at Father Torda. My anxiety increased at the confrontation. The church was silent. Knowing not what to do, I knelt. She put a firm hand on my shoulder, "Stay still, I say."

After that day, the "God's will be done" liturgy kept appearing in my daily life. Once toward the end of August, when I was by the well, a curious child asked, "Why is that woman, Mari, alone, Da?"

The father replied, "Just see. The Divine does its own work. She will die with no one by her bed."

As we sat around the kerosene lamp one night, cracking nuts, Mari told me, "It used to be easy to smile before Izsák left. Welcoming smiles, and kind smiles, too."

Though she wanted to conceal her sorrow from the glassy stare of Szigliget, she could not. Once she burst into tears while lifting water from the public well and had allowed the bucket to fall with a resonant crash back into the dark depths.

She felt cheated by life, I came to see, something distorted and perverse, like the fungus on the corn that the villagers ripped off and burned to prevent contamination of the crop. After a while, she did not try to smile, nor did she feel shame, but merely said in a soft whisper, which I heard from time to time, "Mortals' thoughts should be of this world."

I often heard her muttering that way, as though she had memorized portions of the Bible for wise sayings. But more often, she talked to herself about Izsák.

"I am lonely and the work so hard," she would begin. "I have nothing of yours, Izsák, but the memories."

I learned much later that memories can soothe loss. To have been loved and to have loved can be sustaining. But Mari was one of those souls, gnarled like the wild apple, for whom memory heightened pain. Yet she persisted in recalling memories of Izsák, often confusing them or forgetting the sequence of events.

"*Shabbat* at dusk with a bottle of wine and Izsák toasting the stork that roosted on the chimney. The young ones making their first flights in looping circles around the cottage."

"Or were we on the path from the field?" She tried to recollect. "Was it then he stopped and pointed at the stork? One legged, still as a statue, among the tall grass and the poppies, the bill wide open. 'It is yawning,' he said."

"*Na, az élet,*" she kept saying over and over as her memories expired. "The life. What to say of such a life?"

She was forty when she married, she confided. Yet by forty-five, three years after Izsák had been taken with the Second Army to Stalin's front in the Ukraine, she had reconciled herself to solitude. She let herself be absorbed by the farm chores, coming out only for water and the two weekend services.

She invented things to do, cleaned the coop many times, wove green onions into long garlands and hung them arching like bunting from the rafters in the attic. The garlands were longer than the need of winter months. When they sprouted in the spring, she felt ashamed and threw them to the she-goat so they wouldn't be wasted.

I slowly learned her habits, and I rose with her before daylight to tend the cow and go to the field. I also learned her fears and slowly gained her trust. Once, after we were returning from Badacsony after the day had started to darken, a curtain fell across the sky. We saw a wizened man, well into his eighties, approach us on the road. He was carrying a satchel slung over his back that weighed him down. He crossed to the left side of the road, we to the right. As he neared, Mari greeted him: "*Jó estét.* Good evening."

He did not even look at us but muttered audibly, "*Sie ist zuruck-gekommen zu Yiddischkheit.* She returns to her faith." He just kept walking, a stranger we had never before seen. Almost an omen, with his graying locks, passing us while the crescent moon swung like a scythe in the twilight. And that is how Mari took him. As an omen.

"*Yiddischkheit. Yiddischkheit,*" she worried, seeming to understand the word.

Our pace quickened. When we reached home she searched through a copy of the Old Testament, and at the Book of Isaiah pulled out a letter. As she opened it the center fold frayed apart. She looked at the two pieces dumbly, confused, and finally held them edge to edge, as though nothing had happened. I was standing behind her trying to read along in the dim light when I noticed that the book had been marked up with a pencil. Phrases were circled, dark lines drawn here and there, and arrows connected circle to circle.

> Sing to the Lord a new song,
> praises from the end of the earth!
> Let the sea roar, and all that fills it,
> for those who go down to sea.

This passage was marked darkly. And next to it was written the numbers 792. It was apparent that she was reading along silently because she soon turned to that page.

> I will apportion the desolate heritage,
> saying to prisoners, "Come forth,"
> to those who are in darkness, "Appear."

Here a red mark curved onto the next column, with the point of the arrow heavily marked.

> But Zion said, "My Lord has forgotten me."
> Yet I say unto thee,
> "Can a woman forget her sucking child, that she
> have no compassion on the son of her womb?"

She closed the book and held the pieces of the letter awkwardly, close to her eyes. I could not understand why she did not read the note fragment by fragment. Finally, giving up, she began reciting from memory.

"The walls of Voronezh are crumbling. The whole lot of us

are trapped. There is no time to bury the dead, so we throw them into the pits made by the shelling."

The light of the kerosene lamp tinted her face as she rested on the back of the chair, chanting the letter like a lullaby.

"Dearest Mari, were I with you. I feel like a leaf blown by this Russian winter and I do not even know what this wind is. It is night now and I am writing by the light of Miklós's lamp. He keeps telling me to hurry. I love this time of day. After dusk the shelling stops and the silent twilight turns velvet. Each night I return to you."

After reading the letter she sang the *Kiddush*, the prayer of remembering: "It was evening and it was morning . . ." and I said, "Amen." And when it was evening again, and she had given me the lit candle, she cried the *Havdalah*, the blessing for the close of day: "Blessed art Thou who divides light from darkness and the seventh from the sixth day." And we slept, and the next morning she began her work.

"It is Sunday, Mari," I reminded her, having put on my long pants for church.

But she said nothing.

Kneeling by the stove, she hardly noticed me. She scraped the ashes onto her apron, the gray soot clinging to the moisture in the folds of her hand so that her palms grew dark. Ashes rose into the air, stinging our nostrils with a sharp carbonic odor. Mari pressed the joint of her thumb against her watering eyes and smeared her forehead with a tainted finger.

The day passed as she worked in silence, cleaning the ceiling-high enameled stove in the bedroom, which was connected to the oven door in the kitchen. She went back and forth all day with the long-handled brush that fit down the flue. It finally grew dark.

Mari lifted her apron, and the thin fabric sagged under the weight of the soot. She walked out and threw the ashes onto the dung heap.

She removed her apron then and took off her worn sandals.

She made her way down the hill between the rows of sunflowers and grapes toward the lake. I listened to her singing. "My dear mother, my dear mother, what did you bring into this world?"

She seemed more supple than I had ever seen her. As she walked, her arms swung loosely and her broad hips churned as I had never seen in her gait. Her heart had behaved like a well-trained animal, but now she seemed to regain a lost passion as she sang. I had never heard her sing. She continued with her ancient melody: "Instead, you should have held me, held me. . . ." She had been silent for so long, I knew. This, the fifth year since the Don.

The dark outline of the hills behind the cottage rose like a mask before the face of the dying sun, and the far shore of the lake blended into the mist. The clouds sifted the pigments of dusk—orange, finally violet—and the shallow waters of the lake reflected the transformations of night. The lake, finally clothed in evening, subsided to sleep. The path narrowed as it neared the shore, and the sunflowers along the trail bent in dark arches above Mari.

I could see the first stars of the night between their leaves as I followed behind her. The wind picked up, raking the acres of tall reeds that grew by the bank. Crowds of black reedlings bunched into the air. Mari turned to watch the rackety cloud as it drifted over the cottage, then fell sharply to the left, returning again to the reeds.

I caught up to her then. "Where are you going?"

She loomed over me, as a protector. "It is a matter of time and the time is now."

"Velvet night," Izsák's letter echoed. She, like I, knew he had been at the front with the labor brigades. Likely, as a Jew, at the front of the front.

Then she spoke to me. For the first time she spoke into my eyes.

"It is good to have you here, Pisti." She stroked my face kindly, with a tenderness I had never before known. Her rough-

hewn hands, toughened by labor, seemed more gentle than any I
had ever known. Her face smiled openly.

I said to her, perhaps in gratitude for her touch, "You are a
kind and good woman, Mari."

She raised a hand to her face, as though ashamed. But I knew
it was not that. I saw her catching her breath. *"Baruch ata Adonai,"*
she said, echoing my special phrase that had endeared me to
Annus. She hugged me close. And then to my surprise, she went
on. *"Elohainu melech ha-alom."*

She looked down at me. She smiled. "Now, you make a wish."

I was about to wish for a new soccer ball, but she covered my
mouth. "No, not ask for something, but wish that someone be
blessed. In the blessing only will your wish come true. You must
always bless first. And foremost you must bless G–d."

"Bless Mother and Father," I said.

"Nah, you picked one I don't know yet."

"Well then, you say a blessing."

*"Baruch ata Adonai elohainu melech ha-alom, hamavdil bayn kodesh
l'hol, bayn or l'hoshech. . . ."* Her voice trailed off.

"Do you know what that means, Mari?" I asked, for I surely
did not.

"I must take on the yoke," she replied. "Blessed art Thou, Our
Lord."

She turned quickly then, past the sunflowers, pushing the
reeds aside until she stood by the bank of the lake and saw the
reflection of the metallic moon on the water. She peeled the dusty
clothes from her huge body and entered along the belt of light
until the argent waters washed around her waist. As she fell
backward, Balaton lifted the ashes from her hands and face. Her
head bent back, pulled by the roll of her eyes, and the water
muffled her ears.

I heard her singing again as I sat on the shore, just a few
meters away, and when she opened her eyes, I knew she was
looking at the August darkness, smeared by the galaxy. All around
us was a speckled void, and her song came tender.

The lake is stirred by the touch
of a young shepherd girl,
and fleecy flocks bunch
in whiting waters, tinct of pearl:
  where lake-locked snail-clouds curl.

Then she fell silent as though her song did not matter. She stood up in the lake, the water streaming in lines from her hair across her full breasts and rounded nipples. I had rarely seen bared breasts. Only those of Anyu, and then they had excited my curiosity about our differences. But now, with Mari's nakedness, I felt a new warmth. I felt a glowing warmth in my stomach and felt closer to her than ever.

From the road above the lake came the distant sound of peasants returning from the fields.

"I tell you, he was from the countryside . . ."

"Sure, for sure. What's a first secretary do anyway . . ."

"I heard different. He, a grocer's son . . ."

"Why, *you*, you could be the premier as it is . . ."

The lumbering of the ox-drawn wagon faded into the distance. A thin whistle, the bark of a dog, and Szigliget slipped into silence. A vast stillness grew around Mari and myself, like seaweed slowly covering the shallow waters of the lake. She seemed to be at peace, floating on the smooth surface of the water, all black spirits within her fallen silent. I knew she had changed, but I did not know how. As I sat among the reeds watching the moon wavering on the lacquered water, it hardly mattered what I knew or did not know. *Semmisem lényeges*, I thought. Nothing matters. We were both dreaming of a southern sun in this August dead of night.

8

The Blessed 1955

József returned to Pest from the countryside soon after Liberation, having spent the last months of the war in the woods of the mountains of western Hungary. In the quiet of our kitchen, as he ate smoked tongue and jellied beef, the red roosters printed on the wall seeming to play above his head, he told of having fallen aside on the 8 november 1944 forced march to Hegyeshalom. "Decree Number Nine-seventy-five had 'loaned' the Jews of Hungary to the Germans." He spit out the numbers. He had ended up as a conscript with the Air Defense Labor Services, 109/20. He shouted the numbers again. "Can you imagine being reduced to numbers like that?" Soon after we had lost contact with him in April, the family had been dispersed.

"We were to build an 'Eastern Wall' around Vienna as a defense against the approaching Allied and Russian-Romanian troops."

I imagined the defense as best I could, like our snow forts in winter, equipped with tunnels and rising chest high, a barricade from which we could repel the onrush of any enemy. József soon clarified what sort of wall he was talking about.

"Trenches, tank traps, fortifications." He continued to eat with zeal as he spoke. "All sorts of defenses along the Vág Valley to Styria, following the Austro-Hungarian border. The forced march quickly came to be known as a death march. We had no shelter and only three or four meals for the seven-day ordeal.

When I collapsed, the Arrow Cross, the Hungarian fascists, need I say, who organized the march, thought me dead. An old warrior gone kaput, they must have imagined, I'm sure, for they didn't even bother with the customary head shot," József mused.

Though he was tall and his face chiseled when I first saw him in the weak light of our kitchen, he was also one of the few men in Hungary who had come out of the war well fed, thanks to the help of a shepherd.

He remained, as always, a favorite uncle. He joked with me and made me laugh, just as if we were old fishing friends again and he was taking pleasure in my reeling in a fine black bass.

During the war, we walked down the length of Damjanich Street, near the park, József telling me of his hunting in the Bakony and Gerecse mountains. His tales of adventure were soon elaborated into stories of trips to the Sudan or South Africa in the 1920s.

"It was only you and the beast," he said one day, a dreamy haze over his eyes as he thought back to his youth, decades earlier, when the earth had been his garden. "Elephant or rhino, sure isn't boar," he drooled out between his lips.

"You can kick a boar with good boots. It's smaller than you are. But a rhino, if you misfire and it's charging and your second is in no position to shoot, well, how can you fend off a locomotive?"

I remember laughing. "You never went to the Sudan. You're just fooling."

"I certainly did. It was before your time. Way before you were born."

"No you didn't. When was that?"

"In the twenties, when I was importing cocoa from South Africa. On the way down I'd do some hunting."

Then he crouched and dodged and feinted as though some beast were actually on the sidewalk before us. He chanted rapidly, "Here it is! Here it comes!"

I fired out nervous laughter. "No! No! No, it's not." Suddenly, József ran up and grabbed me in his arms. "Here's the rhino. Yes. The rhino! The rhino!" And as he swept me up, I squealed in fright and joy.

Bit by bit, we got the story of his escape out of him, although Mother snapped at me when I pried. "You're acting like a child, Pisti," she said. "Remember your age."

As it turned out, he had come to on the side of the road, hearing pounding and bellowing all around him. His vision blurred by dust, he realized from the snorting near his head that he was among a herd of cows.

The herder, József learned, was named Dezső, a man in his forties with a huge gray mustache who had been disabled on the Italian front. He used his staff, in part, as a crutch. Having seen the worst of it, he was a kind man who now merely read about the war, and he had been washed of rancor. As mercy had it, he gave József food and a vest and told him of his shed in the Bakony Mountains, part of the Western Range.

After regaining strength, József sustained himself in the woods by gathering and trapping. When it got cold, he took shelter on the mountain meadow near Körishegy, the Ashen Peak, the high point where Dezső's hut was located. The herder had sealed the hut for the season, so József had to pry open the planks covering the windows. The mountain hut was made of logs and sturdy. It could keep the wind and rain out and had a hearth where a fire could be built.

No one bothered him. He collected mushrooms and trapped boar in the Sókor Hills and hare in the Marcal Basin. In late fall, he gathered acorns, which he crushed to a paste, soaked in a stream to bleach the bitterness, and baked into biscuits on hot rocks. He had a knack for getting by.

As I listened to these tales, my awareness of József swung back and forth between the glaring extremes of experience of a Jew who had survived the march to Hegyeshalom and the lighter

desires of a man who now, his mouth full of pickled beef, suddenly
declared his wish to remarry.

They seemed imponderable miracles.

Of course, getting a wife would not happen because of József's
wealth, for he rarely had money. When he did have change in his
pockets, he was hardly a spendthrift. He usually brought only a
flower or two to give to his dates, carnations at that, never a
bouquet, and if the lady said she wanted a drink, he bought
seltzer, or when lavish, raspberry soda. Never was it a brandy or
cognac.

He once returned from a date with a much younger woman
with his cap mussed, the red-flecked feathers sadly broken, like an
old cock's tail. "Can you imagine?" he bellowed. "Asking if I owned
a car, and was it new, or if I had my own apartment!" The memory
of his first wife, Olga, would prick him then.

But he smiled down at me, "You know, I nearly lived out the
war as an aristocrat. Well, at least a householder, a *gazda*, that is."

He then told of the tale of the *suba*, which is a sheepskin
cloak exclusive to the *gazda*, or well-to-do householders. When
the weather got cold and a vest would no longer do, Dezső, who
had once been a shepherd, gave József a brass hook and a
traditional *suba* of thick sheepskin. In part, it was also meant as a
disguise.

Dezső had laughed. "It fits the *gazda* well," József quoted the
veteran. " 'Thou art a regular *gazda*, my lord.' Dezső gave me high
standing by addressing me in the formal voice."

Despite his aging almost overnight and his sporting of a truly
aristocratic stomach that belied his empty pockets, József had
married by winter. His good fortune was due to the simple fact
that there were few men his age anywhere in the country,
anywhere at all. The Second Army had been lost, an entire
generation of Magyar.

"My friends have been pushed over the edge," he quickly
pointed out to lady friends. "But I do not take advantage of
another's loss, my dear." The women understood him.

And though he could have had his pick, he married Véra, a stocky Jewish peasant from Keszthely whom he had learned to trust. She had no dowry to speak of, just what she had salvaged from the closet in her cottage, a few linens and a handful of embroidered pillows. "Not much to build a future on, József," Anyu had chastized him.

But Vera bore him a son, Jószi, within the year. "That Vera," he used to go about saying. "Some kind of a woman. She could do it by will. Bear little ones even in the cabbage patch."

Still it was not all bliss. He had always been moody, and with the birth of his son, his initial euphoria gave way to melancholy. Anyu and Apu, as the godparents, did not take it seriously at first, mocking him about having 'woman's blues' after Vera gave birth. "You were always the sympathetic sort," Anyu used to say.

But his symptoms grew severe. He was sleepless, gained even more weight, and was continually depressed. His condition was not even sad or peculiar anymore. It had grown frightening.

He finally took to bed. All sorts of herbal cures were tried. Finally, he was hospitalized. There he undertook the Pavlovian sleep cure, in vogue throughout Eastern Europe at the time, but after sleeping for three days straight, an IV of sodium solution in his arm all the while, he came to, dehydrated and toxic, on the fourth day. The staff, it turned out, had neglected to give him water.

Vera did not accept that this was a part of the treatment, though the chief of the Unit for Pavlovian Sleep Cures persisted in this argument for some time.

"The good lady, Vera, must understand that these are medical matters." He looked earnest. "All sorts of sleep cures are used nowadays. English. Italian. Even Turkish, although the latter does not yet have significant statistical support."

"And the Pavlov combines dehydration with slumber, huh?"

"Really, madame, you don't understand."

While they argued, József lay in bed experiencing florid hallucinations. He started to wave his arms. "Oh, the fairies. The little fairies," he squealed. "Look, Vera. They're dancing on the sheets."

"*Micsoda?* What in hell is this?" Vera yelled at the doctor. "You call this a cure?"

"The twinkling eyes, so small," József continued, dreamlike. "Come, Vera, look."

"What sort of irresponsible stupidity is this?" Vera yelled at the doctor.

The doctor grew uncomfortable then, and he finally blurted, "As the Lady Vera wishes. I will have the nurses watch him closely."

When they learned someone would be held accountable, the nurses bellowed and gathered around József's bed like a herd at the salting block. József's toxic hallucinations lasted over a week, though mineral waters were prescribed.

Finally, after a period of rest, insulin shock was induced. József regained consciousness in a bed sodden with his own urine, Vera still by his side.

"Who are you?" József muttered at the hand on his shoulder.

"I am your wife," the hand replied.

"Can it be? Am I married?"

"With a son. A little boy."

"What is his name?"

"Why, he has your name."

Silence.

"But what is *my* name?"

At this, Vera again got agitated. She sought out the unit chief and complained, "He can't remember a damned thing."

"But Lady Vera, you must understand that the amnesia is temporary."

"And he urinates all over."

"Lady, lady," the chief went on.

"A saying from my village goes 'Forgetfulness is the kernel of joy,'" she spit at him. "But look, Doctor, he doesn't even know his own name."

The doctor gave her a little time.

And in the end, nothing much worked.

Destitute and desperate, depleted of all funds, Vera, a pragmatic woman whose temper rarely flared, was beside herself, especially when a medical opinion, coming again from the chief, recommended a lobotomy. Adding her own views with all the force of her big-boned stock and charging forward with her voice as though about to bite, she spit out the only words that held any meaning for her by then. *"Frász!"* she yelled. "That's what he has. *Frász!* No one knows what he has." She continued, "The *frász* to you, sir." And she took József home.

Time passed, but his illness persisted. I used to visit often, and I spent part of my ninth birthday with him. On that day, after I tired of squirting my new water pistol into József's courtyard, he chided me about my size even as I munched on my birthday cake. "In order to grow, all you need is willpower," he asserted. "As it is, you're too small for your age." Apu gave me iron pills and milk, Anyu made me schmaltz, but József fed me the bitters of the spirit.

What's willpower? I thought, even as I flexed my bared biceps before the hall mirror. I thought I had some sense of what power was. I stood tall and straight. Could I perhaps stretch to a height appropriate to my age?

József noticed me. "You're practicing to be a cat now?"

"You've become a bitter man," I said to him. "I hope I don't end up that way."

As I learned, irritability was a trait of melancholia, and it colored all my interactions with József.

"By will I don't mean that *Isten akarat* stuff from your father's faith," he'd begin from time to time. "That 'God's will be done' stuff."

"But what else is there, József?"

Here he usually went into Sartre and Camus, and the early existentialists, even Dostoevsky, carefully avoiding Nietzsche, all of which had the impact on me of water poured gently over a duck.

"It's a matter of wanting to be," he once said. "The will to be."

This finally got me irritated. "Come on, József. I just lack iron in my blood."

"The hell you do. You just don't have the will to grow," he snapped back. "That's why you're a runt."

That did it. Ordinarily I admired him, but now my anger burst. "What do *you* mean, willpower? Look at your gut and your rear. You don't have the will to *stop* growing," I yelled. "You have a wattle that dangles from your neck. It hangs in the soup and shakes as you walk."

Now it was his turn to feel injured. Rubbing at his stiff neck, he turned away and rattled his fingers on the table, his face red, especially the wattle.

In the early phases of his illness, József had been a kind and proud man. He had steel-gray hair and a white mustache that stood out from his weathered face and black-blooded lips. After he had returned to the city, he always wore knee-length, finely polished brown boots, a black felt vest with embroidered fringes over a white shirt, and brown tweed pants, even in summer. He wore the feathered cap without embarrassment, even after the feather broke.

But after his illness, his hair grew pure white and rarely saw a comb or brush. His once thick mustache was now constantly scraggly. His once broad smile now flashed a golden tooth, giving him the appearance of a weather-beaten gypsy.

Under the grindstone of melancholy, this glorious man became shrunken and caved in spirit. Where he once had been kind and proud, he was now only kind, and only on rare occasions. He lay in bed all day, staring into empty space. At times he was incontinent; some days he was bound and in pain.

What was worse, he could hardly curl his fingers around the soup spoon, and Vera fed him like a little child. Also, his thoughts came slowly, and he was plagued by demons that ate him with failures past and present, casting a hopeless future and arousing guilt.

And still, on occasion, he stroked my hair and held Vera's hand.

As time passed and one year collapsed into the next, the visits took on a somber air. We laughed less, and now sometimes we cried. Vera's anger was ebbing, increasingly replaced by a hopelessness. She rarely brought cocoa now, not even to make peace during our worst fights.

The contrast between who he had been and who he was now was hard for me to bear. While visiting, I forced myself to recall pleasant memories of times before his illness.

It was only as I matured that my glowing perceptions of József gave way to truth. It came as a shock when I learned of his poverty. Apu would allow me to go with him on home visits, and after he had examined József, I would linger for a time. My visits had grown shorter, and I noticed József enticing me in various ways to stay. He always gave me taffy, though Vera had abandoned the cocoa.

"That's my trophy room," József once said, intently watching me chew the candy. Pointing to a mahogany door at the corner of the room, he repeated to himself, "Full of lions and gazelle and antelope, even a gorilla. If you're a worthy young man, I'll show it to you some day."

My curiosity about the room raced out of control during these visits as József droned on about his losses to Horthy, the dictator who had ruled Hungary between the two wars, and his present preoccupation with Rákosi, the new dictator, a puppet of Stalin, who, he said, wanted to take his apartment and place him in a rest home. "A rest home with bars on the windows, I tell you," he whined on. My thoughts grew tormented. When would this old man finally share his treasures?

Then, one afternoon, József was called to the foyer. I seized the opportunity to satisfy my curiosity. I quickly tiptoed across the rug to the door. To my shock it did not open onto another room but onto a narrow closet, nearly empty. A multitude of loose wooden hangers crisscrossed the rack like tangled driftwood tossed up by the sea; two linen shirts and a pair of neatly pressed flannel trousers hung like flags of permanent defeat. Two cans of boot cream, brown and neutral, lay on the floor by a rag.

After many tiring years at home with no noticeable improvement in József's condition, Vera spoke up one morning. "Enough is enough. I'm off to market."

That day she gathered old twine from local merchants at the open market, and tying the loose ends, instructed József to roll the string into balls on his massive belly. This József was able to do. The rolled twine eventually grew to the size of soccer balls; over time, a dozen were rolled.

Vera then came with crumpled foil, and laying a sheet on József's stomach, she asked him to smooth it out. This, too, he was able to do. She lay down another sheet, and another, until he got the hang of it and could place it neatly to the side by himself.

Neither activity required little more than eyesight and the movement of a wrist. Eventually, he got to the point where he could do it entirely by feel, without even looking at what he was doing.

And that's how it went, twine and foil, foil and twine, for two weeks. Of course József had no idea what was going on, but he had little sense of anything going on. He asked no questions. He just moved his wrist across his belly, just kept smoothing foil and rolling twine across his bloating waist.

Then at the end of two weeks, Vera sold both the foil and the twine at the market, where they were sorely needed. The sale brought great gain—double what she had paid. She returned, full of glee, and surprised József by flinging from behind her back a bread basket full of ten-forint notes, having carefully placed four blue fifty-forint notes on the top to contrast the other green bills.

Well, *Isten áldj meg a Magyart*, which is what József exclaimed, quoting the saying "God bless the Hungarian." How his eyes lit up.

But Vera was smart. She would not let it drop. "See what a good husband you are, József." He smiled for the first time since I could remember. "See what a good father you are to Jószi, my dearest? A good provider. You're so good to Jószi and to me, dear love."

It would be an exaggeration to say that life sprang back into József there and then. But he did shave the next morning, at which point Vera went out of her way to compliment his good looks. In a week he was up and about, gathering old twine by the fishery. And soon he was able to strike out on his own.

Among his many dealings, he bartered empty bottles for bulk wine in the countryside where there was too much wine and too few bottles. He collected dandelion leaves and autumn saffron in the Buda woods for use in salads and sold them at market. He also collected discarded cardboard and resold it by weight (after he had soaked the middle layers). The old tinker in him had revived.

During the holidays, he converted nylon coverings for shirts into Christmas stockings and sold them outside his apartment on the corner of Lenin Körút. It was during this time that he gave me my first blazer, navy blue, British cut, which he had obtained off the back of a young tourist. Mother quickly wrapped it in plastic for protection and I wore it only to church—once a year at Christmas. After the local church we used to attend, Our Lady's, was converted to a warehouse, I was allowed to wear the jacket to parties.

József also sold noisemakers on New Year's, which he made by rolling the paper backing for packaged shirts, and gluing a cheap nozzle to the bottom of the cone. Some of these he colored with paint or pasted with pictures of pretty ladies. The noisemakers with pictures cost extra, and they sold fast.

As József accumulated wealth, I noticed how others in Hungary were frustrated. Father was an internist, yet he had to walk the thirty blocks to work, while József owned a Volkswagen, a convertible, no less. Apu used to meet József in the street, and he would stroke the beige car tenderly, as though it were a cat.

His family had an espresso maker. No one knew where he was getting the coffee. The only coffee our family was able to obtain was from care packages from Ervin. He would send us shipments bundled in used clothing. This would sell for great sums, since the clothes had good color to them. I recall Mother bursting into tears when she once opened a package and saw a plaid skirt on top. All yellow and orange and pink, quite gaudy now that I think back upon it, but worth its weight in gold. She wept openly. "It's like a garden in bloom." She wiped her tears with the fringes of the skirt, and then she burst into laughter, having felt the material. "It's wool, no less. It's wool!" In the middle of the bundle was the can of Maxwell House.

József never sickened again, but would say, "An idle mind makes for illness. Busy, busy, it's best to stay occupied." He was always doing something, going somewhere, fixing or mending or scheming. He was always on the move and always prospering.

He lived to be a wealthy man, a *milliomos*, a millionaire—a millionaire in forint, that is, which is about one-fiftieth of a millionaire in dollars. But that was fine by him. After all, he lived in Hungary where the dollar went fifty times the distance it did in the States.

He also converted his forint on the black market, and rumor had it that he had an account in the West. He had five children by Vera; later, all obtained apartments as soon as they were married. For a short stretch, the family shared two country homes, one on Lake Balaton, in Badacsony, at the base of the flat-topped mountain where the Gray Friar wine, *Szürkebarát*, is pressed. The other was at the Danube Bend, a stone's throw from Czechoslovakia.

He grew grapes for wine and table in both districts. He also enjoyed the luxury of fishing for sterlet in the Danube and for the tender-fleshed and fatty pike perch of Balaton. And he was one of the first to use Orvis equipment, the American fishing gear famous in Europe even back then. Ervin, Anyu's brother in America, sent him two lightweight reels with brass gears when Orvis first developed the line in 1954.

Eventually he also owned a second car; much later, having cashed József's accounts in the West, each of his children owned cars as well. Nothing better than a Trabant Combi or Skôda 105S, but then again, he was Hungary's newest version of a millionaire. In his opinion, a Czech car was far better than no car. It gave him relaxation on weekends at only 5.5 liters for the 150 kilometers to Lake Balaton. At a time when most Hungarians were in awe of the dollar and the freedom of Americans to run after it, he saw great worth in running after forint.

The day I last saw him I was sitting by the window of their apartment and Vera sat in the shade of the far corner. I was surrounded by her embroidery. The matching needlepoints above the mantel offered fruit, baskets of fruit, pink and blue, peaches and plums.

A knock at the door jerked Vera into action. Without even arranging her sewing, just leaving it in a pile, she jumped up, yelling, "Coming! Don't go away. I'm coming!" It reminded me of Anyu's automatic reaction to a knock on the door. With tiny, pattering steps, Vera rushed through the hallway to the door. Opening the side vents, she peered out. Silence. "No one's here, Pisti," she called back to me. No one but a knock, I thought. She opened the door wide, peered out. "It's no one," she said.

Afterward, József put on the flannel pants, and Vera tucked a crisp handkerchief into his suit jacket.

He then turned toward me, unexpectedly, words pouring forth. "The day of liberation, Pisti, 4 április 1945, it was not yet nine o'clock in the morning and I had already finished three glasses of potato *pálinka*," he said.

"You know what *pálinka* is, Pisti? You surely learned it from your Uncle Kálmán who has flown the coop, along with his Ibolya and your friend Pityu. The whole lot of them.

"It's a home-brew," he said. I had already drunk apricot brandy, famous in Hungary, but did not know it could be made at home. My interest grew at the prospect of making my own.

"Made from whatever is at hand—peaches, berries, who knows what. Well, ours was of the who knows what variety, namely potatoes. Which means it wasn't tasty, but it sure had a kick on that special day in April.

"We were in the shed. Soon I could hear voices: 'Freedom . . . Liberation . . '

"Both Dezső and I sat silently as the others grew excited. They finally flew out the door like swallows. The spring air filled the barn, and the odor of the animals lifted. We looked after the group through the light from the open door.

"Then in the distance the shouts rose again. 'Bless the liberators!' " He looked down at me, "So be it."

I was playing handball in the courtyard when József left for the meeting. The murky light of coming night leaked over the buildings and cascaded from the rooftops like stagnant water filling the clear vessel of day.

I did not know that he was to meet with the Council. Judged that very night.

He was taken away two days later. His sudden loss—to wife, and home, and to myself, and to Mother—was never explained to my satisfaction. I was quick to make my elders squirm by pointing out contradictions in the reasons they gave.

His crime was serious, I later learned. He had damaged the proletariat brotherhood. This was in 1955. He must have known an example would be made. He was also Jewish, and who knows what else, maybe a capitalist, or a nationalist, or existentialist.

As he passed in the courtyard, he stopped by me and said, "Remember this, Pisti. Were it up to me, I would sell blood sausage on Park Avenue, the *hurka*. Not to mention *lángos* to go with it, fried dough with plenty of salt. The works. Tasty, filling, fast. Fast is the key, on Park Avenue and that Broaderway. It would be a hit, you better believe, as any hot dog or hamburger. And a tribute to Hungary at that, such fine fare."

"But, József, you don't eat blood sausage," I joked with him, knowing full well that he was far from kosher.

"You're quite right, Pisti," he laughed. "I'd only eat the *lángos*. And only if they were not fried in lard. Leave the *hurka* to you, you little heathen."

Our laughter made us feel important.

9

First Love
1956

Kati and I used to take long walks in Liberty Square. The square, a kilometer wide, ran from the Budapest National Gallery at the north to the sprawling gray tenements to the south. The statue of Stalin rose to the east, a huge monolith reaching past the topmost branches of the aspens in the park. On May Day, the dignitaries stood on platforms flanking the statue's base and waved in unison as though they were puppets. The plaza was paved with cobblestones, heavy rectangles set at an angle. They stood formal and rigid like the men in rows on the podium, but they were far more enduring, although equally lifeless. I did not think of them as such at the time.

I really believed these to be men of good will, just standing there waving as the masses passed with ruddy cheeks, filing past bright and in good cheer so that the leaders could see the health and vitality of the nation they ruled.

I did not think of Kati, my girlfriend, as the daughter of one of the balding dignitaries who sometimes stood near the center of the assembly. She had been my girlfriend since I was fourteen. We had met at the Gundell Pastry Shop on Vörösmarty Boulevard. The pastry shop was old and lovely, with white marble tables and a brass rail running along the base of the counter. At the beginning of that school year, the owners of the shop had opened up the second floor as a place where kids could come after school. The lower section was reserved for adults and for couples who lingered over their espressos and leaned close to each other.

It was only after school that we could have any real fun, but we had few places to go. In class we had to sit rigidly, our hands folded behind us so as to protect our posture. We had to stare at the teacher up front without even as much as glancing toward a friend, let alone whispering to one another. We were punished for the slightest infraction.

Our gatherings became regular, and we got to know one another well. The weather outside grew colder and frost clung to the windowpanes of the pastry shop, beading and rolling down in tiny veins of water that sparkled from the light of the chandeliers. We toasted one another with our bottles of orange soda while from downstairs came the tinkle of crystal wineglasses. We readily called out the names of our new friends as they bound up the stairs: "Hey, Sári. Hey, Kiri. Yoodle-yup."

Kati was one of the first girls to come over from the Ady School for the Humanities, and she and I came to share the same table. I liked her smile, and she had an easy way that helped me overcome my shyness. She had dark hair, darker eyes, and her smile was bright, with full lips.

That first winter, Kati was one of the few kids who had an authentic Russian hat. It was made of mink, and its midnight blackness made the white of her face all the more glowing. Apu had such a fur hat, with a bright red star pinned to the front, and I always looked forward to the day, perhaps when I graduated from *gymnazium*, the high school, when I would receive my first real *sapka*.

I suppose even then, when I was just fourteen, that I was aware of the differences between Kati and myself. Her beautiful hat, the smart look of her brightly flowered skirts—very rare at the time in Budapest—and the bits of gold on her ears and fingers were only some of the things that set us apart. But as winter passed we became friends. I was shy, yet once I got to know someone, it was hard to keep me quiet. And Kati was a good listener as well as a good talker.

We started leaving the pastry shop together to take walks around Liberty Square before going home. Walking in the cold air, which was refreshing after the sweet odors of the shop, we became each other's closest confidants.

Our friendship continued into the summer when Kati and I were assigned to the same youth camp for the Pioneers, the Communist scouts, in the countryside of Zala. Ours was the water scouts, and so we spent our time building rafts and practicing swimming strokes. I invented a cannonball dive with which I tried to splash Kati. Actually, it was more like a torpedo—I would jump in the water feet first, very rigid, clasping one knee. Friends said the resounding splash would fly meters into the air. Sometimes I could drench Kati even as she stood on the raft.

After dinner we ran through the tall grass of the lower field and later danced with the gypsies near the old whitewashed inn at the center of town. The gypsies were riotous, laughing wildly. The violinist kept complimenting Kati's tanned skin, which had turned chocolate from the summer sun. The hairs on her arm were bleached by the summer and in the dawning light glowed gold against her dark skin.

The second summer we spent there Kati taught me the local folk dance and then asked the gypsies to play the fast *csárdárs*. We were sixteen and her hair had grown long and straight. The music was wild and soon grew frenzied. As I held her around her waist she leaned back, laughing as we spun faster and faster. The heavy scent of roses permeated the air. Her head was tilted backward; as we spun, her hair swung out, like the mane of a horse in full gallop. I could smell the rose water she had on the nape of her neck.

Later that night we kissed for the first time. It was by the upper reservoir near the fields of clover. The clover was in full bloom, the entire field alive, but I could smell only the scent at the nape of Kati's neck.

When we returned to the city that autumn of 1955 we were

both looking forward to school. Kati was entering the *gymnazium* and was excited and nervous. Having skipped a grade as a youngster, I would be in my second year, or third form.

Ever since we had met, one of the things we liked most to talk about over and over was our dreams for our life together. For teenagers, we were both ambitious. I had known all along that I yearned to become something more than a *valakivalami*, or something or other, and had set my mind on writing.

"But didn't your mother say you could be a doctor, or lawyer, or head administrator?" Kati said, recalling one of our talks.

"That was when I was in first grade."

"So why not now?"

"That was one of Horthy's decrees. I want to write."

Even though Kati was a year behind me, she had always known exactly what she wanted to be.

"An engineer!" I remember exclaiming when she first confided in me. "You can't be an engineer. You're a girl. And it takes more than that," I continued with assurance. "You need pull to get into the Academy of Science, *protekció*."

This was during one of our walks around Liberty Square. I had only a vague sense of what *protekció* meant. I recalled Uncle Gyula mentioning pull in the purchase of the mulberry trees in Szentendre. I was certainly familiar with the expression, and perhaps Apu had used it when discussing my prospects with me. Even Kati had little sense of what the term meant, but nevertheless she called upon the term when she responded.

"My father says I may consider any career," she began in her polite manner. "That is, of course, if I work hard. He says we have *protekció*."

As I soon came to learn, Kati's father was a publisher for the Party and he did indeed have pull. Although Apu was a Party member, he was not a regular and had joined only reluctantly. Kati's father had connections that my father would never have.

Kati did her part, and her dream of attending the Academy of Science was on its way to coming true. She did well, especially in the sciences, heading straight down the track to the academy with A's in biology and physics. I had never seen anyone work so hard, and even though it was common for students without pull to routinely fail these courses, she had grown so efficient that she actually taped formulas to her dresser mirror so she could review them while brushing her hair. I believed she deserved every A she got, and I was proud of her. Kati's pull, like her beautiful Soviet hat, never came between us.

To a boy and girl, pull hardly seemed to matter. We were working harder and harder though and were able to see each other less frequently. When we were able to meet during the week, we skipped the pastry shop and met at what had become our rendez-vous point, the base of the towering bronze statue of Stalin in Liberty Square.

It was late September a few weeks after József had disappeared when Kati and I met one afternoon under the statue. A warm African wind blew over the city, and a few other couples strolled over the vast expanse of the square. The night before, I had slipped a note under the door of Kati's home asking her to meet me at our usual place because I had something I wanted to talk over with her. It was József. In the time since he had disappeared, I had started to hear things that troubled me. Apu had said things I didn't fully understand. There was talk at school, and I even thought I had heard whispers on the street as I passed.

That afternoon as I waited for Kati, the air had a beautifully clear foretaste of autumn in it. But the square seemed strangely inhospitable, the statue of my boyhood hero looming up at my back foreboding. The couples scattered over the cobblestone plain were dwarfed in the immense space. The soldiers pacing out their rounds in the distance seemed hardly to move.

When Kati showed up I had a surprise for her. It was difficult to hug her as I held it behind my back with one hand. It was a fur hat, exactly like Kati's, that József had given me just before he disappeared. I had planned to wait until the season turned to show it to her, and I felt a little foolish carrying it around in the warm weather. But with József suddenly gone, it somehow seemed important to share it with her.

I buried my face in the warmth of Kati's neck and gave her a little nibble. When she jumped back in a fit of giggling I suddenly held out the hat.

"Pisti," she said through her laughter, "it's beautiful. But I already have a hat. And where did you get it?"

"Oh. But Kati, I'm sorry. This is my hat. It's just like yours. We'll be like twins. József gave it to me before he left."

Kati's face had grown bright as I struggled to dig myself out of the hole I had opened. But when I mentioned my uncle, her smile vanished.

"Have you heard from him?" she asked.

"Not yet," I said as I kneaded the hat in my hands.

"I'm sorry, Pisti. He'll show up, I'm just sure he will."

Smaller statues lined the square at regular intervals. These were of other important figures in the history of communist Hungary, as well as figures representing "the people"—farmers, factory workers, soldiers. Kati and I had our favorites, and we visited these in our walks around the square. It was a game we played. We would pay our respects to them as we strolled.

Kati had studied art in school, and she had told me about what she called socialist realism. The statues were like the large Stalin. Kati described them as strong, erect, and proud. And I would laugh and counter, calling them stiff and lifeless. It was part of the game. Approaching our favorites, Kati would welcome them. "Hello, comrade, you are looking dignified today." And I would call out, "Relax, Mister Peasant, and have some fun."

That day I did not feel like playing, and we walked over the stones in silence. I wanted to talk about József but did not know where to begin. Walking north toward the art museum, I was again struck as I had been over the past few weeks by the number of soldiers in the square. Today in my downcast mood it occurred to me that the soldiers reminded me of the statues, standing stiff and erect, guarding who knows what. I could have teased Kati about it, but I did not.

My favorite statue depicted a small boy embracing the leg of an imposing, stern-looking man. Clinging to the folds of the man's greatcoat, the boy had found a refuge of safety in the man's powerful aura of strength. Standing before the statue, I finally spoke.

"Kati, where do you think he went? My Uncle József."

"I don't know, but I've been thinking about it."

Kati's voice was quiet and tender, her dark brows knit in concentration. She turned away for a moment and just as suddenly turned back. Reassuringly, she said, "But you know your uncle. He was always doing things, going off and coming back with another thing to sell and another story to tell you."

"But this wasn't one of his trips. His wife Vera didn't hear him mention it once. He's been gone for weeks now. And she has begun to despair."

"He'll come back. I just know he will," Kati said with forced hopefulness.

"I don't know, Kati. I've heard that József did something wrong. That he was in trouble with the authorities. Like we've both heard about other people."

"But he wasn't that kind of man at all. My father says that only the worst sorts of people get into trouble. Enemies. And József is one of the nicest men I've ever met."

"I know. But I have these bad feelings," I said. And then, half-heartedly, I added, more to cheer Kati than myself, "Who knows, he might have come back today. News could be waiting for me when I get home."

Kati and I lingered at the statue of the small boy as the sun fell toward the mountains beyond the western edge of the city. A pink hue spread over the square, and our shadows stretched out long before us as we made our way home. In front of Kati's apartment, I kissed her long and hard.

When I returned to our apartment, it was quiet. My heart

sank immediately. I hung my fur hat on the peg next to my father's military cap. He had removed the red star from above the brim, leaving a dark spot that looked like a stain. I would never have noticed the star itself. Only its absence was remarkable.

If József had returned, the apartment would have bustled with activity. But no one greeted me, and as I entered the living room I found Apu sitting alone in his chair. Apparently he had removed the star only moments earlier, for he still held it in his hands. He stared at it intently as he twirled it by its post. He barely looked up as I entered.

"Any word about József?" I asked.

"I'm afraid not, Pisti." Apu's eyes remained fixed on the spinning star.

"Why did you take the pin off your cap?" I asked.

"Because."

"What?"

"It needed polishing, that's all."

I saw then how my father's eyes had changed since the war. Before, they had been clear with smooth skin at their corners, no wrinkles, no dark circles. It was more than age. Apu spit on the star and rubbed it against his trousers.

Apu had hinted that the local committee had had something to do with József's disappearance. He had let that slip out once and never brought it up again. And he never responded to my repeated questioning. I felt it unfair and was secretly hurt that he would not discuss it with me. I felt that I was old enough to enjoy his confidence.

But Apu's mood had soured since József's disappearance, and he had grown increasingly preoccupied. When we played chess, I could beat him over and over in a few moves by using the queen's bishop opening. What surprised me was that he hardly seemed to care. He just looked at the board, a clear checkmate, and without raising a brow would say, "Oh, you won again."

When I did venture to press him for his thoughts on József, I risked his anger. On a few occasions he had noisily closed the evening's paper to scowl at me over its top. "Learn to read between the lines, Pisti."

This evening my questions had to wait because Anyu came through the kitchen door. The mingled smells of our dinner followed in her wake. She folded my face in her wet hands and bent to kiss me. She asked me where I had been.

"It's late and the city isn't as safe as it once was, Pisti," she said.

I told her that I was where I usually was when I didn't come directly home from school, with Kati in the square. My mother and father had met Kati dozens of times and liked her well. When Apu first met her he whispered into my ear, "Good taste, my boy." And then he winked at me. But Anyu loved Kati almost as her own daughter.

"And how is Kati? We haven't seen her it seems for ages," Anyu said.

I told her Kati was fine, but that she was working so hard she didn't have as much leisure time.

"But you should see the grades she's getting," I bragged.

Apu had retreated behind his paper. As I finished speaking, he put it to the side and looked up.

"Well, I should hope so," he said with uncharacteristic sarcasm. And then he added seriously, "Pisti, we've never talked about Kati's family, her father, but let me just say that he is an important man. And in this country important men have certain rights we normal mortals don't enjoy. Don't be too impressed with her grades, and watch your step."

Bitterness had crept into my father's voice, and before he had even finished speaking, Anyu was remonstrating with him.

"Apu, Apu!" she almost shouted. "How can you say such things to Pisti. Don't even imply them. You have no right. They are in love and that is that."

I had never seen Anyu so furious. She took me by the hand and hustled me into the steam-filled kitchen. Our evening meal was simmering on the stove. It never saw the table that night.

Anyu was so mad at Father that she refused to serve it. She fumed in the kitchen, "And just watch, I tell you, he's too proud to even apologize. A head as swollen as on any horse, that's your father." And she was right. He did not put his head through the door to inquire about the meal.

Anyu and I kept to the kitchen, where we ate directly from the pans on the stove, sopping up the juices with thick slices of dark bread. Apu's words had confused me, but Anyu would have nothing to do with helping me sort them out. Instead, she talked about love, and despite her anger at Father told me again of how she and Apu had met, their romance, and how they had surmounted their differences to come together as man and wife.

She talked and talked, never letting me get a word in, speaking with an intensity that frightened me. It was only late at night as we began making motions toward going to bed that she finally consented to respond to a question, a question that formed itself in my mind without my thinking. It surprised even me. "What is happening in our country?" I asked. She answered immediately, without pausing to consider her words, so I trusted them as the truth.

She told me calmly, "You will know more freedom in your lifetime. Things are changing for the better. But as with everything else, all good comes with a little bad."

"Does Father think that the government had something to do with József's disappearance?"

"Yes, Pisti, that's what your father thinks. But I'm sure he's wrong. József will turn up. You just wait and see."

We returned to the parlor, and I saw that Father had been drinking. A half-empty bottle of bourbon sat by his chair. He was playing with the star again, twirling it about before his empty gaze. The green light from the shaded lamp next to him cast deep shadows across his face. I saw for the first time how his eyes had aged since the war. Before, they had been clear with smooth skin at their corners, no wrinkles, no dark circles. No, it was more than age. He spit on the star. He rubbed it against his trousers. He looked up with pulpy, grief-shadowed eyes. "The star is red as wine, as *Bikavér*, the blood of the bull to spill," he said. "And she's a Red. Kati's Red, I tell you. Watch out." That was all he said. He lolled and dozed, and his head fell to one side.

József did not turn up. Autumn came and went and an unusually frigid winter swept down from the north. No word came from József and we all gradually gave up hope. We did not talk about it. Every time the subject was broached, Apu let it be known that there was nothing to talk about. But if there was nothing to talk about, what was left unsaid was clear enough. Somehow, the government had played a part in my uncle's mysterious disappearance. What exactly that role had been, however, was impossible for me to determine, and no one seemed able to help me.

Kati and I talked about it endlessly, and like myself at first, she refused to believe the government had anything to do with it. Kati never was able to see, and it became one of the few things we would argue about. As a sixteen-year-old going on seventeen, I had no idea what to think. I was sad about József and terribly disturbed by the thought that the government might have had anything to do with his disappearance. I became convinced that the government had played a role. Just what that role had been though was hard for me to fathom. And raised the way I had been raised, it was equally difficult for me to believe that the government did not have reasons. They always acted in the best interests of the people. Perhaps József had done something wrong? Perhaps. I just didn't know.

My life, at any rate, hardly changed. I was working hard in school and playing soccer every day. With József gone and my father growing more and more remote, I came to depend more on my Uncle Oti, who had taken me for sherbet on Saturdays ever since I was a little boy. Oti, who had been Father's chauffeur at Kaposvár, was a jolly fellow and one of the least political Hungarians I knew. But he was of little help to me in getting to the bottom of the József mystery. We enjoyed each other, and he was one of the only men I knew to whom I could talk at the time.

As school wound to a close, Kati and I saw each other only rarely. But when we did get to meet we had the fun of being able to think about our coming vacation. We grew excited talking about our plans, what old friends we would see again, what we would do. As in summers past, we would both be staying in the town of Zala, and our imaginations drew vivid pictures from past memories of what lay ahead. In the shadow of Stalin's statue, we practiced the dances we had learned the summer before and counted the weeks and days remaining before we would be breathing the country air.

All our wonderful plans were dashed in a moment. Kati appeared beneath the statue one evening with tears in her eyes. She would not be going to Zala that summer. Her father was sending her to a different camp in a town farther to the east. I was disappointed and on the edge of tears myself but tried to comfort her as best I could. "It will only be for a month," I said. We could write letters. It would not be all bad.

Not many days after our last somber meeting under the statue of Stalin I found myself walking three or four paces behind Kati and her father on Damjanich Street. It was Saturday afternoon, and the street was thronged with people. I was on my way home from a soccer match in the park and came upon them in front of the OSzT. Kati and her father were laden with packages and had evidently just come out of the store. The OSzT was a special store that catered to important Party members. The store's windows were a riot of bright color, more colorful still compared to the grayness that characterized the rest of the street, and for that matter most of Pest. The exotic merchandise displayed in the OSzT windows, nearly all of it from the West, only hinted, tantalizingly, at the riches that lay inside.

Though Apu was a Party member, we had never set foot in the store. He had not been issued the special pass that would have allowed our family to use the store. Only later did I learn that Apu had been denied a pass because he "was not active enough," which

184 / László Petrovics-Ofner

meant that he did not attend the weekly meetings to extol Stalin and praise Rákosi.

On the sidewalk before the store's bright windows, the crowd pressed ahead, shoulder to shoulder. Three bodies in front of me, Kati walked arm and arm with her father, packages bumping at their sides. Having just come from a soccer match in the park, I was splattered with mud from head to toe and hesitated to greet them. My hesitation turned to reluctance when I edged closer and got a better look at Kati's father. I had met the man only once and was awed by his burly appearance. He was barrel chested and looked even larger in his heavy coat. His square face was pocked with craters, and although the day was overcast, dark glasses covered his eyes.

He was an intimidating man, but he was also Kati's father, and as he tipped his head to speak to her his face softened. I resolved to greet them and began to snake my way closer. But I was brought up short when I came close enough to hear the words that passed between them.

"That Pisti fellow is a fine boy, Kati, but he's not for you."

"Why not, Father?" Kati asked, tugging on her father's arm. "You've said that before but never given me a reason."

I could not believe what I was hearing. Panic shook my body. I nearly stumbled. I wanted to run but only pressed closer.

"He's not of our kind," her father continued after a few steps. "His father is just a doctor and refuses to attend Party meetings. A small enough matter, you think, but the lapse has consequences."

"But I like Pisti. We've spent so much time together. You can't say this, you just can't," I heard Kati plead.

"Kati, Kati. I insist that you never see Pisti again. And please note that I am not stooping to bring up the matter of the boy's uncle. I'm sorry, but I am firm. You will see, it is for the best."

Kati's eyes brimmed with tears, and her father bent to embrace her. The surrounding crowd flowed around them. Angry, confused, my face burning with rage, I was swept along and away.

* * *

That night I wrote a note to Kati asking her to meet me at the statue. Early the next morning, I slipped it under her door. After school I rushed to the square. It was a beautiful day. Spring was at its peak, and the leaves of the chestnuts had unfolded to their full greenness. Despite the warm breeze, the square was nearly deserted. I took up my position under the towering hulk of Stalin and strained my eyes in the direction from which Kati would come. I was early and my thoughts raced in confusion. I began to pace at the base of the statue, back and forth, back and forth. Movement seemed to calm me, to allay my hurt and still my confusion.

On one pass before the statue's base, I happened to look up as a bit of red caught the corner of my eye. Craning my head back I saw that someone had stuffed a flaming red rag up Stalin's left nostril. Whoever had done it had been quite a climber. I didn't pause to marvel at the deed. Defacing public monuments was a common enough occurrence and was becoming commoner by the day. Nonetheless, I was surprised when I laughed. It was a deep bellowing laugh that was perhaps my first experience with the *röhög*.

I was surprised not only because I was so far from happiness then, but also because I had always loved Stalin. I had always winced at such sights before. Even over the past year when my friends had begun to lend their voices to the growing criticism of the Russian presence in Hungary, even with József's disappearance, I had continued to venerate the man. How could I not? From as far back as I could remember, I had been taught to love him. In particular I recalled one film, one piece of propaganda, vividly, almost like a dream.

In the film, the Russians liberated Hungary from Hitler, and the downtrodden peasants were asked to write to the new government about their problems and the things they desired. The next scene showed a number of planes dropping cargo on parachutes. The peasants ran to their fields and gazed in disbelief as tractors, sewing machines, and combines fell to the earth before them. The peasants danced and wept, and a song started playing with a voice talking over the music about the future promises of socialism and about the care and concern Stalin held for the common folk. The song was our anthem. It ended, "The nation has paid the sum for sins of past and of days to come."

I had always loved Stalin, and my love would die only slowly, but on that warm spring day as I turned back to my anxious pacing, it suffered a nearly fatal blow. Kati never did show up. I waited until the sun had fallen behind the hills, then made my way home with tears in my eyes.

That night, I hid in my room until my mother came to see what was the matter. My anger had subsided, and I felt weak with sadness and humiliation. I did not want to talk to anyone, least of all her. But she stood at my door until I let her in.

"What's wrong?" she asked as she pulled a chair to the edge of my bed.

I remained silent.

"Is it Kati?" she asked, and when I still did not respond, she continued, "It is Kati, yes? I know a broken heart when I see one. Pisti, answer me," she said sternly.

"Yes," I blurted. And then I lifted my head from the pillow. "Her father told her not to see me anymore."

"Why was that?"

"I don't know," I half lied.

"Don't you?" she persisted.

I looked up at her. Her graying hair was untidy and her thick glasses magnified her eyes. I didn't know what to say, so I said nothing.

"Will you let her go? Just like that?" she said, her voice impatient now, edged with anger.

"What do you want me to say?" I suddenly yelled at her. "What am I supposed to do?"

"You're nearly a man," she yelled back.

"Kati's father—he said something about József."

Anyu suddenly grew silent, visibly withdrawing from my gaze.

It was I who persisted. "That is what he said. Something about József. Nobody told me the truth about him."

"He is gone," she said after a moment.

"So is Kati!" I yelled.

In the weeks that followed, I wrote Kati dozens of letters. I thought her father might try to intercept them, so I dropped them off at her school. Later I posted them through the mail. I went to Stalin's statue every day and paced the large cobblestones at its base. Later I haunted the square when I knew she could not possibly be anywhere near. I was drawn to the place that used to be our own. Heartbroken and sad, I thought of little else but Kati for weeks, barely aware that the rest of the world went about its business, that things were happening. I didn't care.

Summer and the country brought relief from my sadness. I kept busy. I played sports and took long hikes through the forest and open fields. I made new friends and we would talk late into the night. There was much to talk about. From the city came news of protests, demonstrations, arrests. The papers displayed in the camp reading room contained none of this news. But the information filtered in through letters, deliverymen, distant radio waves in foreign languages. To my surprise, I learned from my new friends that these disturbances had been going on for months. I wondered how I could have missed them. I was there at their very center. It was only then that I realized how heartbroken I had been. It was only then, too, thinking of Kati and not feeling the old hurt, that I realized how far I had come.

When I returned to Budapest at the close of summer, I nonetheless felt drawn to our old meeting place. Everything about the city reminded me of my old love. Nothing seemed free of associations. The ice vendors' calls weaving with the early dawn, the songs sung by women as they hung out their sheets in the alley, the tolling of the big bells from St. Stephen's Basilica. All of these things and many more evoked painful memories. But I was determined not to give in to these feelings and tried to keep my mind on other things. Above all, I consciously avoided the square.

Then one day in October, I found myself walking toward the square. I hadn't thought about a destination. I was just out walking, enjoying a particularly beautiful day, when I realized I was following the route I used to take on my way to meet Kati. By the time I made this discovery, it was too late to turn back. I was only two blocks away and had just turned onto the broad boulevard that led to the center of the square. The street was thronged with people chanting slogans and singing songs. Electricity crackled above the stream of dark bobbing heads, above the uplifted fists. There seemed to be no end to it. For a moment I hesitated, standing at the edge of the onrushing flow of bodies. And then I became part of the flow.

Other streams, from every corner of the city, flowed into the square. I had never seen so many people. Every foot of the square's vastness was packed with bodies. Some climbed on shoulders. Dozens clung to the smaller statues. The branches of the trees at the square's edge were heavy with young people. Banners waved. In the distance, at the base of Stalin's statue, someone addressed the crowd through a megaphone. The noise that went up was constant, a low buzz that was nonetheless deafening. The words of the speaker were lost in the collective murmurings of the crowd. And then, miraculously, a profound hush settled over the square.

I strained my eyes toward the statue. The man who had perched on Stalin's shoulder high above the speaker had rappelled down using one of the many ropes that fell from the statue's neck. As I looked on, the ropes seemed to lift themselves from the front of the statue. They angled out and became taut. The quiet broke and shouts went up. I could not see the arms that had taken up the ropes, that began to strain against the huge weight of the statue. Crushed in the sea of bodies that had begun to press ineluctably forward, my voice became one with the voice of the crowd. It took only moments. The statue buckled at the knees and toppled to the cobblestones. Later I learned that only Stalin's bronze boots had been left. The rest had been sold as scrap before night was through.

10

The Last Sunday
1956

The chestnuts were ripe but had not yet fallen. Refusing to yield to oncoming winter, dead leaves clung to the branches of the oaks. A killing frost swept the countryside after the statue of Stalin fell. It was an omen, for the cold rotted the squash, and the hail of northern rains pelted the land in sudden sweeps. The laurel on the hills of Buda, overgrown where the Germans had once dug in to fight liberation, bent sharply in the wind. Their dried leaves rattled like bones, then righted.

Although in revolt, the country maintained a precarious balance, never knowing when the Russians would tip the scales of power in their favor. They were gone now, but no one knew for how long. We expected the tanks any day, and Budapest quietly braced itself for the attack.

Cobblestones were ripped from the streets for barricades and machine guns lined the walks. The roofs were readied with seltzer bottles filled with gas or kerosene. Like toy trains after rough play, yellow trolleys lay on their sides, blocking the entrance to the Chain Bridge where the initial attack was anticipated.

But for the very old and for the young, life went on as usual. Enterprising peasants drove their oxen through the few streets left intact, and their withered wives in plain kerchiefs peddled fresh produce, pears and autumn peaches, as their old "lords," as they called their husbands, drove the carts on to the drinking cellars.

Aging milkmen came daily to deliver their watered-down milk, and when anyone objected, they quickly changed the topic to the general shortage of feed grain. Grandmothers crowded the open markets and dragged home bushels of apricots, which they stored for winter.

My grandmother saved the pits from the day-long stewing in a printed bowl. Steam from the large cauldron had made the air in our tiny kitchen damp and close. I wanted to know what was happening outside and was constantly wiping off the glass, but my tiny portals fogged up as soon as my hand left the pane. Frustrated and anxious to be outside, I contented myself with cracking open Grandmother's huge pile of apricot pits. Angi and I ate the bittersweet seeds by the fistful.

It was the second Sunday of the revolution, and I wondered if Oti would visit me. Oti was my fat, bearded uncle who came by every Sunday. He had been Apu's assistant during the war. Once a week, I became his son for a few hours. This had been a tradition we preserved from our days at Kaposvár where he had served as Apu's chauffeur. Today, Oti would be my excuse to go outside.

When we had first returned to the city, József had been my main connection to the adult male world. When he disappeared, I sorely missed our confidential talks about girls and about life. Out of necessity, I began to rely more on Oti.

In the country, Oti and I had collected mushrooms. In the city, we fashioned our outings to accommodate the season. During cold months, we went skating in the park. During the spring, we went to the soccer games, and I particularly looked forward to the matches held on May Day. That day we went first to the ceremonies at the huge parade grounds of Liberty Square. A multitude of flags rippled in the warming breeze, throngs from the glass factory marched with a giant lightbulb, and the machinists displayed a three-story papier-mâché screw. Thousands of balloons were freed, along with swarms of white doves.

At the May Day soccer matches when I had been younger,

Oti had dressed in his old greatcoat and military hat pinned with a star that dangled loosely to one side. When we would arrive at the stadium, walking past the ticket collectors, who also had stars on their blue conical caps, Oti would salute: "*Elvtársaim*. Happy holiday, my comrades." Looking in amazement at a bearded soldier, they never bothered to look down at his four-legged overcoat. Now we still went to the matches, but I no longer fit under his coat, and we spent much of the time arguing about the merits of the various players.

I was not disappointed the day of the apricot stewing, for Oti arrived in the early afternoon, rescuing me from the tedium of daily work. A boisterous, outspoken man, he burst into our apartment with laughter and hugs and wet kisses. He kissed me last, and his soaked beard rubbed against my face like a mop. I endured his soppy affection. He brought presents—wine for my parents and a switchblade for me. Our old friend Dr. Tóth would not have approved, but when my mother objected, Oti said, "For God's sake, he's nearly a man. And he may have to protect himself soon enough." My mother stood silent, amazed. Oti patted my shoulder and ushered me out.

It was a warm day, and my light jacket flapped in the wind. We were going to a place on Hársfa Street. Oti liked the manager there. He would give us an extra scoop if we found ice in the sherbet—and somehow, Oti always did. That day, as usual, the ice had mysteriously melted by the time the manager came over, but the man winked and gave us another scoop. Oti looked down at me and laughed. "He's a good man, a poor proletarian, but a good man. Your mother would say a *mensch*."

"Oti, what's a *mensch*?" I asked.

"I told you now three times. It's a good person."

"I used to hear Anyu use the word." I recalled her talking to Grandmother that way. "How do they say 'bad person'?" I was looking for the ice in the sherbet.

"I don't know." He was looking for some ice, too. "You'll have to ask your mother. I'm not sure Jewish people really see others as bad. They see them as dullards, or lazy, or losers, but not really as bad. Perhaps even evil, but not bad."

"Kati was evil then."

"What do you mean?"

"She won't see me anymore."

"How come?"

But I was not sure what to say. So I just went on and said the right thing. "Have you ever forced yourself onto a woman?"

"Well, not exactly. What do you mean?"

At that moment I found a huge chunk of ice in my mouthful of sherbet. I quickly spit it out before it could melt. "Waiter! Waiter!"

"Oh, you found some ice." Oti looked up from his dish.

"Waiter! Another scoop, please." The waiter came over with the sherbet without having first checked my find. He smiled down at us. Oti winked up at him.

"See, it's just that," he said, winking at me after the waiter had left. "It's called flirting. That's all you have to do, Pisti." He winked four or five times, the side of his face wiggling energetically. "Just wink."

"What will that do?"

"It will give a signal."

"For what?" I was often annoyed with Oti's cryptic way of speaking.

"Well . . ." Here he trailed off, as though teasing.

"Well what? Tell me." I grew irritated.

"That's right, that's right." He grew excited. "See, you read between the lines. I told you nothing."

"What?"

"You just felt it. And you trusted your feelings. I was teasing you."

"But what has that got to do with it?"

"That is what flirting is. Sending little signals and then reading between the lines. You can't just go up to some girl and say, 'Do you want to have sex?' "

The waiter listened in on our talk while he finished a cigarette at the next table. He was slow in crushing it. He smiled.

"And you should know, Pisti. Much of the world is that way. Reading between the lines."

"Like what?"

"Rákosi will be dead in short order."

I sat shocked. How could he say something like that? Was my Uncle Oti going crazy? The premier of Hungary would die?

"How's that?"

"The Russians called him a king. You're the king of Hungary, they said. Heard it on the radio. Honest. To be the king in a communist country at this time means certain beheading."

"But he has fled to Russia."

"I know. But *you* do not know yet. I can read between the lines." And here he winked.

"Off with his head, and let's to our walk." He laughed.

Hársfa Street is narrow and lined with oaks. During summer evenings, their high branches arch across the road, and the light above the trees is filtered through the foliage, casting a green hue softly down the length of the street all the way to Liberty Square. Nothing contented me more than eating sherbet in the outdoor café at dusk and watching the reflection of leaves dancing endlessly in the summer breeze. By October, bare branches claw at the metallic sky, and ripe acorns lie in sodden heaps along the gutter, rotting in the autumn rain.

That Sunday, as we approached the end of one row of trees, excited university students wearing colored armbands rushed by us shouting something about a traitor. A bare-chested man had been hung by his legs and was dangling over a small fire. Someone told us he was an AVO, a member of the secret police.

"His pockets were filled with *százasok*, hundred-forint notes," someone yelled.

People then ripped at his pockets, and the loose notes caught the updraft from the flame and flew about.

"Blood money. The blood of our people." The old woman raised her fist and wept and shouted in a way I never imagined. "They took my daughter to the station. Now she can't have children." The woman wept and screamed and cursed loudly at the corpse. "Blood money, blood money. Eyaaa!" She waved her arms in the air. The red bills scattered about.

I had rarely seen the hundred-forint note, but I knew they were red. I now saw that they were red. The phrase "blood money," hypnotic and crazed, rang down to me from what seemed an impenetrable darkness. Blood money had sounded like reparation after the war. Apu used to diagnose those who survived martyrdom, such as Eva, and she got gold. But what did it mean? Blood money! Whose blood?

A student shouted at the corpse. "Where is my father? Where is my mother?" And the feeling swept over the crowd. "Swine! Rotten animal!"

From where I stood, I saw the crowd spit, their thick saliva leaking down toward the dead man's throat where it overflowed his face and eventually sputtered into the fire.

The crowd grew more wild. I saw Oti become angry, his face red. I felt myself growing tense. Then something snapped. Oti, intoxicated by the hate of the crowd, began threatening the corpse. I also began to move toward the AVO. But it was as though I were no longer conscious, acting in a dream. Someone kicked the body, and it pivoted above the flame. Ashes from the burnt clothing slowly rose into the air. The skull, charred by the heat, split. The flame sputtered, then died.

I again saw Oti. I looked at the flame. I heard Oti panting. His face was red and sweating, his lips quivering. The red of his face soon paled, and the sweat disappeared. He walked slowly. I ran ahead of him, kicking at the dead oak leaves. When I returned, I noticed that his lips had stopped quivering.

Oti took me home by taxi but did not come up to our apartment. He told me to tell my parents that he was in a hurry to leave. My parents asked me where we had gone. After I told them, they retired to the lounge and talked in whispers for a long time.

I sat in the kitchen, playing with my new knife. It would not be much good for whittling, a hobby I had continued since childhood. I had become adept at carving and would make little figurines from sticks. I would stain the wood after letting it dry and then polish it with wax. I had made József such a figure, a stout peasant carrying a huge bundle on his back. I pretended he was a scout for György Dózsa in the peasant uprisings of 1514. But József disagreed with me. He wanted the statue to be Petőfi, the poet laureate of the nation.

I slipped the new switchblade into my pocket and took my whittling knife from the drawer where I kept it. The new figure I was carving had a knot on his side. It was a figurine I was to give to Apu. I tried to smooth the knot, but the blade went deep and cut into his arm. The left arm, the one holding a small rifle, cracked and fell off.

Apu heard my cry of dismay and brought adhesive to glue the arm back, but it would not hold. He soon gave up. He just looked down at me in a sad way. Darkness hung from the corners of his eyes. I could no longer stand the intensity within me, and I rushed to him, clutching at his shoulders, weeping like a young child. *"Semmi tartós,* Pisti. *Semmisem,"* I heard between my wails. "Nothing lasts."

11

Soot-Black Washed-White
1956

A few days later, I found the entire length of Damjanich Street stripped, the cobblestones piled, mound after mound. These were to impede the tanks, in case the country was attacked. I learned from a worker struggling with a stone that the tanks were already massing on the eastern border.

"Do you really think we'll be attacked?"

The soldier continued with his task, ignoring me. Then he paused and spoke again. "The piles are thirty meters apart, so the tanks will have to go up and down, and then, when they come to those piles close together down there by Hársfa Street," he pointed, "they will get stuck between them. And that will be the end of that." The man lifted another cobblestone.

I scrambled up and down the hills formed by the cobblestones, breathing the sharp autumn air. I piled the stones up wherever I saw that they had fallen. I was alert and alive, ready for action.

At the base of the craggy peaks of cobblestones, facing the sidewalks, grenades lay in piles. They were the old-fashioned Russky kind, with fat stems and big bulbous heads, that had been stored away for years. They looked like overgrown suckers imported for OSzT, the special store for Party members.

Four revolutionaries had cordoned off the gas pumps at the end of the street, where they now stood guard. One was a squat, fat man, another a taller, thin man with sharp features. Both had ruddy faces and tiny veins marking their noses. The other two were young, one with spectacles, the other with pocked skin.

Around the men, piled high, were empty seltzer bottles. There was a shortage of bottles, yet here were hundreds of them, piled neatly. I helped fill them with gas and collected rags from a neighboring building with which to plug them tight. We then stacked them against the wall, row upon row, higher and higher.

The excitement of my afternoon was touched with sadness only when I noticed the quiet of the street, which, though crowded with people bargaining for milk or bread or the produce peasants had driven in by oxen, was a street in wait.

The sun had lost its warmth and now cast a cold eye through a layer of low clouds. The dried leaves of the chestnuts, which only weeks before had hummed in the wind, had disappeared. My playful preoccupations turned in the bite of November's wind. I had no jacket on, I realized, and was shivering.

Rumors trickled into the city from the countryside. Tanks, divisions, as many as the dried thistles of this autumn, the peasants were accustomed to say, had crossed the border. "What do you mean by thistles, old man?"

"Near as many as we had against the Germans." He spit in disgust through the gap left by a missing tooth. "Nearly two hundred thousand, and of the divisions, three-quarters are armored." The bristles under his chin grew down onto his neck.

When I arrived home, Apu was upset. "Eisenhower has not learned from World War II, it is clear." He muttered as he paced around the back rooms. "How could we possibly have expected a nation raised on checkers to stand up to one raised on chess? The opening was there, a weakness in defense, but now it is closed. That is that."

"What is what?" I asked.

"What do you mean, what is what? It's just that."

I had never played checkers. I tried to explain away my confusion. "What do you mean, checkers?" I asked.

"See. There it is." He confirmed my hunch. "You already know the Möller Defense. That's all it took. The strength of two mere bishops could have done it."

But Apu's joy revived when he huddled by the radio. We heard Premier Nagy, in a swift tactical move, declare Hungary a neutral nation as of the first of November. "That Imre, what a head! There's a gambit, I say. Who ever heard of attacking Switzerland?" Apu chortled. "What a stroke!"

On my next outing I was determined to partake in the preparations. The tourist district was nearly empty. I walked past the stores, past the windows displaying bright orange furs, the heads of foxes still dangling intact like dried red peppers, past the privately owned shops with Western shoes and silk neckties, toward the underground at the Vörösmarty terminal.

As I turned onto the square, I saw a crowd at the pastry shop, crates of orange soda piled four high on the sidewalk. Nearby, an enterprising peasant was doing a brisk business in fried dough.

Suddenly a roar cut the sky, low overhead, and the metallic canopy of the hovering clouds flickered with leaflets. The crowd around the pastry shop dispersed, many still drinking soda. The peasant left his stand with great urgency and quickly plucked a leaflet from the ground, then scurried back without reading it. "*Lángos!* One forint," he started at once. "Good buy, I say. Salted *lángos!*"

No one responded to him. He lifted the leaflet with greasy fingers, and I saw his lips moving as he tried to decipher the print.

"Szokialist . . . tonks . . . comrides . . . ," the peasant muttered under his breath. His mustache muffled the nostrils of his huge nose as his lips bobbed with the incoherent words. "Jesus and Mary, who in God's life can make this out?"

Finally, with an easy gesture, he tossed the leaflet over his shoulder as though fending off an omen or seeking luck for the harvest and began chanting again. "*Lángos! Lángos!* Fills you up. Salt is free for freedom fighters. A very good buy."

I had not yet read the leaflet myself.

"Uncle Lángos, how about a little dough and I'll read you the leaflet," I tried my luck.

The peasant cheered at once, apparently seeing great benefit in the barter, his round cheeks brightening. "There's a young soldier for you," he said, as he threw a wad of dough into the hot lard. "I'm lost without my glasses, to tell the truth," he lied.

I scanned the page as he spoke and knew at once that the barter was a loss. But the old man continued his prattle, apparently unaware of any changes in my expression. "It's not that I can't read, mind you. Only the letters keep jumping." He took the paper out of my hands. "Take this for instance. Is this 'tonk' or 'tunk'?" Unbelievable, I thought, this old man, blind to words, blithering so he would also not hear.

The vendor's pace quickened to the point of frenzy. He actually grabbed at passersby as though snatching flies and pleaded, "How about the *lángos*, sirs?" They quickly brushed his hands aside and muttered angrily at the grease left on their shirts.

"You better believe it's 'tanks,' " I finally blurted.

"Sure it's not 'tonk'?" The vendor's denial persisted.

"That's the *o* and this is the *a*, old man, *a . . . a . . . a*, and stands for *alma*, you must remember? Or Amerika, perhaps in your time," I said, my earlier sympathy giving way to ridicule. "But here it stands for tank, not tonk," I taunted. "And cannons of tanks, not conons of tonks," I mocked.

The old man was startled. "Jesus of Mary, that's got nothing to do—"

I read aloud to him.

MAGYAR COMRADES!
FRIENDS OF THE SOCIALIST REVOLUTION!
Our fraternal ally, the Soviet, has been enlisted to aid the nation against the irrational counterrevolutionary forces.

These forces are really servants of Western influence. Our
true friend will be massing tanks and armored vehicles outside
Buda to prepare for the liberation of the city.
ALL RESISTANCE WILL BE SOFTENED!

I threw the *lángos* onto the tracks of the tram as I hopped on
the underground. I wondered about the leaflets. It was old news,
really. The peasant was probably alone in his ignorance. But
hardly anybody cared.

An African wind had swept the land, and everyone was
enjoying the new warmth, eating fried dough and drinking soda,
mixing in the square, older girls smoothing their brown hair,
meeting boys' eyes, and flirting openly on the promenade, postur-
ing and swaying.

I looked about the antique compartment of the train with its
stained wood and brass fixtures. I always liked to ride the Vörösmarty underground because it reminded me of a well-preserved
toy.

Then I noticed a billboard of Stalin who smiled quietly while
a salami-sized penis drawn above his head ejaculated onto his
proletarian cap. The one truth of propaganda posters was that
they would be defaced, often minutes after they went up. I recalled
the spring I was in second grade, a week before May Day, when
ten portraits of Stalin in his greatcoat had been glued to the facade
of my school, all in a row and all with the inscription

Soldiers in the field,
Sailors manning the decks,
Airmen in the skies.

All students bent over books.
Sharpened minds are weapons.

STALIN LOVES YOU ALL.

By the time I was released for lunch, I noticed that each of
the pupils of Stalin's eyes, row on row, had been poked out. The
portraits looked like troops of blind beggars hovering by the wall
instead of the hero I thought Stalin to be. The eyes now detracted

from the earthy smile that accompanied me everywhere and looked down from the wall of every classroom, encouraging diligence. And what was a tyrant anyway? I had wondered back then. Now I knew—the boot pinning the landed fish, the cry of fish upon the shore, a silent scream. I recalled what it must have been like for the Jews to be isolated and marked. At least I won't be killed, I hoped.

My gaze returned to the poster. I looked closer still. Neatly etched over the stars on Stalin's lapel were two swastikas. So this is what a tyrant is, I thought. Someone like Hitler. The thought frightened me, for I realized at once that had there been no war, we would not have inherited Stalin. Somehow the war loomed in the background behind the revolution.

Then the lips on the poster became fixed, losing expression, looking like the lips of a dead man after the undertaker has twisted them into a thin smile. I thought, Keep on smiling, Uncle, friend of boys bent over books. I now know who you are.

The underground rattled along, my thoughts racing over the plans for resistance. Trolleys overturned at the entrance to the bridges. Gasoline stored on strategic rooftops. Single-fire military rifles from World War I. A few machine guns with a little ammunition. Need we more? A sprinkling of old grenades that should still go off. Two bazookas to be delivered from Debrecen, it was rumored. They *will* arrive. And we've plenty of muscle, plenty of people. Ferenc, our super, had said that was the key. All my friends agreed. We were anticipating the confrontation.

Ferenc, a leathery, worn man with a handlebar mustache, told me of these defenses when he allowed us access to our roof. My friends and I weighed the question in our minds: Can we fight tanks? We had long arguments. And finally we agreed. Yes, we had to.

The excitement and certainty of the moment—like in a snowball fight when a dozen or more hard-packed balls have been piled in rows and one is poised behind a hedge, alert, anticipating attack, and confident—drove doubt from my mind.

I suddenly felt hungry, my appetite renewed, and sorry for having thrown away the *lángos*. A grand snowball fight, I said to myself, drawing a comparison to the only battles I had known.

It was dusk when I surfaced from the underground. The street was now littered with leaflets. As the clouds in the rectangle of sky between the buildings lost form, the sheets of paper showed in patches against the sidewalks. I imagined them as gauze pads, big enough to cover a knee.

The kitchen window of our apartment was open, and through the embroidered curtain I heard my parents talking.

"Didn't we live with an open door then? Always ajar? Did you ever ask who knocked?"

"I am always haunted by good Jenő," my mother said.

"These are different times. I can protect you far less."

"I can hear the shots just outside the doorway," Mother continued, deaf to Father's words, talking to herself.

"You remember Jenő, and I remember old Béni with his bad leg, limping along and yelling, 'Doctor, Doctor, they've knocked your door in.'" Father seemed impatient. "*I* often wonder what happened to Béni when he got back to the building."

"But it was a blessing about Eva's baby," my mother went on, still deaf to his words. "Even christened. Eva was safe."

But then she turned abruptly. "I just don't know how to ask for anything without grabbing. Eva had known Jenő since her teens."

Silhouetted by the curtain, I saw them embrace.

"To tell the truth, I think you're mourning Laci and Ibolya and all your kin in Zalavég and from the plains," Apu went on, trying to soothe her. "They are shadows. Jenő was the only one you actually saw."

My father cupped her head. "Don't you think I see you running to the knock at the door? It's not to let strangers in now, but someone from Canada, or New Zealand, any of twenty-five souls walking the globe. An extended family."

My mother pulled from his embrace as though troubled by his interpretation.

"And where are you? Are you free of guilt?" she asked.

"I'm not. I'm not, and you know that." Mother looked alarmed by his response. "I could have helped him, just as you asked. But I was afraid we'd be caught. He was an opera performer."

Father continued pacing. "All of life is before us—Angi, Pisti, a continuing life. Now Eva has arranged a guide to take them to the mountains."

A silence fell then. My father sat down at the table onto which Mother placed both her hands, bracing herself, something she often did when her thoughts were churning, as though she were trying to secure them.

"I'll talk to her," she sobbed.

"Tonight."

"Yes."

"By Wednesday the children should be in Vienna."

I realized I had been standing mute before the door, unaware of time or place, intent on their dialogue. Vienna, I thought. *Disszidálunk*. My mind raced with a new word from the street: *fleeing*.

As Anyu left the kitchen, I heard Apu call after her. "I got the candles this afternoon. We had best stock up on canned goods on the way to Eva's. We'll have to go to the cellar early. The bombing is expected to start by noon."

I understood.

That's how we would get it first. I recalled the leaflets: "Soften the resistance."

And I understood.

The threat of bombings had reminded them of the war. They were sick of it. Sick of two world wars and two civil wars and now a revolution. I recalled Apu once describing Hungary as the crossroads of the wars of Europe. "Huns, Turks, the Hapsburgs, the Nazis," he droned. "What the hell."

They wanted out, to be back in the woods somewhere, far away from the trafficking of horror.

I let my knuckles fall onto the door then and heard Anyu running.

"Coming," she called out. "Don't go away. I'm coming."

The warp of the door stuck, and in her zeal to release it, she yanked energetically. "Here I am. Just a minute." It finally yielded and sprang free, hard against her chest. She greeted me with puffy eyes.

"My vagabond son," she chided. "Coming at night like a vagrant traveler. Give us a hug, my little one, and maybe I'll forgive."

I stepped across the threshold into her arms, but the turn of her phrases, many the same as Apu had used to describe her absent relatives, left me uneasy. I recalled that when I knocked, she did not ask who it was, but seemed certain it would be a familiar face.

Feeling like a child again, I pressed my head against her shoulder. I asked myself, Was it me she was expecting? Who else but me? I wrapped my arms around her, trying to squeeze away uncertainty. But doubt lingered.

Anyu stroked my hair and muttered the poet Attila József's lullaby: "Chit, chit, little one. You are home now."

Was she really trying to comfort me or herself? I wondered. She recited the lullaby in full. But I was plagued, and tenderness turned to fear even as I clutched her.

We would be bombed tomorrow, and she said nothing about it. There was no urgency, not anywhere. Not in the streets, nor the city, not even here at home, except for what *I* felt. My mind leapt. Which building would be hit?

"What troubles you, Pisti?" I heard.

Her recognition came too late.

No kind word or affectionate embrace could keep the fabric over my mind from tearing and letting history flood free. It had not been Stalin alone, I realized, but also the Nazis. I wondered how many cousins I would have had, playmates for adventures in the woods by Zalavég, and uncles and aunts to greet me, to celebrate the holidays, my confirmation, or my name day.

I saw Hitler rise across the decades, grown from the empty and oppressive boots of Stalin, the Bootmaker, as he had been dubbed, left standing on Liberty Square. In his life he had brought genocide, and in his death he had brought cold war, a mistrust for any human caring and mutual dependence.

History suddenly gained a grown form, and I saw Hitler's black shadow fall across the past into my present, not as some storybook adventure or a propaganda horror, but real now, darkening my life.

My thoughts leapt again. *Disszidálunk.* Fleeing.

Vienna by Wednesday.

And today *Shabbat.*

As my parents were leaving, their apparent deception prevented me from expressing my fears and my sadness. I grew enraged that I should be excluded from this moment, a moment so important to us all. So *I* lied to them. It was the first time ever out of anger.

I said I would invite Jancsi up to play chess. The words rolled leaden from my lips, heavy and lifeless: "I will play chess."

But my real intent was to disappear, to run away. I would stay out late and make them worry. I gloated over my plans for revenge—I pictured my parents' anguish. Dearest God, tonight of all nights. Why didn't we tell the little one?

Jancsi was my friend, a blond-haired, tanned boy who was well developed for seventeen. He had started the second form before school was closed this fall. I was ahead of him, having skipped a grade in elementary school.

I approached Jancsi on the balcony, where he was shooting his French slingshot with the brass handle, which was molded in the form of a small rifle with a built-in trigger. He was firing marbles into the courtyard darkness. They hit against the opposite wall, and we heard them shatter with a crash. "Tried to find you earlier," he said. The slingshot was a rarity in Budapest, every bit as rare as ballpoint pens. It had been smuggled in from Vienna by his aunt.

"I went down by Váci Street."

"Any luck?"

"Only a *lángos*," I said, not wanting to talk about the peasant. "Did you see the leaflets?"

"They're sickening," he answered. " 'Soften the resistance,' Father said. 'You'd think they were kneading dough'—that's just what Father said."

"Apu said they're going to bomb," I lied. I was angry that we had not discussed it. They should have thought me grown enough to share our mutual danger. "My parents are stocking up now to go to the cellar in the morning."

"I've never heard a bomb explode."

I looked at him in anticipation.

"My father said we'd have to rise by six," Jancsi said. He continued to fire his marbles.

So there it was. *His* parents had spoken with him.

I fell mute.

He was my good friend, my best friend. And *I* could not even speak to him. Just to say good-bye. I would just disappear from his life. A helium balloon that had slipped his fingers and drifted away.

I dared not raise my concerns but instead asked him to sneak out to the playground with me and to tell his mother we were going upstairs to play chess.

"But it's dangerous," he replied. "Especially at night."

"Who gives a damn?"

We hopped down the stairs three at a time, thrilled by the anticipation of danger. After all, it was the night before we would retreat to the cellars. My mind jerked to Jancsi's rhythmic steps. No more chess with Jancsi or summers in the country.

Behind the wall to the playground, the lights of the nightclub were lit, their many colors dancing across the night sky. They dangled from the bare branches of three huge birch trees, draped like a many-stranded necklace. Women in high heels and pastel gowns danced the rumba with their men as the gypsy violinists stood idly by. The hit tune of the summer, "Mambo Italiano," started, and a cheer went up as the dance floor filled.

The gypsies shuffled in place, muttering among themselves, gesturing with the violins tucked behind their backs. The head of the group was pudgy; the buttons of his black jacket pulled taut, and the violin hardly covered his rump. We skirted the club by way of the field next to the mansion to the right and sat overlooking the playground from the top of the wall near the swings.

Soon two figures approached between the buildings, scurrying in the shadows close to the facade. They each carried a bundle wrapped in a raincoat, and Jancsi immediately knew their intent. "Say, Pisti. They've got guns."

"What makes you say that?"

"It's too late in the season for fishing poles. And they aren't skis. What the hell would they bring skis here for?"

We sat quietly on the wall, blanketed in darkness, as the men undid their bundles by the swings.

"Just hand over that machine gun, Zoltán," the fat man said.

"*Csak nézzen ide, Börönd barát.*" It was clear Zoltán was tipsy, as his nose, beaked like a loon's, swung in the air. "Just look here, Börönd buddy, it's the damned cocking rifle's got to go first. Heavy as hell."

"Look, look, we'll bury both of them," the fat one asserted.

But a problem soon arose.

"You got the shovel, Börönd buddy?" Zoltán could hardly talk.

"Now hold on, you fool. *You* were supposed to get that, goddamn it. You were supposed to get the damned shovel."

"Now what you mean, good Börönd?" Zoltán was slurring his words. "What you saying?"

"For Christ's sake, Zoltán. You got too damned drunk to think of the essentials," the fat revolutionary spit out. "Just look at us, you fool. Sitting in a playground surrounded by weapons. What the hell are we supposed to say if someone comes by?"

"Well, let's bury them quick."

"You fool. You didn't bring a shovel." Börönd smacked his own head. "We need a shovel, damn it."

At this, Zoltán got up, dejected from the abuse, and scratched his neck. He sauntered to the sandbox, sat down in defeat, and unscrewed his flask.

"Look at you!" Börönd shouted after him. "What a fool you are, seated in a sandbox like a child, drunk as anything."

It was only then that Zoltán felt the sand. He pondered on the sand trickling through his fingers for some time. Finally he spoke. "Good buddy. I have not brought a shovel, and for that I am sorry."

"What?" Börönd seemed amazed. "You joking with me? Don't you think I *know* that we don't have a shovel, you fool?" He started wrapping up the guns.

"But look here," Zoltán exclaimed quickly, standing in the sandbox and kicking the sand.

Fat Börönd ran over to view their good fortune, and with great enthusiasm tried to embrace his thin friend. But Zoltán, already tipsy, fell over. Börönd stood over him. "Zoltán, thou art a genius." He spoke in the formal voice out of sudden respect for his friend's find.

And soon both men, thin and fat, were on their knees, digging in the loose sand like dogs after bone. When a trench had been formed, they placed the guns side by side and piled the sand back over them.

"Börönd, are we free, good friend?" Zoltán drawled. "I ask, are we clear?"

Börönd crawled out of the sandbox on all fours. "Yes, we're clear. Clear as clear and nothing to fear." And then he started laughing, his fat stomach, silhouetted against the park light, bobbing as he chortled. "Clear and free." He took Zoltán's flask.

They staggered into the open light between the buildings, arm in arm, singing an army song.

> *The big dog does it to the little dog,*
> *Kingo-dingo ding.*

> *The big dog does it to the little dog,*
> Jaj piri, *hey* piri, *ding.*

After they had rounded the corner, Jancsi and I quickly ran to the sandbox. The machine gun still contained a full clip, and the rifle turned out to be an old ornate hunting gun. A single bullet, still unused, at least eight centimeters long, was secured in the chamber. The barrel was decorated in brass and copper work, and the stock was carved in a dark wood, inlaid with ivory. We both wanted the heavy elephant rifle, which is what we imagined it to be. In the end, we had to choose.

"One to four . . . one to four," Jancsi chanted, flicking out his fingers one at a time. "Shoot."

The rifle was mine, since I knew Jancsi always went for two.

On the way back to the building, I slid the gun through the window and down the shaft to our bin for tinder, facing the street across from the 43 Damjanich apartment building.

Of course the bombers never came, although we all rose early that Sunday and went to the cellars, a regular exodus in the stairwell, with women carrying pitchers of milk, burnt strudel, and crying infants, and the men loaded with blankets and flashlights, utensils of all kinds piled high—pliers, jackknives, and hammers—anything for any emergency.

We made our way to the cellar but backed up at the entrance where the passageways to the storage compartments for coal and tinder narrowed. Several of the smaller children began to cry in the melee. The compartments were lit only by candlelight. After we had made a place among the coal, I was quick to go to our second bin, where I buried the exposed rifle among the tinder.

But soon a rumble was heard, and Apu wondered if it was aircraft. "It's peculiar. It just doesn't sound like it," he puzzled. "It's a drone, not a buzz."

Just then word came down the passageway, like a baton

passed unwanted from cubicle to cubicle, that the bombing had been a ruse, that the city was now overrun with tanks. Stalin's tanks, I thought. The entire populace had sought shelter or was sleeping and was mounting only token resistance.

I was outraged. Dogs of darkness, wild jackals, my mind raced.

Then we heard the first blast, a one-two, firing and explosion, as the shell tore into some building. And then another blast. And another.

I slunk back to our second bin, which faced the street, and shinnied up to the window.

The street was covered with debris, the air thick with particles of dust from the building across from ours, number 43. Two tanks, side by side, like a team of work horses, fired volley after volley, their guns recoiling, the tanks rearing backward. I watched for what seemed a lifetime but what was merely a lick of the fire's tongue. And then a boom and rumble deep as the tanks lurched backward.

The facade of the building cracked, revealing rooms on the top four floors, blue and white, tilting, with pictures still dangling from the walls. The facade leaned and fell, clouds of dust darkening the sky. The noon sun, now a blue eye, tinted the street as at twilight, night soon to come. Three people spilled from the front rooms.

The square pattern of the interior now naked to the street looked like Angi's dollhouse. I stared at the lacerated structure. Seven stories up, a little boy held onto the leg of a piano that was wedged by a couch. Loose on one hinge, a door swung freely, lapping lazily at the noon darkness.

The screw that had tightened my thoughts as I watched the scene was stripped of its threads when I realized that I could be the little boy. It could be me on our fifth floor clutching our grand piano. For the first time, I knew I could die. Really die. As Margit had, Dr. Tóth's widow, who grew very thin, and Apu put her in the hospital, until one day she died, and we went to the cemetery, the black horses neighing and everyone walking slowly and deliberately. As I looked up the seven stories, I knew at once I could die, loss, my guardian, come too soon.

A white light overcame my mind then, pitiless white, all-encompassing and brilliant. I imagined never seeing Mother. That's what death meant. Never seeing Anyu or Oti, or Kati or Jancsi. I looked at the mesh of the screen on the window. Tiny squares. Crisscrossing. Rusty at the edges, worn through. I ran my fingernails across the grating. Heard the rasping sound. No touch or endearment. A dreamless sleep. Dust on the ledge. Loose tinder. The dust piled in lumps. Just alone. And white light, nothing but white, as when awaiting an operation, on the table, waiting, no one there, no doctor or nurse, but a catholic light.

Wanting to run, yet frozen, I remained alert in the tiny cubicle with the strained vigilance of the roe downwind from the hunter.

Then the piano jarred loose and slid from the slope of the parlor floor, pulling the rug and a lamp and turning once lazily in the air before landing upside down on the heap of bricks, living-room furniture, two bathtubs, and all the belongings that had spilled from the building. When the piano shattered, a resonance louder than the shellfire broke the momentary silence, broke my trance. The legs of the piano extended upward and out, like those of a dead horse. The rug caught a breeze and, gaining buoyancy, landed across the street.

As the tanks moved to the next buildings, the lead tank caught on a pipe in the rubble on the road, jamming the left tread, preventing it from moving forward. The driver ground the engine into a roar, forcing thick exhaust to belch, but the tank could not move in a straight line. As the pipe set deeper, the tank spun counterclockwise, blocking the second tank.

Suddenly streams of flame fell from the dark sky, first two, then three more, then many at once, showering down, the darkness yielding a rain of fire. The flames exploded around the crippled tank, to the left, to the right, until it was surrounded by a blaze.

The second tank was also hit. It tried to back away, lunging from side to side, knocking a lamppost on the right side of the street, its turret burning in pockets of fire. Thick smoke from burning gasoline billowed into the air. By the time the tank escaped to the avenue, its crippled comrade was entirely ablaze. The hatch soon opened. I thought of them as Stalin's soldiers, even though I knew Stalin had died three years earlier. Three of Stalin's men scrambled out. They had replaced the Russian troops familiar to us, and, as Oti had warned, had been sent with a single command: "Destroy."

At once the air was torn by fire from small arms, pelting the tank and pinging as the bullets hit the metal frame. The last Russian out was hit even before he was off the tank, and he drooped over the turret like a rag hung to dry. As volley after volley hit him, he jerked about in spasms until he loosed and slid to the ground.

The first two soldiers rushed from the tank across the avenue toward our building, the gunfire eating at the cobblestones by their feet, until one soldier fell. The bullets continued their unrelenting dance around him.

Like a trapped animal, I scratched the wire mesh covering the window. Death blooms poppy-petal red. I had never seen such flames.

The other Russian made it to the safety of the stoop of our neighboring building. He was no more than twenty meters from my cellar hideout, and luck had stood him well—the stoop provided good cover against fire from the roofs. The sides of the solid railing arched over and protected his head, while a huge oak tree guarded him from the left. He crouched between the tree and stoop, motionless and waiting, rolled like a beetle when it has been touched. He could not see me as long as he stayed like that, I thought, and we both waited, and the rooftop waited.

A silence fell over the street, punctuated by the sound of

debris falling from the ravaged building. The frightful silence bloated my lungs, which wanted release. I tried not to breathe but felt myself panting. Fire still sputtered on the burning tank.

The heavy blanket of silence was penetrated again by grinding. When I looked out the small opening, I saw four tanks slowly turn onto the boulevard. Stalin's four soldiers had yelped for help, I thought, and the cowering comrade would be saved. Saved to do what?

As he turned his head toward the sound, the soldier spotted me and at once crouched lower, firing his pistol. I ducked, and bullets showered from the roofs in his direction, chipping at the concrete railing above his head and splintering the oak tree.

He knows where I am and thinks I am a sniper, I thought. The animal fear again rushed forward. Stabbed with cramps from the intensity of my vigil, I doubled in pain and staggered from the tinder. The white dream returned, a whiter shade of gray, like death.

I burrowed to the center of the pile on my hands and knees, like a frantic animal, and retrieved the heavy hunting gun. I dragged it back up the woodpile, my soiled clothes hampering movement. I climbed backward, lifting the weight of the gun with both hands. Once at the top, I heaved the gun against the ledge. Peeking out, I saw the Russian as a beetle, burrowed to pith, hunched and fearful of the rooftop fire.

Raising the stock with both hands, I pushed the gun onto the ledge and under the screen. I clicked the safety off. The Russian still crouched, and I pointed the gun toward him, mechanically reviewing my practice with Jancsi the night before—line the sights, hold your breath, ease the trigger. I balanced the muzzle on the sill to steady the big rifle, but my hands continued to tremble. The rumbling from the approaching tanks grew louder. The soldier heard it too as he moved about, lifting his head some. He would have to wave or somehow show himself or the tanks would go by. I knew this much.

I had only one bullet. I waited, the point of the gun waving.

The Russian crouched—also waiting. Then as the quiet of the dead settled into my limbs, all energy spent, my grip steadied. The gun balanced on the ledge and grew still. I sighted the gun, watching the copper aiming pin at the front slowly fill the valley of the rear sight. I focused my aim on the beetle's hunched back and pleaded with myself, Just hit him. Hit him anywhere. It's an elephant gun. And I held my breath as the rumbling grew.

But my finger betrayed me. It curled around the brass trigger but remained paralyzed. Again I sighted, held my breath, and again could not move my finger.

Then flicking out his head from the safety of his hole, the Russian saw me again and shot with his pistol. His attack freed my paralysis at once.

The boom resounded and the rifle recoiled, leaping from my arm, flying past the pile of tinder. The shot ripped a slab as big as any baker's loaf from the oak by the side of the Russian's head. Desperate, spinning from cover, the whites of his eyes showing as if he were blind, the soldier scrambled for the road, waving wildly, the tanks still at some distance. Again the rooftops erupted. He looked unreal there in the road, jumping and dancing, scrambling back to cover with tiny steps.

But he never made it. He fell dead, stumbling no more than a meter from my window, the turtle-shell helmet rolling to the side. And I saw that he was a youth, smooth skinned with a clear complexion the canary yellow of the star mother had worn long ago and ripped from Rózsi's chest, and Cili's, and forbidden them to wear. She had stamped her feet back then: "There is danger in shame."

Volley after volley pelted the young Russian. I slammed down the cover of the window and hid in the darkness. "Der springt noch auf," I heard above me. "This will rise." Behind and above me, the bullets danced staccato. I barely heard them.

Then the roar of the tanks was before our building. In my mind's eye, I saw the first tank move past the stoop and the second. Then the next two. I pictured their movements, slow and deliberate.

I pictured Stalin's four tanks side by side swing their turrets toward the building nearest where their comrades lay and heard *"Der springt noch auf"* sound above while I pleaded, lie still lie still I say when patience blooms to death where love once paced washed-white peaks now fear and doubt appear lie still lie still as soot-black dust clots the ear.

12

The Living

Grandmother had lived through two great wars. She knew that they were real, not made up. She had also lived through three revolutions and knew that they were hardly different from wars. Her son, my father, had lived through two wars and two revolutions. He was convinced no war could be won. "Just look at us," he'd say. "Millennial servitude is our only lot." In turn, his wife, my mother, had lost twenty-five of twenty-eight relatives, all in one war, the Good War.

Mother did not actually know the full depth of her losses until 1953, when she sat down with Rózsi at the kitchen table one summer's day, pencil in hand and a sheet of paper before her on the oilcloth of the kitchen table. I sat at the head of the table, salting goose crackling and mounting the stamps I received from Ervin in America in my stamp album. I gazed at the red roosters painted on the wall and imagined them crowing in the early morning.

Anyu and Rózsi did not notice me, intent as they were on drawing the family tree. The many branches hanging down reminded me of a willow. The trunk hung with a thick branch from Zalavég meeting two boughs from the Hortobágy. Then circles were drawn for women, squares for men, with dotted lines between couples and solid lines falling down from between them, like climbing ropes, to which children clung. The squares and circles continued downward. X's marked the dead and the missing.

Finally, after about an hour, they sat back, Rózsi in awe. "It's a tree that's shed its leaves, my dear," she said to Anyu. "Nearly no one's left."

But Mother, from whom I had learned how to turn gloom into hope, did not despair even then. "We can't be sure, can we Rózsi?" she said. "Only three are actually known dead. So why need we be pessimistic? Maybe the others are only missing."

"How can you say that? Where would they be missing?" Rózsi argued. "Are they missing in *action?*"

"Maybe they're in Canada, or New Zealand," Anyu persisted. "Or Israel. Simply gone somewhere."

Rózsi finally saw her point. "The autumn foliage of our sad tree blown across the earth."

"It is not certain that they are irretrievable, nor that we should be forlorn," Anyu went on.

They then returned to the graph and, methodically, next to the twenty-two X's that they were not sure represented irrevocable loss, put a question mark.

Sure enough, questions soon prevailed. It was now a tree cast in doubt, but *only* in doubt, with question preferable to certainty in this case.

They got up from the table, Rózsi considerably rejuvenated. She left the piece of paper lying on the checked cloth. For a while I kept sorting my stamps, but soon my curiosity got the better of me. I picked up the sheet, smudging the lower end with the goose fat. I saw the many names—Berend(?), Ofner(?), Ofner(?), Balázs(?), Waldman(?), Ofner(?)—and their many offspring dangling down from the horizontal lines, like hangers from a closet, also punctuated by question marks.

I recalled that Mother had been hopeful even before the chart was devised. Even before Liberation, she had fought against uncertainty in the hope that the autumn foliage from her small tree had been blown by friendly breezes, not ground into the soil on some unmarked trail. The grease from my hand smudged the lines of the pencil, tainting my fingers with lead.

Apu and I deduced her hope from the manner in which she answered the knock at the front door, a simple event that always held out a moment of promise. Each knock was adopted as an orphan, arousing in her the anticipation and excitement of becoming a parent yet again—or, at least, a relative.

I recall a time in my childhood when I sat on the Oriental rug with my marbles and toy Skôda. I had lined the marbles up side by side in a spiral so that the path between them made a road, winding across lush valleys of the Persian design. The rug was worn, which made it ideal for my purposes, since the car could roll freely. At intervals I had placed red marbles, the old kind, made of clay; when I came to these, the car had to stop to obey the traffic signal. I would then carefully replace the red marbles with my green snake-eyes, the go signals of the game.

In this fashion, I drove around the flatland of the rug, chanting, "Put, put . . . Stop!" And, "Go! Put, put."

Mother was writing at the desk, and she looked up, smiling. "Why are you 'put, putting,' Pisti?"

"The car has to stop and go."

"Why can't it just go?"

"There are stop signs."

"Well, take them away."

"I can't do that."

"Why not, Pisti? You made them."

"I did not."

"Well, tell me who did?"

"God makes all stop signs. Even these. I just put them there."

She began to laugh.

"You can laugh, Mother," I went on. "But it's true."

Then came the knocking. Three quick raps. And she jumped up, much as I had seen Vera do from time to time, all traces of her earlier mirth replaced by urgency.

"Coming, coming," she yelled. She tried to fit on her slippers in a frenzy. "Don't go away. I'm coming."

The embroidered slippers would not hold to her feet, and she

kicked at them energetically, toes down. "God above," she ago-
nized. "What a time for this. Let's hope they don't go away."

Finally, one slipper clung to her foot. Giving up on the other,
she grabbed it in her hand, running out, off balance, the slippered
foot clomping with her eager stride. "Don't go away. This is me.
The former Miss Tildy, of Soroksári Street, Seventh District." The
slipper clattered at each step. "Who are you?"

"Beg pardon, madame, the super reported a leaking pipe,"
came the confused reply from the far side of the door.

"Oh. Oh, yes. I recall now. Please do come in."

I knew how she would return—defeated, her shoulders more
hunched, her child of faith lost. And on this occasion she also
came back barefoot, a slipper in each hand, the bunion on her left
foot exposed, her face burning with indignation at hopes rudely
dashed.

I tried to renew our earlier discussion, feeling responsible for
her happiness. "God made red lights," I resumed, exaggerating my
child's tone. "We always have to stop, don't we, Mother?"

"What?" She was lost in thought.

"But _I_ make green lights," I said, taken aback by her remote-
ness but persevering in hope.

She did not hear me, and I returned to my game.

The flecks of dust in the dark rug sank deeper as the toy car
pressed over them. I looked up. I looked at the lace tablecloth. It
was faded, yellow in hue. The glass doors of the cabinet shone
across from me. The pictures and decorated cups and painted
cigarette boxes on the cabinet shelf marred my reflection in the
glass. I looked up. A solitary crack ran across the diagonal of the
ceiling, like a river on a map with tiny veins as tributaries along
the sides. I turned my head. Anyu was weeping silently. I pressed
the toy car into the rug.

"Put, put . . . Stop!"

"Go! Put, put."

* * *

The morning we left was like any other morning. We rose at six and had a heavy breakfast of assorted meats. The packing had been done days earlier, and Angi and I had been warned to talk to no one, or if we had to, to say simply that we were off to Uncle Kálmán's. I had never forgotten Kálmán's homing pigeons, exercising them each night. But to say I was visiting him made me uncomfortable, since he and Ibolya had escaped twelve years earlier.

I had a slice of black bread and pepperoni with yellow peppers. Apu commented that the peppers were full of vitamin C. "That's a blessing in a land short on citrus fruit," he said. "Tomatoes are excellent, too."

Anyu got the *pogácsa* from the oven, the traditional meat biscuits for leavetakings. There were twelve in all. Four were overdone, and she scraped their bottoms with a knife. The burnt pastry soiled the white porcelain of the sink. She ran the water to wash away the ashes, spreading the water along the sides with a cupped hand.

I was finally given a five-hundred-forint note folded into a tiny pillbox and told the name of the man we were to meet at the Bakony station. He would be disguised as Mr. Red, White, and Green.

The family then trudged down the stairwell, which was shot up and pocked from weeks before, the plaster missing in huge chunks. We entered the street. The buildings were scarred by bullet and shell holes from the T-54 tanks.

Apu carried my satchel. Angi hardly brought anything in hers. My sister and I walked in front of the adults, uncles and aunts and our parents, two lonely goslings before a gaggle of gooseherds.

Our satchels were totally unnecessary, it turned out, and I wondered why they had been readied days earlier. The bags served only for show, to make us appear like normal travelers. Their only use was to hold the dozen meat biscuits that Anyu had baked, meant as good wishes for the trip.

It was still early. The train would not leave until eleven o'clock. A mist hung over the streets, curling into doorways and passageways, like the tongue of an alley cat, licking at the open wounds of the bullet-ridden facades. I kept looking backward at the adults. They were there.

Would we see one another again? I wondered. Would I ever see my friends? Jancsi? Kati? Would their names fade? The names of streets, the look of the avenues fade? Would I forget the language? Would I find love where we were going? And where was that?

I turned back to the adults. "Where are we going after the Bakony Mountains?"

"Your sister knows."

"Where are we going, Angi?"

"Where money grows on trees and gold lines the sidewalks."

I was incredulous, stirred by sense of unease, but it sounded good. "We are fleeing," I knew. "To the West." The word *diszidálunk,* "to escape," reverberated from a few days ago.

"Money grows on trees there," Angi repeated. My tensions eased at her faith in magic. Gold-lined gutters sounded good.

It was not until we reached the station that a pallid sun, white as my shirt, crawled high into the sky and slowly ate at the haze. I then saw looming before me the giant glass dome of Nyugati Station, white and hunched, like the ash-dusted elephant I had seen kneeling in the Magyar State Circus years earlier.

Once in the station, we were again warned not to talk and were hurried onto the train. It was as though the gooseherds were trying hard to quiet the geese, making shushing sounds and walking about with fingers pressed to their lips. Of course, this was all done discreetly, for if a policeman happened by, all shushing stopped, fingers were clasped behind the back, and true silence fell.

I pulled myself up by the handrail. I had to reach high up, pulling myself stiff armed. I felt the cold metal against my palms.

I saw the dirty lamp above the entranceway, which had collected several flies. Only one of the flies buzzed, trying desperately to escape the oval bulb of the lamp. The smell of coal from the warming locomotive bit my nostrils.

Angi had to be helped onto the train because she could not pull herself up. I mocked her, "And you didn't even carry anything in your bag."

I saw that she was distressed. For the first time that I could recall, her head gave a sudden jerk to the left. She closed her eyes. Her head jerked again.

"What's wrong?" I was confused. The terror of solitude was suddenly overwhelming, as though I were to be cast into the ocean miles from shore with no ship in sight and the waves heaving. I took out a meat biscuit.

"Nothing's wrong. Nothing," she went on. Her head jerked again.

"It looks like you're shaking your head no."

"No, I'm not."

We settled into the first available compartment. I leaned out of the train window, my fingers rubbing against the oil of the latch. Mother, who saw me, ran over, looked about hurriedly, to the right, to the left, and then standing on tiptoes, whispered up, "*Ott jobb az élet.* Life is better there, Pisti. You must believe me."

"*Ott gazdagadhan az ember,*" she continued to mutter, and she started sobbing at once. "You can prosper there." A policeman happened by just then, and she tried desperately to hide her tears, lowering her head and rubbing her eyes vigorously as though irritated by soot.

"Why are you crying, Mother?" I asked her after the man had left.

She looked up, her face red and wet. "Just keep quiet, dear," was all she said. "Don't say a word." And a silence descended on me that weighed for decades. It was the beginning of my broken tongue, the beginning of a choked-up feeling that I could not express what I wanted—love. You know I love you.

* * *

The fields we passed were all plowed under, stark and bare, except for an occasional half-harvested cornfield in which one or two overgrown sows rutted. In the past, I had traveled mostly in springtime when the fields were rich green and buttercups mixed with blue flowers among the tall grass. Ox-drawn wagons with fat rubber tires could be seen in the spring, carrying piles of tools for the groups of peasants who worked at the outskirts of town.

Once in a while, especially if I traveled in late afternoon in June, I would also see a horse-drawn wagon, maybe a four-horse rig driven by a dandy, as bachelors were called, wearing a fine-feathered cap and a cape that billowed as the horses charged on, the dandy smacking and lashing the air with his long whip as he balanced precariously in front of the seat.

Now, in December, there was hardly any life. No herd or herder, no flock or goose boy. Only the chilling wind through the open window, the smell of the coal from the engine, and a gray-metal sky from which all traces of the sun had leaked long before.

The conductor looked into our compartment. "Aren't you two due for Győr?"

Angi and I said nothing. He repeated himself: "Are you due for Győr?"

We looked out the window. I took a bite from a meat biscuit.

"Please," he begged. "What say you?"

We looked up at him, dumb.

"Surely, the two of you go somewhere."

We were terrified.

"You go to Győr."

"No. We visit Uncle Kálmán," I said finally.

We got off the train at the Keresfalu station. It was a small depot serving the Bakony hamlet. There wasn't even a sign there, and because we had doubts about where we were, my sister and I stood on the steps of the train for some time, wondering if we should get off. Finally the conductor came by and nearly kicked at us.

"Keresfalu! Keresfalu! Yes, yes, it is this. Uncle Kálmán for sure here lives. You two at last arrive," he yelled in the countryside manner, drawling the vowels and inverting grammar. "Don't you think the train must go on?"

I remember clearly how the embankment there was made of tar. There was no platform at all. We had to jump off the steps, probably a meter and a half. Angi jumped first and landed on both feet, collapsing into a slump. I followed her but landed more awkwardly, falling and rolling over, and I slid down the slope of the rocky embankment, scraping my back.

I scrambled to the top again on all fours, my back stinging, and saw that Angi was sitting on the tracks. I joined her and sat surveying the fields from our vantage point, my back throbbing with pain. I looked across the withered sunflowers, broken at angles from when the seeds had been harvested. I saw the dry stalks of corn, here and there a loose ear still dangling, as though forgotten by both animal and man, but not by the clamoring blackbirds. I looked down the length of telephone wires, sagging from pole to pole. The blackbirds flitted loudly between the cables.

We had been sitting on the track for an hour when the train from Szentendre, an express, sneaked up on us. It was probably a hundred meters away when I spotted it, but the engine was huge and charging headlong. It seemed only twenty meters from us. Angi ran to one side, and I sprang up but fell again, scraping my back a second time. When I was able to stand, I shouted, "Run! Run! It will hit you, Angi!" Then the train rumbled by and the steam hit my face and I feared Angi had surely been hit, but after it passed, I saw her waving to me from the other side of the slope. She ran to me and took hold of my hand.

I had grown increasingly tense. "Damn it. Damn you. Why don't you take care of yourself?" I pulled from her embrace.

"I'm all right."

"Goddamn it. Take care of yourself."

* * *

We did not know what to do. We ate some more meat biscuits but no longer sat on the track. A man wearing a red hat, white shirt, and green pants was to meet us and take us to Bakony. Apu had been terribly afraid we would forget the disguise and kept repeating, "Don't forget, he's Mr. Red, White, and Green." I finally told him there was little likelihood of my forgetting as these were the colors of our national flag.

It struck me as an odd disguise, such a loud clash of colors like a clown would wear. But when I finally saw a man drive up in a horse-drawn wagon, sporting a maroon hunter's cap and green workman's pants, he hardly seemed odd. The colors were muted, and his clothes did not appear boorish.

He turned the wagon around and motioned for us to come down. As I neared, I saw that his face was distorted. His smile was much too broad, like it had been painted on by a young child. And his complexion was too pale for the life of the countryside, as though it had been powdered with flour, like the face of a buffoon.

He spoke in gestures, vocalizing only once: "The envelope?" I sensed his self-interest at once but did not know how to defend myself.

After he had looked through the contents of the pillbox, he chortled, "*Jó, édes apám.* Good, good, dear father mine." He then motioned us into the pile of hay at the back of the wagon, indicating that we should cover ourselves. "Good this bit-bite medicine. For me good."

The ride was endless. It seemed like we rattled on for days. And under the dark covering of hay, there was nothing to do. We could hardly breathe. Neither could we sleep, the ride was so bumpy. As night fell, which I could only tell from a thickening darkness through the hay, words came to me for a second time, as during the bomb scare in the city: "Who will drive me home, along the bumpy road, past flowing fields?"

Father's words came back. "Take care of each other, children." Would we drive ourselves home? And in what? A coughing Trabant? Or a regal Mercedes? Or only in our dreams?

Finally, the wagon stopped and the driver whistled for us to get out of the hay. Angi and I got off the wagon. But the man remained seated. In the moonlit night, as I looked up at him, the face of Mr. Red, White, and Green glowed silver, and I could see his face screw into a broad grin, as though it were in spasms beyond his control. He spoke again, for the second time. "Travel you by night. In haystacks do not sleep. On fire often are they set," he warned. But he maintained his smile.

As he spoke, I realized he was talking in some ancient Magyar dialect, perhaps in a broken tongue. Or was he using a voice from the time when Hungary was still composed of clans?

Then raising his voice, he shouted at the horses, "Put! Hut! Put! Hut!" Cracking his whip, he shouted back as an afterthought, "Across the mountains the West is." He then sped into the darkness. "Home I go. Homeward ho!"

We were alone again.

Angi's neck had continued to turn and jerk. It was as though she were saying over and again the very phrases I wanted to shout: No. No.

Finally she spoke. "I wonder what we'll do there?"

"Where?"

"Maybe I'll become a nurse. Or a nun."

We groped around for some time. Achieving any sense of direction seemed hopeless in the night. We appeared to be surrounded in every direction by bushes and heath. We sat down and ate another biscuit.

Clouds had blanketed the moon, and the night, dark and deep, seemed dead, except for the liveliness of evening insects. We huddled together, restless, unable to sleep, though we had been awake now for more than a day. The words again spoke to me: "Who will point with a whip to the green-hued house among birches and rowan?" And the words continued, as a wish: "Who will wait up for me? Who will cry out in the hallway?"

Angi and I finally fell asleep, arm in arm, as light leaked softly from the east.

* * *

The forest that covered the mountain was dense and dark. Our supply of biscuits would not last long. If we followed the stream up the mountain, staying near the moist soil, we felt sure we would find mushrooms. But I kept looking at the trees instead. On either side of the stream, thick oak trees grew in the sea of scrub clothed in autumn foliage. I saw four varieties of oak, which I remembered from the ragged book on trees József gave me after he quit writing so long ago, before the war. The turkey oak, which József called the scrub, had rough black bark, deeply furrowed into irregular ridges. I also saw many black oaks, sometimes called yellow oaks because of the color on the underside of the leaves.

My thoughts turned to József's notebook, but I should have paid closer attention to the ground, for we found no mushrooms, none at all.

We were soon down to our last biscuit, having eaten several during the course of the day's journey. Angi still scurried up and down the bank, refusing to give up.

At last, I decided to shell acorns and crush them to a paste. I knew that if I let them soak in the running water overnight, wrapped in my shirt, they would be bleached of bitterness by morning and would be edible.

We would eat, but our movement toward the top of the mountain was slow. I was humiliated by the thought of our foraging for acorns, day after day, like two pigs.

Night came again and we could see nothing. It grew cold. We piled some leaves in a hollow and huddled together for warmth. Only an animal instinct remained: to survive somehow. Right now, the instinct told me I needed warmth.

Angi felt the same thing. We huddled close, and I felt less pain at our loss. I learned again the lesson from my youth—that only human warmth can allay human pain. I finally fell asleep, Angi's hair entangled in mine.

* * *

I dreamed I was out at sea in the middle of the Atlantic. Nothing was in sight. The ocean was calm. In the distance, clouds were gathering. The waves began to stir. I was treading water. The sea grew colder as the clouds approached. I was growing more tired. But even in my dream, I knew I could at least cling to a hatch cover that was floating nearby. The hatch cover became a door. It seemed inviting. I squeezed through it and was led into a church where there were many friends to greet me. My parents were there, and all the friends I thought I had lost. Kati kissed me at length. A sign above the crucifix read: Just tired. Hungry. Lonely. That's it. Keep it simple. The saviors are all simple and ordinary folk, I thought. I saw Our Father smiling down at me from above the cross.

The next day, refreshed, we continued on, walking further into the darkness. Then a clearing suddenly opened before us.

There, in the center of the forest, I saw a giant spruce on which rested hundreds of many-colored birds, with ornate plumage and elegant markings. Angi and I marveled at the sight of this tree, fully dressed, like a Christmas tree with living decorations. I recalled having learned from Apu that the Christmas tree was really a symbol for the crucifix.

We soon forgot our hunger. Angi kept asking about the birds. I recognized them from the ones Kálmán had kept. "They are homing pigeons," I told her. "All of the Hungarian breeds Uncle Kálmán had." My awareness of longing was reawakened as I recalled what he had said: "They always return home."

"The Komaros whitehead and magpied Körös, up there," I pointed for my sister, chanting the traditional Hungarian names. "And look, there, a highflier from Szeged. You can tell by the bands across its breast, Angi, where it's red and brown."

"Kálmán said they always return home?" she asked.

We grew more enchanted by our living toy, this magical tree. "Let's sing Ibolya's song," Angi suggested. "Maybe we can get home, too."

Magic, I thought. My sister yearns for magic.

I felt sorrow for her. An onrush of sadness. She was as lost as I and just as frightened. Yet I had lost sight of her. I had hoped she would care for me. Now she was just yearning for magic.

The words of the song returned to me, and I pictured Ibolya singing them in the countryside.

> *I wandered in an emerald wood*
> *and saw a violet shaded blue*
> *with feltlike flowers, ink in hue,*
> *and every petal plush.*
>
> *And as it stood*
> *mid darkened wood,*
> *at once it wilted, wanting due. . . .*
> *Veiled and vast, the wild was hush.*

I could not allay my growing unease by such chanting.

Would we ever get home? Where was our home, anyway? Were we heading West? I looked at the sun. Yes, we were heading West.

My anxiety would not subside. I again tried to generate enthusiasm, artless in my desire even with Angi. "Look, Angi," I said. "Look at all those many tumblers, muffed and storked."

I stood before the tree. My cloth bag, empty now of biscuits, hung limp by my side. The words again forced themselves on me. Attila József's simple words: "I have no mother."

The birds took flight, at once and in a flurry.

"I have no father."

The birds were flying, the air alive, and the forest startled.

I watched the pigeons rise high in a cloud, bunching. Then they dove as one, untamed, and fell behind the crest of the mountain to the west. They flew west and disappeared.

I imagined them as the Ofner, the Berend, and the Balázs, all on Anyu's side, unaccounted question marks on the grease-smudged paper of our family tree.

The words pressed down a final time, irrevocable and despairing.

> *No mother, no father,*
> *No God or homeland either.*

Three nights later, we crossed to the West.

13

Returning
1989

And when I return, in my own turning, will there be the sweep of wind and downy flake? Or a bone-dry desolate land? Or has the passage of time transformed this world also?

The land will be full of life. Laughter. The ebullience of a people ripe with living and the cry of suckling infants hungry for life. A new richness crowding the marketplace, stuffed with goods even in winter, slaughtered geese dangling by the leg next to aging pepperoni and hard salami in the butcher shop and imported produce in the stalls, strawberries from Israel and oranges from North Africa.

Until the age of eight I had seen only one orange, never tasted the juice. Angi had been ill much of that time, and someone had come back all the way from the West, which at the time meant Vienna, a full day's journey by train, and had brought her an orange. It was wrapped in paper. I imagined the paper was silk, covering some gem, glowing gold, the size of a fist. It was magic. Orange, the burst of color, the smell of the skin.

The visitor gave it to Angi, for Angi was ill and the orange, I learned, was rich in vitamin C, richer even than yellow peppers. I understood this as the main reason Angi would get the orange, although as yet I had no idea of the importance of vitamin C. Of course, now it is perfectly clear—a fellow countryman having actually won a Nobel Prize for research on the vitamin.

Angi held the orange in her hand and turned it about before her face, and I asked if I could smell it again. But when she handed it to me, I could not contain myself and I grabbed it from her hand and quickly slid under the bed and bit into it as though it were a golden apple from the sun. I did not know oranges had to be peeled.

I just bit into it. And I sucked at the oil of the skin and the juices of the flesh, lost in the odors and the flavor, my lips stinging from the citric acid, and I hardly heard Angi's wailing or Grandmother's yells: "You rascal! You rascal! It's for your sister, damn it. Your *testvér*, your sister, you hear! Don't you know what that means? Your body and blood, damn you, *test* and *vér*."

I bit into the orange again, skin and all, not having yet swallowed the first mouthful because the peel was hard to chew. I felt the juices overflow my mouth and wet my hand. I did not hear all the yelling, nor did I feel the blows of the broom on my back as Grandmother scurried to flush me out. "Out! Out, damn it. Get out from there." I just chewed the fruit, lost in wonder. An orange. An orange, I thought. Sweet as any kiss.

It was later I felt the blows.

By 1976, the stores of Budapest were full of cans of orange juice, even grapefruit juice, and by 1985, there were tropical fruits of all kind.

But orange juice alone hardly makes for abundance. It is only people that can make a land abundant.

So what of the people? The people are joyous, the most life-loving one can find. The women are the most beautiful, with high cheekbones and brown hair and brown eyes. The children are cute and well adjusted. And are they smart? The smartest among them are the smartest in all the world, inventing everything from instruments for medicine and physics to Rubik's Cube, self-psychology, and new forms of music.

And what of the land? Would it remain for me unforgiving,

unforgivable as perpetual autumn, an October of returning again and again? Would life remain just a narrow bridge between some vast expanse of an eternal past and a future abyss?

Over the years, I had become a witness to memory, and memory spoke to me of desolation where the ashes of a multitude, as beautiful, as smart, as cute, as industrious as all the rest, had not been cast onto the balmy waters of shallow lakes or strewn among the ice of the smooth-flowing rivers. They had been spread, the ashes of men, women, and children, on icy roads in winter to keep war vehicles moving, to keep tires on the road and movement, any forward movement of war, sure and firm and forward.

Forward. *Előre*, the statue that replaced Stalin's monolith, stands in contrast to socialist realism. It surges forward sharply. But for the longest time, the question for Hungarians was passed from lip to lip: "Forward to where?"

This would be the land of desolation to which I would return. I knew it as sure is sure. There would be the sweep of wind, and the play of downy flake, and the fields and mires of the western plains where the fall harvest, cut only now, spikes with stubble. Having yielded bountiful harvest, golden grain, and bread for every table, the fields now carry a thin layering of snow.

As though nothing had happened and nothing in the past mattered. Life, a narrow bridge, grown flimsy and more feeble from history in our time.

But the old, the tots, and their ruddy parents now celebrate a new-found freedom. The dance of life is at long last in full revel. The pharaohs, nearly all of them, at long last yielded. Even the Germans, as a river in springtime, stream and flood across the border en masse, green borders of hemlock and aspen and green needles of pine, no longer the minefield, the wired electric fence, or the wall. May there never be any enemy or Amalekite to slaughter the lagging and tired at the rear of the German line.

Each morning's dawn holds new promise for us all.

*   *   *

The flurry sweeps past the border towns where the Germans crossed into Austria on their exodus to freedom, past the rail yards of Hegyeshalom where the tracks crisscross the terrain like irregular stitching on a stomach wound. The cold tracks are bundled in snow. When the rail cars whirl by, the snow billows and blows about and the tracks glisten in the winter-dry air.

The flakes dust the valleys of Transdanubia and wash the earth-toned autumn colors of the plots on the plain. The pregnant clouds move eastward to the woodlands outside the town of four rivers, near Keresfalu, our destination when Angi and I escaped. The feathered crystals dissolve into the rivers and melt near the shore. The waves stream as the rivers meet. Snow falls heavily across the stained-glass windows of the Calvinist villages.

Snow blankets the granaries and the longhorned cattle stand mute against the cold. The racehorses also turn against the wind, their thick winter coats mottled by the forcing gust. In the spa town, the gothic inn Chrystal slumbers. The ornate Fire Tower, where for centuries the warning cry of approaching enemy was raised, is silent now.

The snow falls soft and slumberous eastward, across the Roman ruins for the God Isi, over the Abbey Church, and covers the long, low "peace house" where Rákóczi gave battle to the Hapsburgs; eastward to Buda, blanketing the enormous red star on the tower of János Hill, the War Museum of Budapest with its red star now white, the Citadel from which the Hapsburgs kept watch over this rebel city after the defeat of the War of Independence. Eighteen forty-eight. A full century before communists put up the Statue of Liberty to the south, a monolith for socialist realism celebrating Stalin's "liberation" of the Magyar. Eighteen forty-eight. A full one hundred years before Rákosi decimated the nation, the snow falls over Lady Liberty and the olive branches she holds high, her arms extended and erect.

In the distance I imagine Apu standing under the Statue of Liberty, still laughing in the snow and still wearing his fisher's hat though it is February. I imagine Mother, laughing her usual laugh, telling me I could find him here. I laugh at the sight of him: perpetually an ice fisher as in his youth in the countryside. Nearing evening he is still out, playful as a little boy. But he is laughing in the snow because he knows the irony of the world when one hundred years earlier the cry for independence, "now or never," rang from this very place and would again one hundred and fifty years later, blanketing the wars of the worlds in snow.

I picture that he hugs me as we greet. "My son."

"How are you?"

"*Vagyok.* I am."

"Well?" I worry for him.

"Well enough."

We turn to leave, and arm in arm we walk from the sculpture.

I say, "Let's leave this outdated statue and go see *Előre*. Now that's art. The masses surging forward in a mad dash. I want to take a picture of the statue in the snow."

"*Előre* is not outdated?" he laughs cynically. "You think that sculpted worker is surging ahead toward some flag?"

"Now that he's free, he'll likely rush headlong toward any good-looking woman he can find."

Apu's laughter pulls his arm free from my embrace. He doubles over and as he comes erect finds himself facing in the opposite direction, back toward the statue, still in the shadows of Lady Liberty extending palm branches up to a clearing sky. He looks her over, running his eyes across her rigid and muscular body.

"Not the good-looking woman I was talking about," I say.

"Yay. Nah. Nah." He stands erect again and eyes the statue. "I received a letter from the Jewish Foundation for Righteous Gentiles."

I recall the essay I had been translating for the rabbi. "Are they still good enough to help you?"

He does not hear me but continues with his thoughts. "It is becoming common knowledge that the Jews were not entirely alone during the war."

"Well, you should know, Our Father."

"Don't be foolish. I learned about it in the letter. The rabbi was somber. You should read it. It was even translated. The Jewish community was not aware of Christian Rescuers until the mid-sixties. Everybody still thinks the Jews were utterly abandoned and alone. Some sort of nonsense for young minds to be learning." His face distorts in revulsion. "It was tragic enough."

"The Hungarians have one of the worst reputations. Even the anthem turns on the note of fratricide. The persecuted have all the right to call it such."

"You're still bitter. The truth is that the Jews were preserved by the Magyar much longer than by any other country in the Axis. Acts on behalf of Jewish humanity were largely individual, person helping person." He pulls down the flaps of his hat.

"It wasn't just Wallenberg in Hungary," Apu continues. "We had no time to organize an extensive underground by which to be remembered. Remember Eichmann took over in the spring of forty-four, and by autumn his work was finished." He pulls tight the strings so that the fur bulges around his ears. He looks like a teddy bear. I smile to myself.

"What does the rabbi want?"

Apu ties the twine around his chin, reaches into his pocket, and hands me a piece of paper.

"You have become an exile, Pisti." He looks at me with a steady gaze. "You are a wandering Jew. I cannot help that. I tried raising you a Catholic, even across an ocean's distance. Your guardians did the best they could. But your earliest memory is probably of walking and walking. No wonder you live by backward glances. It was not my wish. Yet where there is hope there is life. And one can prosper, even by wandering. It is not the worst of things, to be wandering. Each morning holds forth a new promise." He points to the paper.

"Read it. Read it," he nearly shouts. "A ruined place is forever in only one way—life cannot be regained, the clock turned in our turning twenty or thirty years back to a past somehow restored. I used to think exile or banishment was the only profanity. Oblivion is the only profanity. And these are the rescuers, mostly all forgotten. We do not even know if they are in body or if they are in need."

He notices the star hovering above Lady Liberty's head, like a halo. He makes a sweep with his hand. "See that star?" he laughs. "There used to be yellow stars, and red stars, and now they are of the past, covered with snow, the white of winter's silence."

He looks up. "Snow-covered stars," he laughs again. "Stars frozen in time. Best to believe in the nights of August, the white-peppered galaxy when I met your mother."

I unfold the letter.

1. Sándor Antal, Kőér Street 3, Budapest X
2. Dr. Lajos Aczél, Dobi István Street, Budapest X
3. Imre Bálint, Lenin Körút 115, Budapest VI
4. Málvin Bokor, Váci Street 22, Budapest V
5. László Berend and wife, Rákóczi Street 55/b, Budapest VII
6. Gyula Csermely, Lenin Körut 53, Budapest VI
8. Dr. Pal Karkas, 21 Bayview Lane, Montreal, Canada 15411
9. Dr. Dezső Szömöry and wife, 56 Park South, 4-A, NY, New York

Nine names, I think. When I join them it will be a *minyan*. Hungary will be a garden called Earth.

I turn to walk toward Lady Liberty. Apu shouts after me, "Remember the living!" I walk through the snow and I do not turn back. His voice alive and ringing in the crisp winter air, Apu calls again, "Remember the living, my son."

Acknowledgments

I thank Slavie, who knows he kept me going long after I had started. In 1977, I had interviewed him for a biographical sketch: S. R. Slavson, the father of group psychotherapy. Group therapy had its roots in the Self-Culture Club he formed in 1911. Among the children exposed to his influence were Ben Shahn, painter, Louis Hacker, historian, and Joseph Freeman, novelist.

When I met him in his eighties, this feeble man said to me one day, shaking with urgency, "Look, László, you should write. Always do what you're best at. Write, I tell you. Write it."

He searched through his shelves, moving things about, until he found *Leaves of Grass* by Whitman. It was to make a point, as he turned to a marked page. "This is how I have tried to live."

> STRANGER! *if you, passing, desire to speak to me,*
> *why should you not speak to me?*
> *And why should I not speak to you?*

"We remain silent because of guilt," Slavie muttered to himself.

He sat in the stuffed chair, waving his mottled hands. "Go write. Go write." He started to doze and handed me the book with a tired grasp. "You keep it," and he slept. How I loved his sweet and kindly nature. No one could enter the circle of his friendship without feeling his aura, a stronger presence. But his strength was benign, as the firm hand stroking one's hair. I took the book. 1855. One of the first editions. Inscribed by Whitman to his new publisher, David McKay.

I thank my mentor, Frank Gado, professor of English at Union College, Schenectady, N.Y., for the start he gave. Frank taught creative writing by first teaching us to read authors in depth. I still remember his first criticisms of an overly romantic style.

I had gone to a maternity waiting room, of all places, to write a realistic sketch of anxious fathers lined by the pay phone. For my last paragraph, I developed a scene from oncology, one floor below obstetrics. I thought it a remarkable insight, providing irony—birth and death in discord, etc. Frank rapidly inured me to criticism—Romanticism the foible of not just Yeats, but many Hungarians. His arguments, irrefutably based on text, taught me to distinguish the grain from the chaff.

I am also indebted to a number of historians and archivists. While preparing this manuscript, I was preoccupied with historical accuracy. Then one text stated that Hungarian Jews were emancipated in 1866, another in 1867, and a third in 1868. If a simple fact as a date (yet one so crucial) is subject to interpretation as textual reality, memory and awareness also gain validity as means to claiming an individual interpretation for historical reality. For those for whom the Chaos of Being lies with the Holocaust, the need to undertake such interpretation is essential to personal peace.

Of historical works on the Hungarian Holocaust, one seemed to stand far above others. For the authenticity that clarified the oral histories and twice-told tales that form the basis of *Broken Places* and provided much of the details that lend life to the novel, I am grateful to Professor Randolph L. Braham's meticulous and scholarly works, the two-volume *Politics of Genocide: The Holocaust in Hungary* (New York: Columbia University Press, 1980). Here little is based on memory, much on awareness, a discernible quest for objective truth about a period of darkness unknown in the millennia since the Magyar migration.

The members of the writers' group 3E, composed of William Melvin Kelley, Sondra Spatt Olsen, Terese Svoboda, Carol Pearce, Shirley Morgenstein, and Margaret Haller, provided invaluable support. The group, organized in 1983 from members of The Writers Community of New York where Willy was writer in residence, met at Carol's studio, 3E, every other week. Criticism was always supportive and of high quality.

The group helped me shape a work that started in 1969 in Budapest as studies in socialist realism and evolved into oral histories of my extended family, friends, and acquaintances. The work continued to evolve with six more trips to Hungary, becoming finally the story of my family's dispersion, our *Magyar diászpora*.

I also want to thank my editor at Atlantic Monthly Press, Anton Mueller, and my agent, Laura Gross, for their patience and care given freely.

Of the religious organizations that were most helpful, I am indebted to the Lubavitch Community, to P'nai Or of New York, and to St. Stephen's Church in New York.

8 március 1990
Berkeley, California
LPO